U0153279

超實用
生活英語分類單字
Practical Daily English Vocabulary

李普生 著

書泉出版社 印行

INTRODUCTION
前言

人類溝通時的主題可以說是無窮盡；雖是無窮，但依然可以將所有語言使用者，不論他[她]的母語為何，會使用到的語言主題做一大膽預測。本書編輯的前提是以英語文為主要使用工具，提供讀者不同主題領域相關的字彙及片語。

本書所分單元包含：

- 食物烹調及進食
- 家居場所及活動
- 衣著服飾
- 隨身用品
- 家庭及人際關係
- 動植物飛禽走獸
- 身體心理及情緒
- 餐廳旅館銀行及商店
- 休閒運動及娛樂
- 醫療保健
- 美容美髮及個人保健
- 工作行業

★ 生老病死人生百態

在使用本書時，讀者一定要記住：天下絕對沒有「絕對」的事；這本書裡所列舉出的字彙絕對不是僅有的字彙，所有用法也絕對不可能是唯一的；所列字彙足以進行日常對話，但若要進行深入的討論，就必須借重專業書籍了。讀者透過自己的日常生活，只要發現是屬於某個特定領域或範圍的生字或片語，您就要自己動手，把它加入現有書冊中所列舉的名單中；也只有如此，您才能真正地活到老學到老，也只有如此，您才能真正成為一名辯才無礙的溝通者。

CONTENTS 目錄

前言
INTRODUCTION

民以食為天 001
EVERYTHING YOU NEED TO KNOW ABOUT EATING

蔬菜	VEGETABLES	/002
水果	FRUIT	/005
麵包	BREAD	/007
盒裝食品	PACKED GOODS	/008
調味料	CONDIMENTS(SEASONINGS)	/009
肉類, 家禽與海鮮	MEAT, POULTRY & SEAFOOD	/010
乳製品	DAIRY	/012
甜點	DESSERT	/013
香料	SPICE & FLAVORING	/014
飲料	BEVERAGE	/016
餐盤、餐具與餐室	DISHES, UTENSILS & DINING ROOM	/017
烹飪器皿	COOKING UTENSILS	/019
烹飪技巧	CULINARY SKILLS	/021
片語慣用語	IDIOMS AND EXPRESSIONS	/023
中文英文大不同	A WORLD APART	/026

金窩銀窩比不上自己的狗窩 027
EAST OR WEST, THERE IS NO PLACE LIKE HOME

房屋式樣	HOUSING	/028
房屋細部	PLACES	/030
客廳	LIVING ROOM	/032
臥室	BED ROOM	/033
廚房	KITCHEN	/034
浴室	BATHROOM	/036
育嬰房	NURSERY	/038
房屋外觀	OUTSIDE APPEARANCE	/040
家居瑣事	HOUSEHOLD CHORES	/042
片語慣用語	IDIOMS AND EXPRESSIONS	/044
中文英文大不同	A WORLD APART	/046

佛要金裝，人要衣裝

FINE FEATHERS MAKE FINE BIRDS

衣服	CLOTHES	/048
鞋類	FOOTWEAR	/053
片語慣用語	IDIOMS AND EXPRESSIONS	/055
中文英文大不同	A WORLD APART	/057
隨身用品	PERSONAL BELONGINGS	/058
片語慣用語	IDIOMS AND EXPRESSIONS	/064
中文英文大不同	A WORLD APART	/065
化妝品	COSMETICS AND TOILETRIES	/066
片語慣用語	IDIOMS AND EXPRESSIONS	/071
中文英文大不同	A WORLD APART	/072

父母子女；言行應對進退

FAMILY & HUMAN RELATIONSHIPS

家庭	FAMILY	/074
人	PEOPLE	/078
人生階段	STAGES	/081
人格特質	PERSONALITY QUALITIES	/083
片語慣用語	IDIOMS AND EXPRESSIONS	/088
中文英文大不同	A WORLD APART	/091

身體部位器官

KNOW THYSELF

身體內部/外表	BODY(EXTERNAL & INTERNAL)	/094
疾病，症狀與受傷	DISEASES, SYMPTOMS & INJURIES	/099
體檢和治療	PHYSICAL CHECKUP & TREATMENTS	/104
藥品	MEDICINE	/106
片語慣用語	IDIOMS AND EXPRESSIONS	/107
中文英文大不同	A WORLD APART	/110

天上飛的、地上走的、土裡長的

ANIMALS, BIRDS, PLANTS & TREES

動物	Animals	/112
棲息地	Dwellings	/120
單位	Groupings	/121
幼獸	Young Animals	/123
鳥類	Birds	/125
片語慣用語	Idioms and Expressions	/131
拈花惹草	Plants and Trees	/135
片語慣用語	Idioms and Expressions	/143
中文英文大不同	A World Apart	/145

七情六慾 147

Emotions

相關名詞	Nouns	/148
相關動詞	Verbs	/152
相關形容詞	Adjectives	/154
片語慣用語	Idioms and Expressions	/156
中文英文大不同	A World Apart	/158

做甚麼哪裡做 161

What to Do and Where to Do It

工作	Jobs and Work	/162
片語慣用語	Idioms and Expressions	/175
中文英文大不同	A World Apart	/177
各行各業	Stores & Shops, Agencies & Services	/178
中文英文大不同	A World Apart	/186

醫藥保健 189

Medicine and Health

地點處所	Places & Areas	/190
設備	Equipment	/192
醫事人員	People	/194
治療過程	Processes	/196
藥品	Medicine	/198

醫療問題 PROBLEMS /200
疾病和狀況 DISEASE AND CONDITIONS /203
片語慣用語 IDIOMS AND EXPRESSIONS /207
中文英文大不同 A WORLD APART /210

211 運動比賽
SPORTS AND GAMES

名稱 NAMES /212
裝備 EQUIPMENT /215
場所 AREAS /217
片語慣用語 IDIOMS AND EXPRESSIONS /218
自娛娛人 AMUSEMENT /220
片語慣用語 IDIOMS AND EXPRESSIONS /237
中文英文大不同 A WORLD APART /238

人算不如天算
MAN PROPOSES, GOD DISPOSES

天災人禍 DISASTERS /240
片語慣用語 IDIOMS AND EXPRESSIONS /245
中文英文大不同 A WORLD APART /246
能源環境 ENERGY AND ENVIRONMENT /247
中文英文大不同 A WORLD APART /252

大江東去，淘盡多少風雲字
DO YOU KNOW THAT WORDS COME AND WORDS GO!

總筆劃索引

英文索引

Unit 1

民以食為天

EVERYTHING YOU NEED TO KNOW ABOUT EATING

蔬菜	VEGETABLES
水果	FRUIT
麵包	BREAD
盒裝食品	PACKED GOODS
調味料	CONDIMENTS(SEASONINGS)
肉類，家禽與海鮮	MEAT, POULTRY & SEAFOOD
乳製品	DAIRY
甜點	DESSERT
香料	SPICE & FLAVORING
飲料	BEVERAGE
餐盤、餐具與餐室	DISHES, UTENSILS & DINING ROOM
烹飪器皿	COOKING UTENSILS
烹飪技巧	CULINARY SKILLS
片語慣用語	IDIOMS AND EXPRESSIONS
中文英文大不同	A WORLD APART

002

VEGETABLES

中文	英文
山藥	Chinese yam
冬瓜	butternut squash
冬蔥；紅蔥頭	shallot
包心菜	cabbage
玉米	corn
甘[番]薯	sweet potato
（小）白菜	(baby) Bok choy
（大）白菜	Chinese cabbage
竹筍	bamboo shoot
芋頭	taro
豆；蠶豆（例：紅豆，大豆，四季豆/泛指豆筴可食用的豆類，菜豆，皇帝豆，黑豆）	bean(small beans, soya beans, string bean/kidney beans, lima beans, black beans)
豆芽	bean sprout
芽甘藍	brussels sprouts
芹菜	celery

VEGETABLES 蔬菜

▸中文	▸英文
花椰菜	cauliflower
金瓜	acorn squash
青花菜	broccoli
青椒	green pepper
青蔥	scallion, green onion
南瓜	pumpkin, squash
（珍珠）洋蔥	(pearl) onion
秋葵	okra
紅洋蔥	red onion
胡蘿蔔	carrot
苦瓜	bitter gourd
茄子	eggplant
韭菜	Chinese chive, leek
香菇	mushroom
馬鈴薯	potato
瓠瓜	battle gourd

004

VEGETABLES 蔬菜

中文	英文
甜椒	bell pepper
甜菜	beet
朝鮮薊	artichoke
番茄	tomato
菠菜	spinach
黃瓜	cucumber
萵苣	lettuce
蓮藕	lotus root
豌豆	pea
蕪菁	turnip
蘆筍	asparagus
櫻桃[迷你]蘿蔔	radish
蘿蔔（大根）	Chinese radish/daikon
韮黃	leek sprout(s) [shoot]

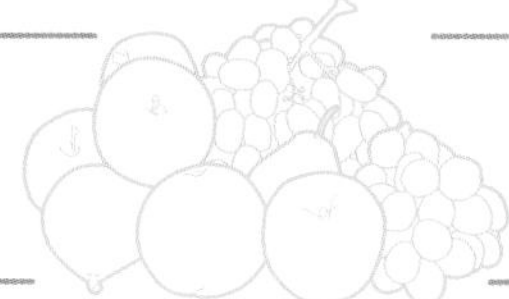

FRUIT 水果

中文	英文
木瓜	papaya
西瓜	watermelon
李子	plum
杏子	apricot
芒果	mango
奇異果	kiwi
油桃	nectarine
柳橙	orange
香瓜	muskmelon
香瓜，哈蜜瓜	honeydew
香蕉	banana
洋香瓜，哈密瓜	cantaloupe
桃子	peach
草莓	strawberry
梨子	pear
棗子	date

FRUIT
水果

中文	英文
無花果	fig
萊姆	lime
椰子	coconut
葡萄	grape
葡萄柚	grapefruit
葡萄乾	raisin
酪梨	avocado
蜜棗	prune
鳳梨	pineapple
蔓越莓	cranberry
橘子	tangerine
檸檬	lemon
藍莓	blueberry
覆盆子	raspberry
蘋果	apple
櫻桃	cherry

BREAD
麵包

▸ 中文	▸ 英文
丹麥麵包	Danish pastry
牛角麵包	croissant
奶精	cream
玉米麵包	corn bread
烤麵包（片），土司	toast
甜甜圈	doughnut
蛋糕粉	cake mix
麥片	oatmeal
焙果	bagel
圓麵包	(hamburger) bun
餅乾	biscuit
穀類	grain
薄煎餅	pancake
雞蛋餅	waffle
鬆餅，馬芬	English muffin
麵包	bread
麵包捲	roll

008

PACKED GOODS
盒裝食品

中文	英文
白米	rice
通心粉	macaroni
義大利麵條	spaghetti
餅乾	cookie
穀類食品	cereal
薄脆餅乾	crackers
麵條	noodles

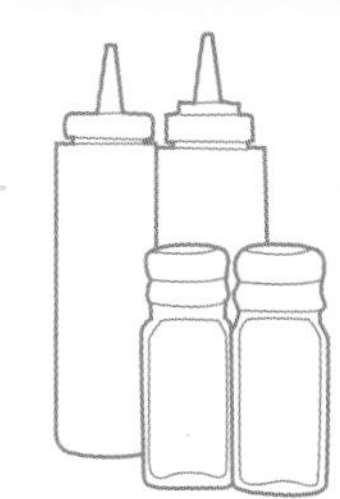

CONDIMENTS(SEASONINGS)
調味料

▸中文	▸英文
莎莎醬（墨西哥料理用沾醬）	salsa
沙拉醬	salad dressing
芥末醬	mustard
美乃滋	mayonnaise (mayo)
胡椒	pepper
料理油	(cooking) oil
番茄醬	ketchup
醋	vinegar
醃漬類開胃食品（例：酸黃瓜，橄欖）	relish (pickles, olives)
橄欖油	olive oil
醬油	soy sauce
鹽	salt

MEAT, POULTRY & SEAFOOD
肉類，家禽與海鮮

▸ 中文	▸ 英文
大比目魚	halibut
小蝦	shrimp
火腿	ham
火雞	turkey
牛肉（例：碎牛肉，烤牛肉，腰肉菲力；腰肉紐約，牛小排，肋眼）	beef (ground beef, roast beef, tenderloin/ fillet, sirloin/New York, spare rib, rib eye)
羊肉（例：羊腿，羊排）	mutton (leg of lamb, lamb chops)
肉丸子	meatball
明蝦	prawn
扇貝	scallops
蛤蜊	clams
煙燻肉	bacon
漢堡肉	hamburger/meat patty
熱狗	hot dog

MEAT, POULTRY & SEAFOOD 肉類，家禽與海鮮

▸ 中文	▸ 英文
蝶魚片	filet of sole
豬肉（例：豬腳，豬排，五花肉）	pork (knuckle, pork chop, pork belly)
鴨肉	duck
龍蝦	lobster
鮭魚	salmon
雞肉（例：雞胸肉，不去骨雞腿，去骨雞腿肉，雞翅）	chicken (chicken breast, chicken legs/drumsticks, chick thighs, chicken wings)
蟹	crabs
鯰魚	catfish
鰈魚，比目魚	flounder
鱈魚	cod
鱒魚	trout

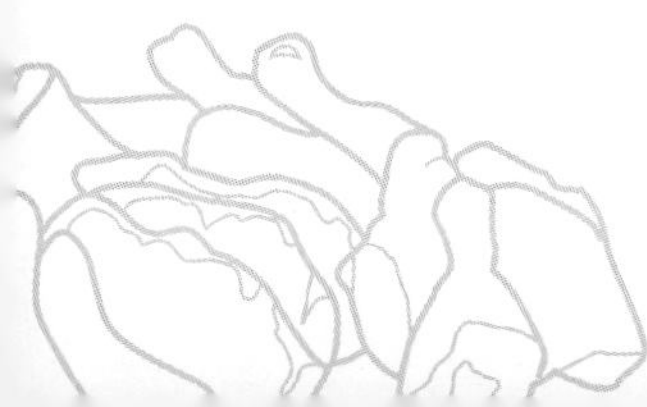

012

DAIRY
乳製品

▸ 中文	▸ 英文
牛奶奶油混合乳	half and half
奶油	butter
奶油乳酪	cream cheese
奶精	cream
冰淇淋	ice cream
低脂牛奶（牛奶，脫脂牛奶）	low fat milk ((whole) milk, skim milk)
乳酪	cheese
植物[人造]奶油，乳瑪琳	margarine
鄉村起司	cottage cheese
酸奶（油）	sour cream
優格	yogurt

DESSERT 甜點

▶中文	▶英文
布丁	pudding
布朗尼（內有乾果的一種巧克力糖糕）	brownie
肉桂[果醬，蛋糕]捲	cinnamon [jelly, desser] roll
杯子蛋糕	cupcake
法式捲餅	crepe
泡芙	puff
派	pie
捲餅	turnover
蛋糕	cake
聖代	sundae

SPICE & FLAVORING
香料

中文	英文
丁香	clove
大蒜	garlic
小茴香	cumin
月桂葉	bay leave
可可	cocoa
肉桂	cinnamon
咖哩	curry
芥末	mustard
洋香菜，荷蘭芹	parsley
紅椒粉	paprika
香料植物，草藥	herb
香菜	coriander
迷迭香	rosemary
荳蔻	nutmeg
紫蘇，羅勒，九層塔	basil
奧勒岡・牛至（烹飪用屬薄荷性的植物）	oregano

SPICE & FLAVORING 香料

▸ 中文	▸ 英文
蜂蜜	honey
鼠尾草	sage
辣椒	chili pepper (cayenne pepper)
蒔蘿	dill
糖	sugar
糖漿	syrup
薑	ginger

016

BEVERAGE 飲料

▸ 中文	▸ 英文
不含酒精的飲料	soft drink
水（礦泉水）	water (mineral water)
可樂	coke
白蘭地	brandy
汽水	soda
咖啡	coffee
果汁	juice
威士忌	whiskey
烈酒	liquor
茶	tea
啤酒	beer
麥酒	ale
無咖啡因的咖啡	decaf. (decaffeinated)
葡萄酒	wine
綜合果汁酒	(fruit) punch
檸檬水	lemonade

DISHES, UTENSILS & DINING ROOM
餐盤、餐具與餐室

▸ 中文	▸ 英文
大淺盤（通常為橢圓形）	platter
大湯匙	tablespoon
大碗	serving bowl
大盤	serving dish
水壺	pitcher
奶油[喝咖啡用的奶精]壺	creamer
奶油碟	butter dish
托盤	tray
沙拉碗	salad bowl
咖啡壺	coffee pot
胡椒瓶	pepper shaker
桌布	table cloth
（紙）餐巾	(paper) napkin
茶杯托盤	saucer
茶匙	tea spoon

DISHES, UTENSILS & DINING ROOM
餐盤、餐具與餐室

▸ 中文	▸ 英文
茶壺	tea pot
馬克杯	mug
瓷器櫥櫃	china cabinet
糖罐	sugar bowl
餐刀	knife
餐叉	fork
餐桌，餐椅	(dining room) table, chair
餐盤	plate
鹽瓶	salt shaker

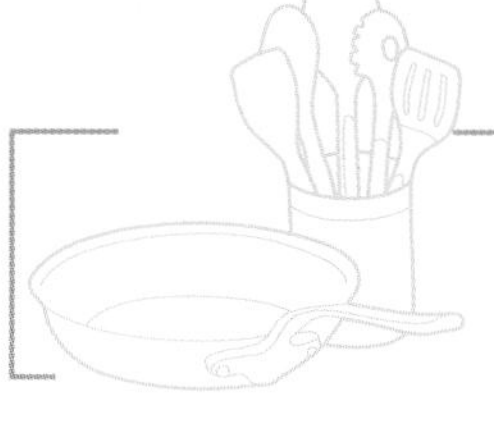

COOKING UTENSILS
烹飪器皿

中文	英文
大碗	bowl
平底鍋	pan
打蛋器	eggbeater
削皮器	peeler
食物處理機	food processor
食譜	recipe
烤肉用具	broiler
烤盤	baking pan
烤箱	oven
砧板	chopping board
桿麵棍	rolling pin
烹飪用書	cookbook
壺；鍋	kettle
量杯	measuring cup
開罐[瓶器]	can [bottle] opener
煎鍋	frying pan

020

Cooking Utensils
烹飪器皿

▸ 中文	▸ 英文
漏匙	draining spoon
蓋子	lid
燉鍋	stew pot
壓力鍋	pressure cooker
鍋鏟	turner
濾網	strainer
爐子	stove, burner
麵包模	bread pan
攪和器，果汁機	blender
攪拌器（打蛋用）	whisk
攪拌器（如拌沙拉用）	mixer

CULINARY SKILLS
烹飪技巧

▸ 中文	▸ 英文
切	cut (up)
切丁	dice
切片	slice
切柳	fillet
切絲	shred
文火慢烤	roast
文火慢煮	simmer
水煮	boil
加入	add
打破；折斷	break
扒	fried-simmer
白灼	scale
刨絲	grate
剁碎	chop (up)
拔絲	caramelize
炒	stir-fry

CULINARY SKILLS 烹飪技巧

中文	英文
削皮	peel
炸	fry
紅燒	braise
倒	pour
烘培	bake
烤	broil
烹煮	cook
搗成糊狀	beat
嫩煎	sauté
蒸	steam
燉	stew
燒烤	grill
攪拌	stir

IDIOMS AND EXPRESSIONS
片語慣用語

▸ 中文	▸ 英文
13個	baker's dozen
一人吃兩人補；懷孕	to eat for two
一文不值	to not worth a bean
一箭雙鵰	to eat one's cake and have it
人多手雜	too many cooks spoil the broth
上流社會	upper crust
心不在焉	out to lunch
充實的一餐	square meal
加強	to beef up
可疑	something fishy
再多再好也不要	not for all the tea in China
吃的很少	to eat like a bird
吃相難看	to pig out
忍氣吞聲	to eat humble pie

Idioms and Expressions

片語慣用語

▸ 中文	▸ 英文
性急地問問題	to pepper with questions
空談不如實證	proof of pudding is in eating
很容易	as easy as apple pie
思考反省的事	food for thought
挑嘴的人	a picky eater
洩露祕密	to spill the beans
為已發生的事難過	to cry over the spilt milk
狼吞虎嚥地吃	to wolf down one's food
鬼扯騙人，一派胡言	baloney
貪多必失	to bite more than one can chew
陳舊[陳腐]的	corny
魚和熊掌兼得	to have one's cake and eat it
發牢騷	to beef about

IDIOMS AND EXPRESSIONS
片語慣用語

▸ 中文	▸ 英文
集中風險	to put one's eggs in one basket
愛炫耀的人	hot dog
禁果	fòrbidden fruit
節食	to be on diet
精華	cream of the crop
酸葡萄	sour grapes
慫恿	to egg on
養家活口	to bring home the bacon
壞人	bad egg
關係密切	like two peas in one pod

A World Apart
中文英文大不同

因為思維不同，語言的使用也有差異；中國人說「喝湯」，但在英文中我們說「eat one's soup」；中文用「我們一起吃午餐」，英文則用「Let's do lunch sometimes.」。

有時，英文中在特殊節日也有應景的用字和說法，例如「clam bake」，美國東北角的各州在國慶日（Independence Day）時，在海灘以燒烤海鮮來替代傳統的烤肉；感恩節（Thanksgiving）也大不同，一般人吃火雞但在某些地方則有「chiduckey」（chicken duck turkey），先將雞置入鴨中，再把鴨子放入火雞肚中；三雞一吃，不亦樂乎！

最近，常有人把「comfort food」掛在嘴邊；離鄉遊子身居異國，突然發現隔壁店裡竟然有奶酥麵包、珍珠奶茶、刈包和雞排，雖然味道或有不同但卻能在吞食之際一解鄉愁；「慰藉食物」一詞也就應運而生！

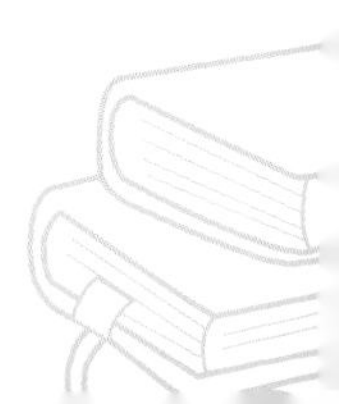

Unit 2

金窩銀窩比不上自己的狗窩

EAST OR WEST, THERE IS NO PLACE LIKE HOME

房屋式樣 HOUSING
房屋細部 PLACES
客廳 LIVING ROOM
臥室 BED ROOM
廚房 KITCHEN
浴室 BATHROOM
育嬰房 NURSERY
房屋外觀 OUTSIDE APPEARANCE
家居瑣事 HOUSEHOLD CHORES
片語慣用語 IDIOMS AND EXPRESSIONS
中文英文大不同 A WORLD APART

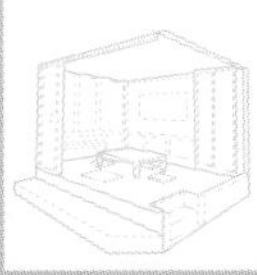

HOUSING
房屋式樣

中文	英文
大廈，大樓	mansion
大樓	building
山中小木屋	chalet
公寓	apartment, (英) flat
分戶出售的公寓	condominium (condo)
木屋	log cabin
冰屋	igloo
別墅；渡假村	villa
拖車式房屋	trailer house
牧場莊園	ranch house
前面一層後面兩層的房子	salt-box
城鎮宅邸	town house
活動房屋	mobile home
皇宮	palace
茅屋	hut
茅草房屋	bungalow

HOUSING 房屋式樣

中文	英文
套房公寓	studio
高級頂樓公寓	penthouse
高樓	high-rise
帳篷	tent
船屋	houseboat
莊園	manor
單戶住宅	house
鄉間宅邸	country house
農舍	cottage
摩天大樓	skyscraper
樓中樓；雙層公寓	loft
樹屋	tree house

PLACES
房屋細部

▸ 中文	▸ 英文
土間；玄關	mud room
工作室	utility room
天井；露臺	patio
地下室	basement
地窖	cellar
有玻璃天花板的室內空間	sun room
衣櫥	closet
私室；小書房	den
育嬰房	nursery
車庫	garage
臥室	bedroom
門廊；陽臺	porch
客廳	living room
洗衣間	laundry room
家人在廚房進餐時的角落	nook

PLACES
房屋細部

▸ 中文	▸ 英文
家庭室	family room
書房	study
浴室	bath (room)
草坪	lawn
院子	yard
廁所	toilet
飯廳	dining room
遊戲間	play room
閣樓	attic
廚房	kitchen
餐具室；食品儲藏室	pantry
儲藏室	store room
廳	hall

Living Room
客廳

中文	英文
小茶几	end table
天花板	ceiling
立燈，落地燈	floor lamp
百葉窗	blind
扶手椅	armchair
沙發	sofa, couch
書架，書櫃	bookcase
茶几	coffee table
帷	shade
窗戶	window
窗簾	curtain
幔	drapes
壁櫥	wall unit
壁爐	fireplace
燈	lamp
雜誌架	magazine holder
雙人座沙發	loveseat

BED ROOM
臥室

▸ 中文	▸ 英文
五斗櫃	chest (with drawers)
床（雙人床，兩張單人床，五呎×五呎，五呎×六呎，六呎×六呎）	bed (double, twin, twin, queen, king)
床架	bed box [frame]
床單	sheet
床罩	bed spread
床墊	mattress
床頭板	headboard
床頭櫃	night stand [table]
枕頭	pillow
枕頭套	pillowcase
夏被	quilt
梳妝臺	dresser, bureau
被子	comforter
毯子	blanket
電毯	electric blanket

KITCHEN 廚房

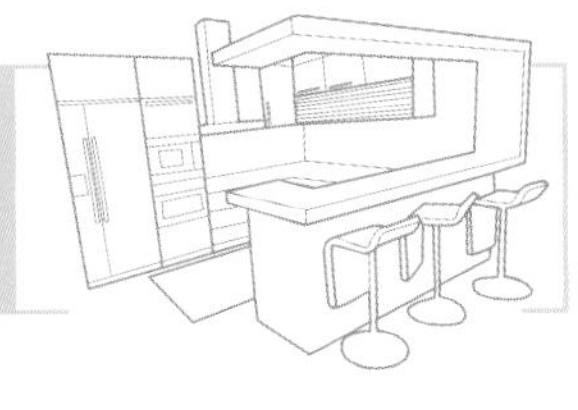

▸ 中文	▸ 英文
小烤箱	toaster oven
水槽	sink
水龍頭	faucet
冰箱	refrigerator (fridge)
有蓋的罐子	canister
冷凍庫	freezer
咖啡機	coffee maker
垃圾桶	garbage pail
垃圾壓縮機	trash compactor
垃圾輾碎機	garbage disposal
抹布	dishrag
洗碗專用洗滌劑	dishwasher detergent
洗碗精	dishwasher liquid
洗碗機	dishwasher
烤麵包機	toaster
紙巾架	paper towel holder

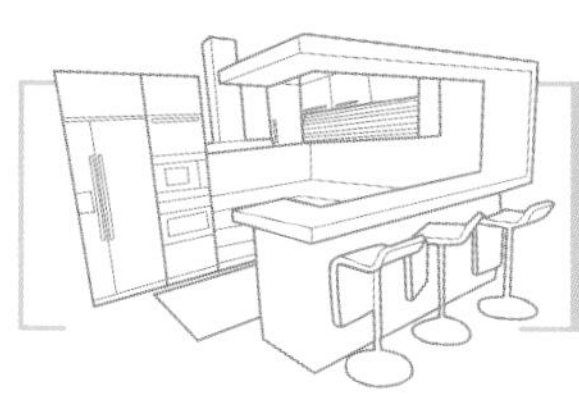

KITCHEN 廚房

▸ 中文	▸ 英文
茶壺	tea kettle
（電動）開罐器	(electric) can opener
微波爐	microwave
碗盤瀝水架	dish rack
隔熱墊	potholder
調味罐架	spice rack
餐桌墊	placement
餐椅，餐桌	kitchen chair [table]
擦碗布	dish towel
櫥櫃	cabinet

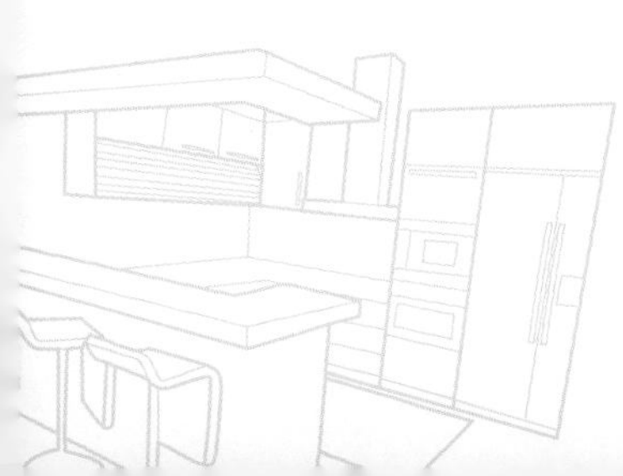

BATHROOM
浴室

中文	英文
毛巾架	towel rack
（電動）牙刷	(electric) toothbrush
吹風機	hair dryer
防滑墊	rubber mat
抽風機	fan
空氣芳香劑	air freshener
肥皂盒	soap dish
按壓式肥皂	soap dispenser
架子	shelf
洗衣籃	hamper
海綿	sponge
浴室梳妝臺	vanity
浴室擦腳墊	bath mat
浴缸	(bath) tub
馬桶（馬桶座，馬桶刷）	toilet (toilet seat, toilet brush)
排水孔	drain

037

BATHROOM
浴室

中文	英文
漱口杯	cup
廢紙簍	wastebasket
磅秤	scale
蓮蓬頭（浴簾）	shower (shower curtain)
藥櫃	medicine cabinet
鏡子	mirror

NURSERY 育嬰房

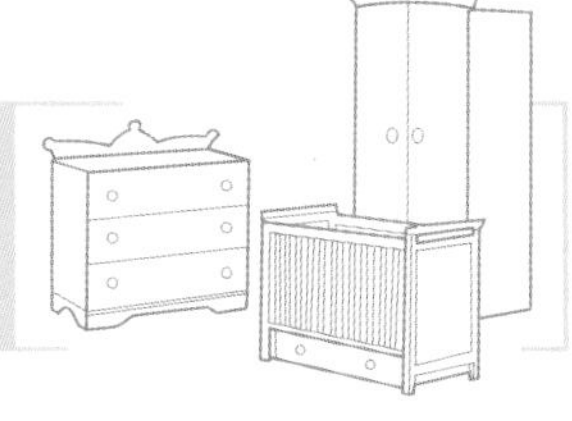

中文	英文
尿布桶	diaper pail
折疊式嬰兒推車	stroller
夜燈	night light
玩具箱	toy chest
前背式嬰兒背帶	baby frontpack
後背式嬰兒背帶	baby backpack
食物保溫箱	food warmer
高腳椅	high chair
掛式旋轉玩具	mobile
換尿布檯	changing table
搖籃	cradle
遊戲床	playpen
學步車	walker
嬰兒床	crib
嬰兒汽車安全椅	baby seat
嬰兒馬桶	potty

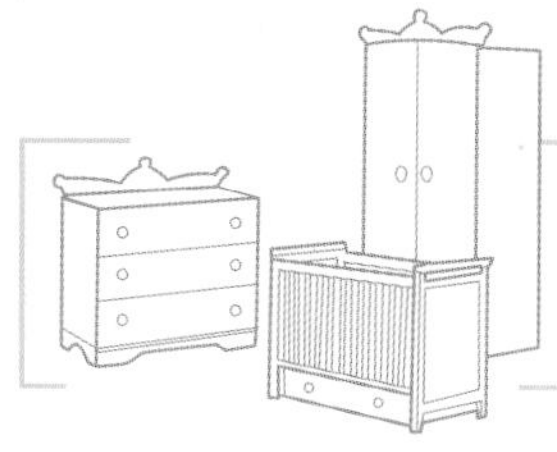

NURSERY 育嬰房

▸ 中文	▸ 英文
嬰兒專用墊高椅	booster seat
嬰兒推車	baby carriage
嬰兒提籃	baby carrier
嬰兒無線監測器[對講機]	baby monitor [intercom]
嬰兒搖鈴	rattle
攜帶式嬰兒床	portable crib

040

OUTSIDE APPEARANCE
房屋外觀

▸ 中文	▸ 英文
工具儲藏室	tool shed
（活動式）百葉窗	shutter
私家車道	driveway
車庫	garage
門把	door knob
門鈴	doorbell
信箱	mailbox
前門	front door
前廊	front porch
前廊臺階	front steps
屋頂	roof
後門	back door
烤肉架	barbeque grill
紗門	screen door
紗窗	window screen
草坪	lawn

OUTSIDE APPEARANCE
房屋外觀

▸ 中文	▸ 英文
側門	side door
煙囪	chimney
路燈（柱）	lamppost
電視天線	TV antenna
衛星接收器，小耳朵	satellite dish
露天平臺	deck
露臺	patio
籬笆	fence

HOUSEHOLD CHORES
家居瑣事

▸ 中文	▸ 英文
打蠟	wax the floor
吸塵（例：吸塵器配件，吸塵袋，手提攜吸塵器，掃地毯器）	vacuum the house (vacuum cleaner attachments, vacuum cleaner bag, hand vacuum, carpet sweeper)
拖地（例：吸塵拖把，乾拖把，海綿拖把，溼拖把）	mop the floor (dust mop, dry mop, sponge mop, wet mop)
洗衣服	do the laundry
洗窗戶（水管，刷子，水桶）	wash the window (hose, scrub brush, bucket)
洗碗盤	do the dishes
倒垃圾（垃圾桶）	take out the garbage (trash can, garbage can)
清掃浴室	clean the bathroom
換床單	change the linen [sheets]

Household Chores
家居瑣事

中文	英文
摺衣服	fold the laundry
鋪床	make the bed
撣書架上的灰塵（例：雞毛撢子，畚箕）	dust the bookshelves (feather duster, dust-pan)
燙衣服	do the ironing
擦亮家具（家具亮光劑）	polish the furniture (furniture polish)
擺設餐桌	set the table
晒衣服	hang out the laundry

Idioms and Expressions

片語慣用語

▸ 中文	▸ 英文
上床睡覺	to hit the sake
大肆整頓	to make a clean sweep of...
大鳴不平	to raise the roof
不周詳的計畫	a house of cards
中要害的，中肯的	to hit home
少了溫馨，房子不是家	a house is not a home
死巷子；沒結果的事	blind alley
災難的前兆	handwritings on the wall
和左鄰右舍較量	to keep up with the Joneses
客主易位，扭轉局勢	to turn the tables on
乘坐帚柄；無遠弗及	to ride the broomstick
掃興[煞風景]者	wet blanket
新官上任三把火	a new broom sweeps clean

Idioms and Expressions
片語慣用語

▸ 中文	▸ 英文
整潔的	spick and span
隱瞞掩飾過失或缺點	to whitewash
變更住址或職業	to pull the stakes

A WORLD APART

中文英文大不同

「A man's house is his castle」，「Home sweet home」；何時說「home」何時說「house」呢？

* 「house」在英文中是實體，實際的建築物。例如：「Welcome to my house!」「Why don't you come over my house for supper tonight?」
* 「home」是個抽象的觀念，它代表了一個想法或某種象徵。例如：「Home is where one's hearts belongs to」，「Home-coming Queen」（學校選美皇后）。

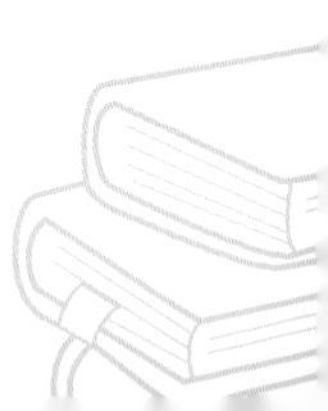

Unit 3

佛要金裝，人要衣裝

FINE FEATHERS MAKE FINE BIRDS

衣服	CLOTHES
鞋類	FOOTWEAR
片語慣用語	IDIOMS AND EXPRESSIONS
中文英文大不同	A WORLD APART
隨身用品	PERSONAL BELONGINGS
片語慣用語	IDIOMS AND EXPRESSIONS
中文英文大不同	A WORLD APART
化妝品	COSMETICS AND TOILETRIES
片語慣用語	IDIOMS AND EXPRESSIONS
中文英文大不同	A WORLD APART

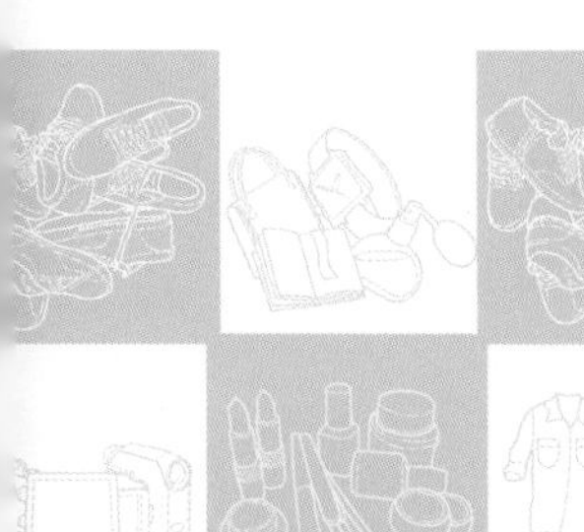

CLOTHES 衣服

▸中文	▸英文
T恤	t-shirt
三角褲	briefs, underpants
上漿的正式襯衫	dress shirt
大衣	overcoat
女用內褲	panties
女用襯衫	blouse
內衣襯衣	underclothes
內褲；襯褲	underpants
手套	gloves
斗篷	poncho
毛衣	sweater
毛線褲	sweater pants
牛仔褲	(blue) jeans
四角[平口]內褲	boxer shorts
（厚重）外套	coat
孕婦裝	maternity dress
尼龍襪子	nylons

CLOTHES 衣服

中文	英文
正式外套	dinner jacket
皮夾克	leather jacket
皮帶	belt
皮帶扣環	buckle
休閒西裝外套	sport coat, jacket
休閒襯衫	sport shirt
吊褲[襪]帶	suspenders
有帽沿的帽子	hat
汗衫貼身內衣	undershirt
羽毛背心	down vest
羽絨外套	down jacket
耳罩	earmuffs
西裝上衣	jacket
束腰	girdle
防水衣，雨衣	slicker
披肩	cape

050

CLOTHES 衣服

▸ 中文	▸ 英文
泳衣	bathing suit
長披肩	stole
長袖運動衫	sweatshirt
長褲	pants, trousers
雨衣	raincoat
雨鞋	rain boots
便褲	slacks
洋裝	dress
背心；馬甲	vest
風衣外套	trench coat
套裙	slip
套裝	suit
浴袍	bathrobe
胸罩	bra
酒會外套（非全正式）	cocktail jacket
高領毛衣	turtleneck

CLOTHES 衣服

▸ 中文	▸ 英文
假髮	wig
晚禮服	(evening) gown
粗棉布的工作服	dungarees
連身衣	snowsuit
連身衣褲	jumpsuit
連指手套	mittens
連帽毛外套	parka
圍巾	mufflers, scarf
無袖背心	tank top
無袖連身裙	jumper
無邊帽	cap
短褲	shorts
絨布寬鬆外套	blazer
滑雪外套	ski jacket
裙子	skirt
運動短褲	running shorts

CLOTHES
衣服

▸ 中文	▸ 英文
（前胸雙排鈕扣）對襟毛衣	cardigan
睡衣	pajamas
睡袍	nightgown
緊身運動衣	leotard
緊身褲	tights
領帶	(neck) tie
領結	bow tie
寬大的工作服	overalls
燕尾服	tuxedo
褲裝	pantsuit
褲襪	pantyhose
襪帶	garter

FOOTWEAR
鞋類

中文	英文
人字拖	thongs, flip-flops
及膝襪子	knee socks
方頭鞋	square-toe
木屐	clogs
牛仔馬[短]靴	cowboy [dress, riding] boots
平底鞋	flats
尖頭鞋	pointy-shoe
帆布運動鞋	sneakers
拖鞋，淺口便鞋	slippers
厚底鞋	platform
娃娃鞋	Mary Janes
後跟勾帶鞋	sling-back
套鞋，包腳鞋	overshoes
高筒球鞋	high-tops, high-top sneakers
高筒橡皮套鞋	galoshes

054

Footwear
鞋類

中文	英文
高跟鞋	high heels
涼鞋	sandals
（北美印第安人穿的）鹿皮軟鞋	moccasins
絲襪	stockings
運動鞋	gym shoes
慢跑鞋	running shoes
網球鞋	tennis shoes
鞋子	shoes
鞋帶	shoelace, shoe strings
橡皮套鞋	rubbers
繫帶牛津鞋	oxfords
襪子	socks

IDIOMS AND EXPRESSIONS

片語慣用語

▸ 中文	▸ 英文
人要衣裝	clothes make the man
小本經營	on a shoestring
打扮漂亮	dolled up
如坐針氈	on pins and needles
存不住錢	to burn a hole in one's pocket
抓住	to collar someone
受母親或妻子的操縱	tied to someone's apron strings
信口開河	to spin a yarn
保持冷靜	to keep one's shirt on
海底撈針，徒勞無功	to look for the needle in the haystack
神氣十足的小人物	stuffed shirt
耗損	wear and tear
強行留人長談	to buttonhole some-one
得理饒人	if the shoe fits, wear it

IDIOMS AND EXPRESSIONS
片語慣用語

▸ 中文	▸ 英文
情勢已經轉過來	the shoe's on the other foot
盛裝	all dress up
設身處地，將心比心	to be in one's shoes
等待最後結果	to wait for the other shoe to drop
暗中傷人	to hit below the belt
溫和地	to handle with kid gloves
輸光	to lose one's shirt
擦亮	spit and polish

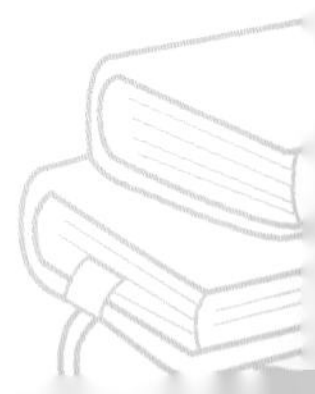

A WORLD APART

中文英文大不同

外國人的穿著相當考究，倒也不是非名牌（brand-names）不可，而是因時、因事而在穿著打扮上有些必須遵守的規則（dress code）；所以常聽人說：「put on one's Sunday's best」（最好的衣裳）。但現在因為新新人類的充斥職場，很多服飾傳統都有了變通，舉例說：「Dress-down Friday」，在週五時可著便服上班；雖然如此，短褲（shorts）和拖鞋涼鞋（sandals）依然是大大地不可！記得：如有穿著上的問題，參考員工手冊「Dos and Don'ts for Employeess」上的規定。

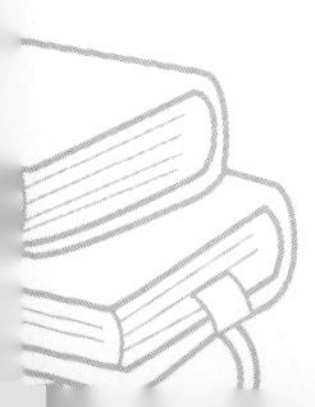

PERSONAL BELONGINGS

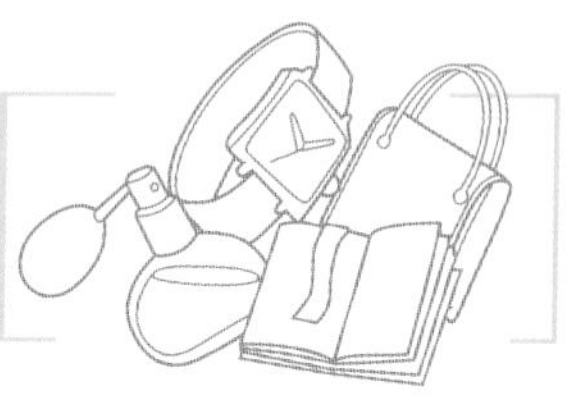

▸ 中文	▸ 英文
MP3播放器	MP3 player
女用胸針	brooch
小物包	barrette
小零錢包	coin purse
公事包	briefcase
手[拐]杖	cane
手[腕]錶	wristwatch
手帕	handkerchief
手持式個人電腦	handheld PC (HPC)
手挽斜背袋；隨身行李	overnight bag
手提或膝上型電腦	laptop computer
手提袋	handbag
手機	cell phone
手鐲	bracelet
支票簿	checkbook
方頭巾	kerchief

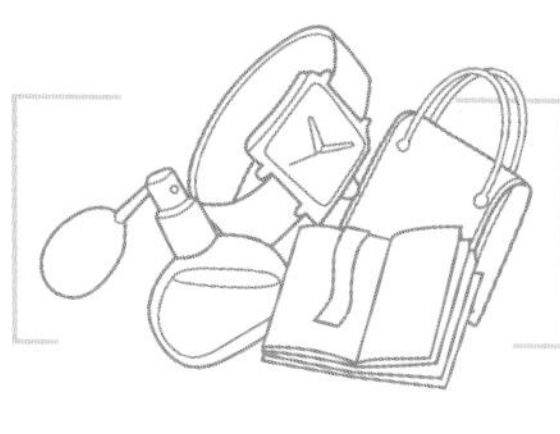

PERSONAL BELONGINGS
隨身用品

▸ 中文	▸ 英文
水手刀，小刀	Jack knife
火柴	matches
打火機	lighter
皮夾	wallet
皮夾子	billfold
名片夾	calling [business] card case
有支架的拐杖	crutches
耳環	earring
別針；大頭針	pin
別針型領帶夾	tin pin
吸鼻煙	snuff
身分手掛牌	ID bracelet
身分證	identification
防狼噴霧器	mace
咀嚼式菸草	chewing [smokeless, dipping] tobacco

PERSONAL BELONGINGS
隨身用品

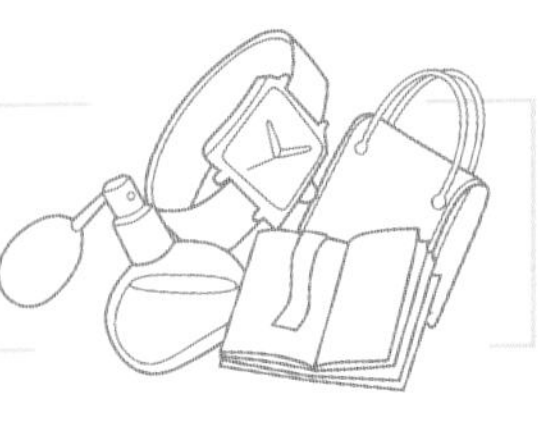

▸ 中文	▸ 英文
咀嚼式菸草袋	tobacco pouch
拔毛器	hair pull
拐杖	walking stick
肩[側背]背包	shoulder bag
雨傘	umbrella
信用卡夾	credit card case
削鉛筆刀	penknife
削鉛筆器	pencil sharper
指甲刀	nail clipper
（懸於項鍊下的）紀念品小盒子	locket
約會記事簿	date book
計算機	calculator
訂婚[學校，圖章，結婚]戒指	engagement [school, signet, wedding] ring
香菸	cigarette
原子筆；自來水筆	(ball point [fountain]) pen

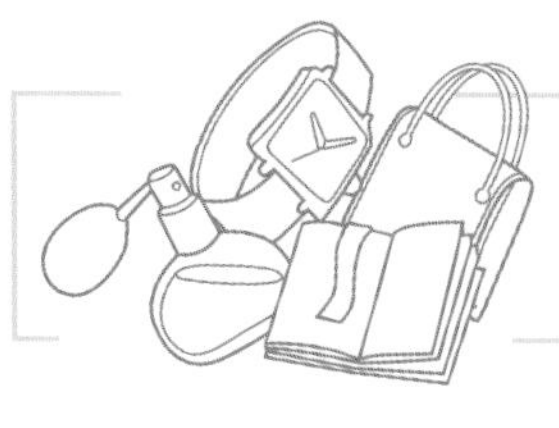

PERSONAL BELONGINGS
隨身用品

中文	英文
梳子	comb
紙巾	tissue
迷你磁碟隨身聽	minidisk player (MP)
掛在浴室的用品袋	hanging (toiletry) bag
眼鏡盒	glasses case
袖扣	cufflinks
袖珍本書	pocketbook
袋子	bag
通訊簿	address book
雪茄	cigar
麥克筆	marker
硬幣	coin
筆記型電腦	notebook PC
筆記簿	notebook
菸斗	pipe
（珠子）項鍊	beads

PERSONAL BELONGINGS 隨身用品

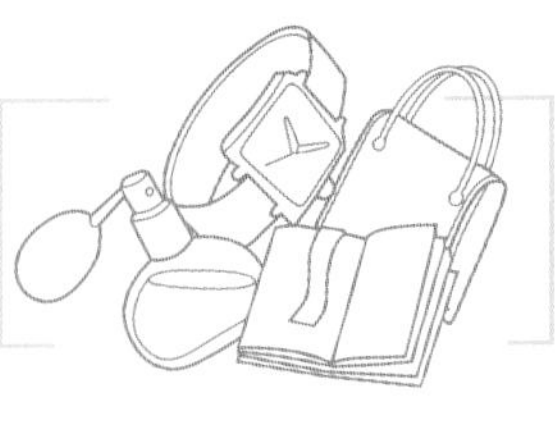

中文	英文
項鍊	necklace
傳呼器	beeper (B.B. Call)
鉛筆	pencil
（掌上）電子助理[萬用手冊]	(palm [pocket]) organizer
電子記事簿	pocket calendar
零錢包	change purse
領帶夾	tie clip
撲克牌	playing cards
髮夾	bobby pin
髮夾	hair pin
髮梳	hair brush
燈筆	pen light
錢包，女用手提袋	purse
隨身聽	walkman, CD player
頸鍊	choker
隱形眼鏡	contact lens

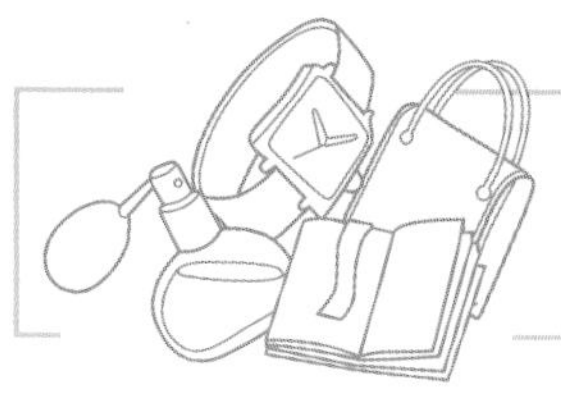

Personal Belongings 隨身用品

▸ 中文	▸ 英文
雙焦距[太陽，老花]眼鏡	bifocal [sun, reading] (eye) glasses
藥盒	pillbox
攜帶型傳呼器	pager
鑰匙圈	key ring
鑰匙鍊	key chain

IDIOMS AND EXPRESSIONS

片語慣用語

中文	英文
市鑰	key to the city
弄清楚	to make heads or tails of...
事事往光明方向看	(seeing through) rose colored glasses
拋硬幣決定	to flip a coin
狀況良好	up to snuff
記載祕密的小冊子；愛情黑名單	little black book
喜歡嗎？（你）好好考慮	to put that in one's pipe and smoke it
搶婦女錢包的人	purse snatcher
照顧的無微不至的，衣著入時的	well groomed
痴心妄想，白日夢	pipe dream

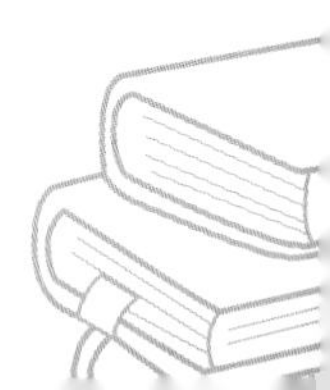

A World Apart

中文英文大不同

「personal」這個字在英語文化中是個不可輕視的字！「It's something personal.」意思：「別問！」。

千萬不要在他人明確告知是私人事情後，仍不斷打聽，「prying」或「poking one's nose into...」，還再三保證絕不會把祕密張揚出去「My lips are sealed」或「Just between you and me.」

「rose」這個字也相當有趣：

「Stop and smell the roses」，因致力投身於工作而忽略了人生中其它更有意義的事，如家人或親情，所以「停下來看看周邊美好的事物！」。

但有時精神不濟或如行屍走肉，此時，「Stop and smell the coffee!」。

COSMETICS AND TOILETRIES
化妝品

▸ 中文	▸ 英文
化妝品（名詞） 化妝（動詞）	makeup make up
手用乳液	hand lotion
手部清潔劑	hand cleanser
牙刷	toothbrush
牙粉	tooth powder
牙膏	toothpaste
牙線	dental floss
去角質	cuticlc remover
古龍香水	cologne
仿晒油	suntan lotion
冷霜，雪花膏	cold cream
沐浴油	bath oil
身體乳液	body lotion
防晒乳	sun block
防晒油	sun screen
刮鬍膏	shaving cream

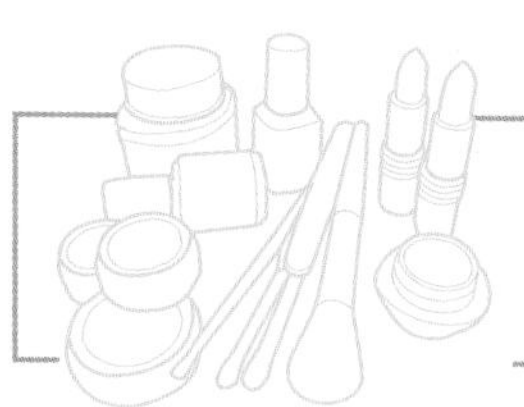

COSMETICS AND TOILETRIES 化妝品

▸ 中文	▸ 英文
刮鬍鬚後用乳液	after-shaving lotion
卸甲液	nail polish remover
拔毛鉗	hair remover, tweezers
泡沫澡	bubble bath
肥皂	bath soap, soap
花露水	toilet water
剃刀（拋棄式，單軌式，安全式，雙軌式）	razor (disposable, one-track, safety, two-track)
指甲刀[剪]	nail clippers
指甲油	nail polish
指甲砂銼	emery board
指甲銼	nail file
染髮劑	hair color [dye]
洗手肥皂	hand soap
洗面乳	facial cleanser, face wash, foaming

COSMETICS AND TOILETRIES 化妝品

▸ 中文	▸ 英文
洗眼劑	eye wash
洗髮精	shampoo
洗臉肥皂	facial soap
眉筆	eyebrow pencil
美容乳液	beauty lotion
美容霜	beauty cream
面膜	facial mask, masque
香水	perfume, scent
唇膏	lipstick
梳子	comb
浴用鹽，浴香粉（使水軟化的）	bath salts
珠光唇膏	lip gloss
紙巾，面紙	tissue
胭脂，口紅，唇膏	rouge
眼影	eye-shadow
眼線筆	eye-liner

COSMETICS AND TOILETRIES 化妝品

▸ 中文	▸ 英文
眼藥水	eye drops
脫毛藥	depilatory
軟膏，油膏	ointment
連鏡小粉盒	compact
棉花球	cotton balls
睫毛膏	mascara
腮紅	blush
裝刮鬍膏的杯子	shaving mug
隔離霜	cosmetic [makeup] base
電動刮鬍刀	(electric) shaver
漱口水	mouthwash, oral rinse
撲粉；化妝用粉	powder
潤絲精	hair rinse
潤膚膏[霜，露]	moisturizer
潤膚霜	body cream
髮刷	hair brush

COSMETICS AND TOILETRIES 化妝品

▸ 中文	▸ 英文
凝膠牙膏	toothpaste gel
嬰兒用洗髮精	baby shampoo
臉部泥膜	mudpack
護手霜	hand cream
護唇膏	lip balm
護膚霜	skin cream
體香劑（滾珠，肥皂，固態，噴霧，棒狀）	deodorant (roll-on, soap, solid, spray, stick)

Idioms and Expressions

片語慣用語

▸中文	▸英文
小夥子	a little shaver
行為漂亮才漂亮	Handsome is as handsome does.
油腔滑調的	to look oily
油頭粉面的人	a greaser
狐臭	B.O. (body odor)
很多	the great unwashed (= many)
美貌只是一層皮；沒內涵的外表	Beauty is only skin deep.
倖免於難	a close shave
情人眼裡出西施	Beauty is in the eye of the beholder.
嗅到麻煩	to smell a trouble
塗了脂粉的女人	a painted woman
愛好清潔是僅次於敬神的美德	Cleanliness is next to Godliness.
鬍渣	five o'clock shadow
嚴厲的懲罰	to wash one's mouth out with soap

A World Apart

中文英文大不同

有太多人投資太多的時間、金錢和精神在外表上；不錯，邋遢的外觀（a sloppy appearance）的確是有礙觀瞻且造成錯誤，甚至於不好的第一印象（poor first impressions），但個人保健（personal hygiene）有時更重要；是否洗澡、是否更衣、是否注重口腔清潔、是否身有異味…，有太多太多實際花費有限，但效果卻不亞於名牌產品加身的作法，不僅能營造良好印象更能讓自己受益良多（with twofold effect），就好像有人先暴飲暴食之後再去減肥中心（fat farm）拚命瘦身；如果日常多留意，不僅省錢而且效果更好！

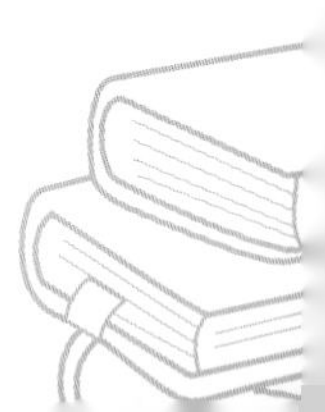

Unit 4

父母子女；言行應對進退

FAMILY & HUMAN RELATIONSHIPS

家庭	FAMILY
人	PEOPLE
人生階段	STAGES
人格特質	PERSONALITY QUALITIES
片語慣用語	IDIOMS AND EXPRESSIONS
中文英文大不同	A WORLD APART

FAMILY
家庭

▸ 中文	▸ 英文
丈夫	husband
女兒	daughter
父親	father
父親的，父系的	paternal
兄弟	brother
未婚夫[妻]	fiancé(e)
母親	mother
母親的，母系的	maternal
同父異母，同母異父，養父[母]	adoptive parent
同父異母[同母異父]的兄弟姊妹	half-brother [sister]
伯[叔]祖；舅公；姑公；姨公	granduncle
伯[叔]祖母；姑[姨]婆；舅婆	grandaunt
（小）弟[妹]	baby brother [sister]
兒子	son

FAMILY
家庭

中文	英文
叔[舅，伯，姨]公，叔[舅，伯，姨]婆	great uncle [aunt]
妻子	wife
爸爸（暱稱）	daddy, dad, pa, pop, papa
姑嬸，伯[叔]母	aunt
姊妹	sis (sister)
孤兒	orphan
岳父，公公	father-in-law
岳母，婆婆	mother-in-law
侄[外甥]女	niece
侄子，外甥	nephew
姻親	in-laws
（大）哥[姊]	(big) brother, sister
（外）孫子女	grandchild(ren)
家犬	family dog
家族，親戚	kin, kin folks

FAMILY
家庭

▸ 中文	▸ 英文
家譜，宗譜	genealogy
（外）祖父[母]	grandparent(s)
（外）祖父	grandpa
（外）祖母	grandma
配偶	spouse
堂[表]兄弟姊妹	cousin
排行中間的孩子；個性較冷漠的孩子	middle child
教父[母]；義父[母]	godparent(s)
第一任先生[太太]（不可充當保證人）	first husband [wife]
（外）曾孫子[女]	great grandchild(ren)
（外）曾祖父[母]	great grandparent(s)
媽媽（暱稱）	ma, mom, mommy
新郎	(bride) groom
新娘	bride
寡婦	widow

FAMILY 家庭

▸ 中文	▸ 英文
監護人	guardian
撫養親屬	dependent
養子[女]	adopted [foster] child
養父[母]	foster parent
親兄弟姊妹	siblings
親生父母	biological parents
親屬	relative
親屬關係，血緣	kindred
雙親，家屬，人們	folks
鰥夫	widower

PEOPLE 人

中文	英文
一行人，一夥人	party
女性友人	female friend
女朋友	girlfriend
友人，舊識	acquaintance
主人	host
古怪的男人	geezer
四肢發達頭腦簡單的人	jock
未婚夫[妻]	fiancé [fiancée]
同伴，伴侶	companion, company
同伴，夥伴	mate
同志	comrade
同事，同行	colleague
同事，朋友，夥伴	associate
老處女	spinster
男性友人	male friend
男朋友	boyfriend

PEOPLE 人

▸ 中文	▸ 英文
怪傑，發燒友	geek
性格軟弱的人	drip
朋友	friend
門徒，追隨者	disciple
信徒，擁護者	follower
室友	roommate
客人	guest
為人老實重義氣的人	square
約會對象	date
哥們，搭檔，好朋友	buddy
書呆子；書蟲	nerd
密友	crony
隊友	teammate
愛人	lover
群眾	crowd
遊伴（青少年的），黨派	gang

080

PEOPLE 人

▸ 中文	▸ 英文
遊伴，玩伴	playmate
夥伴，好友	pal
夥伴，拍檔	partner
對，組，班	team
領袖，指揮者	leader
敵人	enemy
敵手，對手	antagonist
暴民，烏合之眾	mob
親戚	relative
顧問，參事	counselor

STAGES 人生階段

▸ 中文	▸ 英文
十歲以前的孩童	pre-teen
小孩	child, kid
中年人	middle-age
尼特族（即不升學也不就業更不學習進修的人）	NEET
幼兒，嬰兒	infant
幼稚	childish
未成年的人	young adult
未成年者	juvenile
年長者，輩分高的人	elderly
年輕人	youth
成人	grownup
老年人	aged
空巢期（子女成人後離家時的父母）	empty nest(er)
青少年	adolescent

STAGES 人生階段

▸ 中文	▸ 英文
青少年（13-19歲）	teenager
孩童時代	childhood
退休人員	retiree
銀髮族	senior citizen
學步的小孩	toddler
嬰兒	baby
歸巢族，啃老族（學成就業但因經濟問題而返家居住者）	boomerang

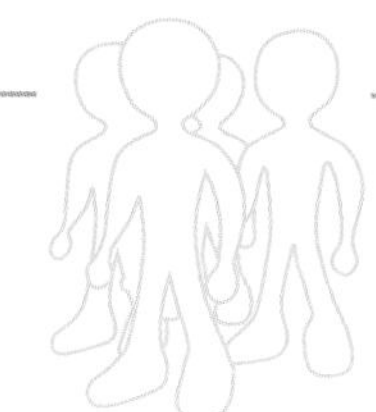

Personality Qualities 人格特質

▸ 中文	▸ 英文
大聲的	loud
大膽的，莽撞的	bold
不自然的，扭捏的	self-conscious
仁慈的	kind
友善的	friendly
令人愉快的，舒適的	pleasant
可愛的	lovely
平淡無奇的	plain
用功的	studious
合作的	cooperative
安靜的，輕聲地，沉默的	quiet
有才智的，有理性的	intelligent
有決心的	determined
有所保留的	reserved
有幫助的	helpful
有禮貌的	courteous, polite

PERSONALITY QUALITIES
人格特質

中文	英文
有藝術技巧[鑑賞力]的	artistic
自私的	selfish
自制自律的	disciplined
自負的，驕傲自滿的	conceited
行為端莊的，文雅的	well-mannered
冷漠不關心的	aloof
冷酷[冷淡，不友善]的	cold
吸引人注意的，迷人的	attractive
志得意滿的	complacent
辛勤工作的	hard-working
刻意迴避的	stand-offish
卑鄙的	mean
性感的	sexy
勇敢的	brave, courageous
幽默的	humorous

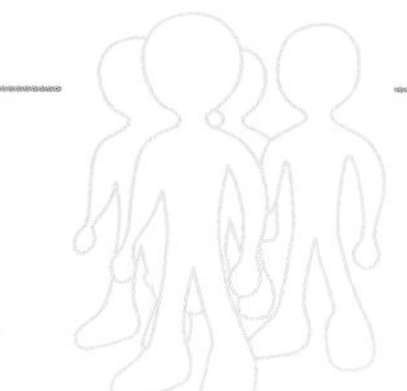

PERSONALITY QUALITIES
人格特質

▸ 中文	▸ 英文
拮据的，經濟狀況不佳的	up-tight
美麗的	beautiful
英俊的；慷慨的	handsome
值得信賴的，可靠的	trustworthy
值得信賴的	dependable
值得疼愛的	loveable
容易受騙的	gullible
浪漫的	romantic
神氣活現的	stuck up
神智正常，頭腦清楚的	sane
缺乏禮貌的	ill-mannered
強烈的，強健的	strong
敏感的	sensitive
清新的	fresh
笨的，愚蠢的	stupid

PERSONALITY QUALITIES 人格特質

▸ 中文	▸ 英文
粗魯的，沒禮貌的	rude
羞怯的，侷促不安的	bashful
羞澀的	shy
貪婪的	greedy
殘酷的	cruel
無恥，厚臉皮的	brazen
無情的，殘忍的	ruthless
無理的	impolite
勤勉的	diligent
嫉妒的	jealous
愚笨的；不願說話的	dumb
愚蠢的	foolish
感情豐富的	sentimental
滑稽的	funny
漂亮的	pretty
瘋狂的	crazy, insane

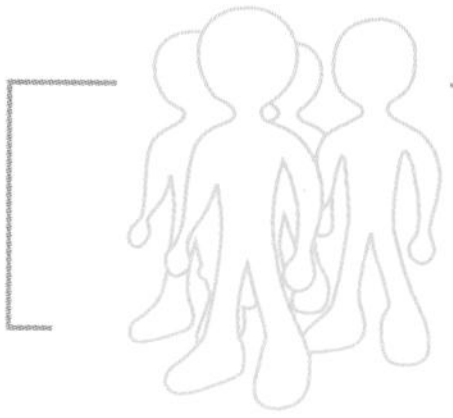

PERSONALITY QUALITIES
人格特質

中文	英文
興高采烈的，心情好的	cheerful
燦爛的，美麗的	gorgeous
膽怯的	cowardly
醜陋的	ugly
懷恨的，惡意的	spiteful
懶惰的	lazy
嚴肅正經的	serious

IDIOMS AND EXPRESSIONS

片語慣用語

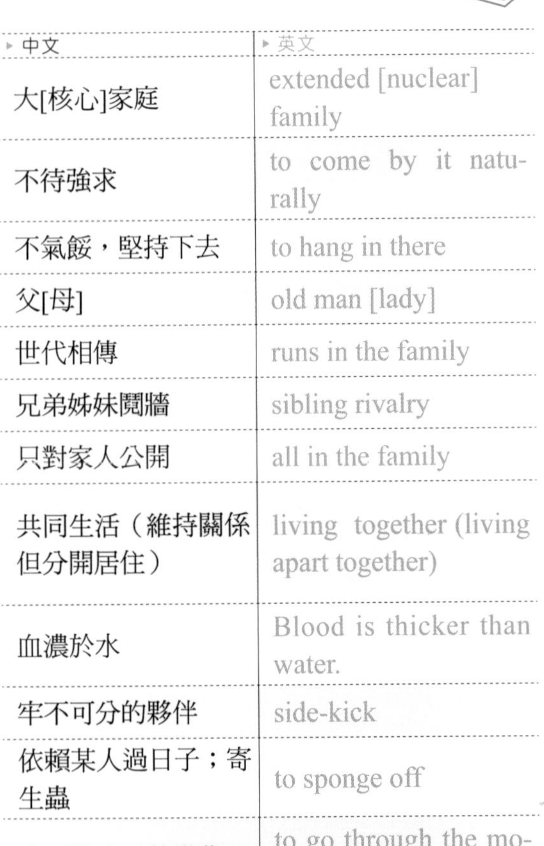

中文	英文
大[核心]家庭	extended [nuclear] family
不待強求	to come by it naturally
不氣餒，堅持下去	to hang in there
父[母]	old man [lady]
世代相傳	runs in the family
兄弟姊妹鬩牆	sibling rivalry
只對家人公開	all in the family
共同生活（維持關係但分開居住）	living together (living apart together)
血濃於水	Blood is thicker than water.
牢不可分的夥伴	side-kick
依賴某人過日子；寄生蟲	to sponge off
表面裝出…的動作	to go through the motions

IDIOMS AND EXPRESSIONS
片語慣用語

中文	英文
近[遠]親	close [distant] relatives
後母	wicked stepmother
拜把兄弟	blood brother
政治寵兒	favorite son
相親	blind date
首領	ringleader
家庭仇隙	family feud
家譜	family tree
容易上當受騙的人	fall-guy
配偶互相稱呼	better half
（總稱）婦女	fair sex
張三李四	every Tom, Dick and Harry
殺銳氣，讓某人栽跟頭	to take someone down a peg
毫不保留地告訴他人你的想法	to pull no punches

IDIOMS AND EXPRESSIONS

片語慣用語

▸ 中文	▸ 英文
許終身，論及婚嫁的伴侶	steady date
絕交，斷交	to break up
像，與…類似	to take after
對某位異性著迷	to have a crush on
輕鬆不受拘束	to hang it all out
酷肖[像]父母者	chip off the old block
緋聞	to have an affair
聯合起來對付某人	to gang up on
簡直一模一樣的人	spitting image
壞蛋；可憐蟲；倒楣的人	son of a gun
關係親密的人	kissing cousins

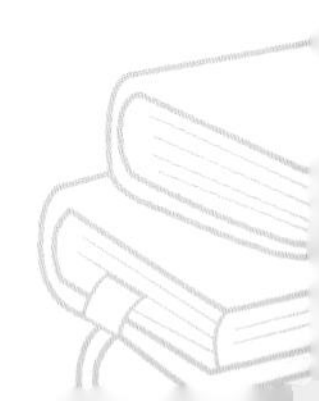

A WORLD APART

中文英文大不同

「Family feud」，（家庭爭執）；只要超過兩個人，就會有兩種意見；「he said, she said」，連夫妻都會起爭執！為爭家產或為表達自己意見「to have a say in...」，或只是為了反對而反對「to fight for the sake of fighting」；若說兄弟鬩牆，姊妹翻臉是人之常情也不為過！但當情勢有需要時，家中大大小小都能前嫌盡棄「to bury the hachets, to patch up」，全力對外才是王道。

「排行」（birth order），根據科學家的研究，對人格的養成也有影響：

1. 老大（first born）：服從性高「compliant」；在意名位「position & prestige」；控制慾強「control freak」。
2. 老么（last born）：創意性強「creative」；野心弱「less ambitious」；欠缺自律「lack self-discipline」。
3. 中間（second born）：競爭性強「competitive」；善解人意，有耐心「being understanding and patient」；缺乏安全感「insecured」。

是不是每個人都能符合上述的說明就見仁見智了！

NOTE 筆記頁

Unit 5

身體部位器官

KNOW THYSELF

身體內部/外表	BODY(EXTERNAL & INTERNAL)
疾病,症狀與受傷	DISEASES, SYMPTOMS & INJURIES
體檢和治療	PHYSICAL CHECKUP & TREATMENTS
藥品	MEDICINE
片語慣用語	IDIOMS AND EXPRESSIONS
中文英文大不同	A WORLD APART

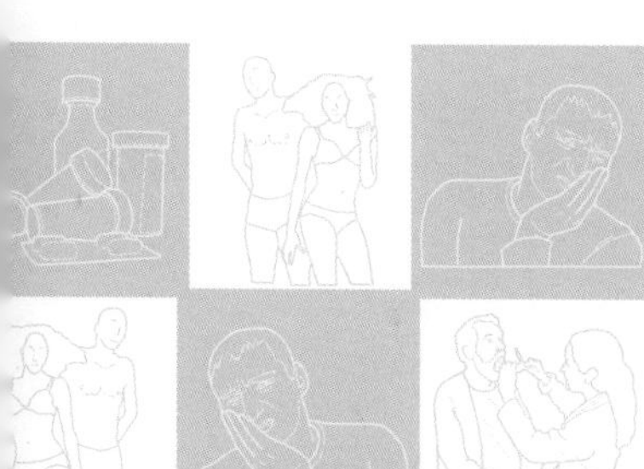

BODY (EXTERNAL & INTERNAL)
身體內部 & 外表

▸ 中文	▸ 英文
大[小]腸	large [small] intestines
大拇指	thumb
大腿	thigh
小腿肚	calf
太陽穴，鬢角	temple
心臟	heart
手（例：拇指，食指，中指，無名指，小指）	hand (thumb, index/pointer, middle/tall-man, ringman, little/pinkie)
手肘	elbow
手指	finger
手指甲	fingernail
手掌	palm
手臂	arm
包皮	foreskin
奶頭	nipple

BODY (EXTERNAL & INTERNAL) 身體內部 & 外表

▸ 中文	▸ 英文
皮膚	skin
耳朵（例：耳垂，中耳）	ear (earlobe, eardrum)
肌肉	muscle
屁股（多用複數）	buttocks
肝臟	liver
乳房	breast
盲腸，闌尾	appendix
肺臟	lungs
肩膀	shoulder
前臂	forearm
指關節	knuckle
背部	back
拳	fist
氣管	windpipe
神經	nerve
胰臟	pancreas

BODY (EXTERNAL & INTERNAL) 身體內部 & 外表

中文	英文
胸	chest
胸腔	ribcage
脊柱	spinal column
脊椎神經	spinal cord
酒窩	dimple
骨盆	pelvis
骨頭	bone
動脈	arteries
眼睛（例：眉毛，眼睫毛；眼皮，眼白）	eye (eyebrow, eyelashes, eyelid, white)
脖子	neck
脛	shin
腋窩	armpit
腎臟	kidney
陽具，陰莖	penis
腰部	waist
腳（腳踝以上）	leg

BODY (EXTERNAL & INTERNAL) 身體內部＆外表

中文	英文
腳底	sole
腳後跟	heel
腳趾	toe
腳趾甲	toenail
腹部	abdomen
腦	brain
膀胱	bladder
鼻子（例：鼻孔，鼻樑）	nose (nostril, bridge)
嘴（例：顎，舌頭，牙齒，齒齦牙床，唇，下巴）	mouth (jaw, tongue, tooth, gums, lip, chin)
膝	knee
踝	ankle
齒齦	gums
靜脈	veins
頭	head

098

BODY(EXTERNAL & INTERNAL)
身體內部＆外表

▸ 中文	▸ 英文
頭骨	skull
頭髮	hair
髭，小鬍子	mustache
臀部，屁股	hip, buttocks
膽囊	gallbladder
臉	face
臉頰	cheek
額頭	forehead
顎	jaw
鬍鬚，山羊鬍	beard
鬢角	sideburns

Diseases, Symptoms & Injuries 疾病，症狀與受傷

中文	英文
人群恐懼症	demophobia
中暑	heatstroke
心臟病	heart attack
水泡	blister
水痘	chickenpox
牙痛	toothache
出血	bleed
出疹子	rash
失去知覺	unconscious
打飽嗝	burp
打嗝	hiccups
打噴嚏	sneeze
耳朵發炎	ear infection
耳痛	earache
扭傷	sprain, twist
抓傷	scratch

DISEASES, SYMPTOMS & INJURIES
疾病，症狀與受傷

▸ 中文	▸ 英文
抽筋，痙攣，生理痛	cramp
昆蟲叮咬	insect bite
服藥過量	OD (Overdose on Drugs)
肺結核	TB (tuberculosis)
肥胖症	obesity
咳嗽	cough
咽喉炎	laryngitis
幽閉恐懼症	claustrophobia
畏寒	chill
疣	wart
胃痛	stomachache
背痛	backache
飛行恐懼症	aeruophobia
凍傷	frostbite
恐水症	hydrophobia
晒傷	sunburn

DISEASES, SYMPTOMS & INJURIES
疾病，症狀與受傷

▸ 中文	▸ 英文
氣喘	asthma, shortness of breath
氣喘所發出的聲音	wheeze
浮腫，腫脹	swollen
疼痛，受傷	hurt
胸痛	chest pain
骨折	break
高血壓	high blood pressure
脖子僵硬	stiff neck
脫臼	dislocate
蛀牙	cavity
貪食症	bulimia
麻疹	measles
割傷	cut
喉嚨痛	sore throat
發燒	fever, high temperature

DISEASES, SYMPTOMS & INJURIES
疾病，症狀與受傷

中文	英文
發癢	itchy
筋疲力竭	exhausted
脹氣	bloated
虛弱無力	faint
感冒	cold
感染	infection
愛滋病	AIDS (Acquired Immune Deficiency Syndrome)
瘀血，瘀傷	bruise
腮腺炎	MUMPS
腹瀉	diarrhea
過敏反應	allergic reaction
電腦恐懼症	cyberphobia
厭食症	aneroxia
嘔吐	vomit, throw up
鼻血	bloody nose

Diseases, Symptoms & Injuries
疾病，症狀與受傷

▸ 中文	▸ 英文
鼻塞	congested
憂鬱症	depression
噁心想吐	nauseous
燙傷	burn
糖尿病	diabetes
頭痛	headache
頭暈目眩	dizzy
擦傷	scrape
癌症	cancer
懼高症	acrophobia

PHYSICAL CHECKUP & TREATMENTS

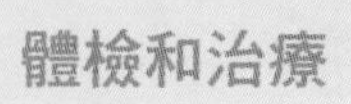

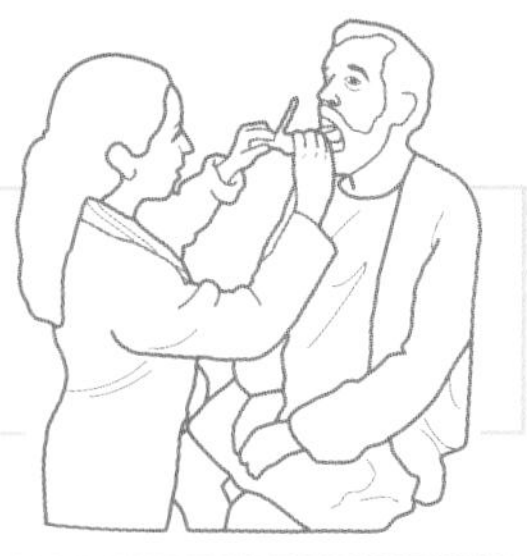

中文	英文
包紮傷口	dress the wound
打麻醉藥	give one a shot of anesthetic
抽血	draw some blood
清洗牙齒	clean one's teeth
清潔傷口	clean the wound
量血壓	check your blood pressure
量體溫	take one's temperature
填牙	fill the tooth
照胸部X光	take a chest X-ray
詢問病史	ask your some questions about your health history
檢查…	examine one's eyes [ears, nose, throat, teeth]
縫合傷口	close the wound

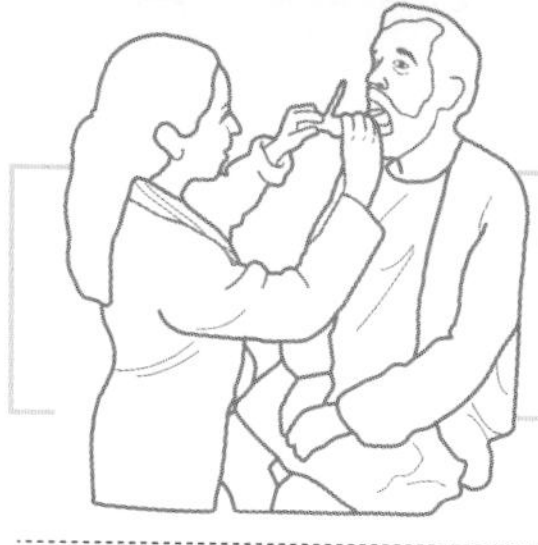

PHYSICAL CHECKUP & TREATMENTS
體檢和治療

▸ 中文	▸ 英文
聽診心臟	listen to one's heart
鑽蛀牙	drill the cavity

MEDICINE
藥品

中文	英文
不含阿斯匹靈的止痛藥	non-aspirin pain reliever
止咳片	cough drops
制酸劑	antacid tablets
阿斯匹靈	aspirin
咳嗽糖漿	cough syrup
眼藥水	eye drops
喉片	throat lozenges
感冒藥片	cold tablets
維他命	vitamins
鼻塞噴劑	decongestant spray, nasal spray

IDIOMS AND EXPRESSIONS

片語慣用語

中文	英文
一時想不起來	on the tip of one's tongue
一動也不動	not to move a muscle
口碑	by word of mouth
小心提防	look over one's shoulder
天生的	in one's blood
心裡緊張	get butterfly in one's stomach
手拙	all thumbs
失言	a slip of tongue
在人背後	on one's back
有使…心服的能力	carry one's own weight
有很多…，很忙	up to one's ears [eyeballs, neck]
血肉之軀	flesh and blood
吵來吵去自相殘殺	at each other's throat
沒問題！	No sweat！

Idioms and Expressions

片語慣用語

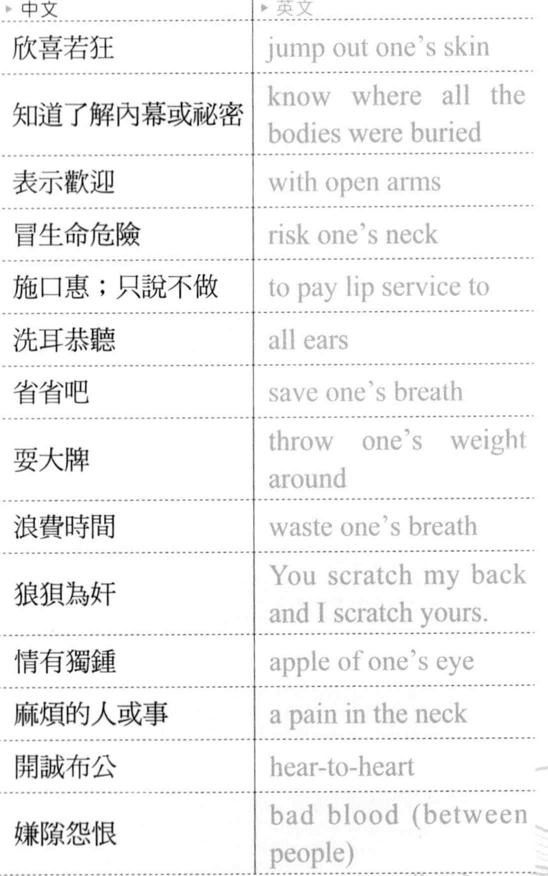

▸ 中文	▸ 英文
欣喜若狂	jump out one's skin
知道了解內幕或祕密	know where all the bodies were buried
表示歡迎	with open arms
冒生命危險	risk one's neck
施口惠；只說不做	to pay lip service to
洗耳恭聽	all ears
省省吧	save one's breath
耍大牌	throw one's weight around
浪費時間	waste one's breath
狼狽為奸	You scratch my back and I scratch yours.
情有獨鍾	apple of one's eye
麻煩的人或事	a pain in the neck
開誠布公	hear-to-heart
嫌隙怨恨	bad blood (between people)

Idioms and Expressions

片語慣用語

▸ 中文	▸ 英文
愚蠢不堪	dead from the neck up
極為悲痛	to eat one's heart out
隨意的	after one's heart
聲音沙啞說不出話	have a frog in ones throat

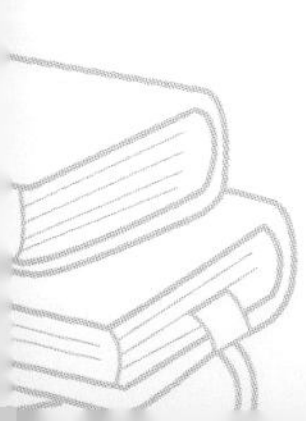

A World Apart

中文英文大不同

遇到事情時，「two heads are better than one」，因為你的夥伴很可能是個聰明人（have a smooth forehead）而且很有智慧（have a lot of brains）！但若是意見相左時，少不得會懷疑或不同意「raise one's eyebrows」；可是真理越辯越明，所以如果對自己的想法信心十足，也就會「not bat an eyelid」了。可是就是有人喜歡把他人的想法或功勞占為己有，所以要小心隔牆有耳（Wall has ears）！也有沒主見的人，凡事你說對就對（led by somebody by the nose），也有人只是嘴上說說（lip services）；做人要誠實，見到不對的事該說就要說（have a tongue in one's head），千萬別成為他人霸凌（show one's teeth）下的犧牲者！當然姿態太高表現過於強勢（force one's idea down other people's yhroat）或過於滑頭（speaks with one's tongue in one's cheek）也不一定是件好事；喜歡帶頭到頭來可會自討苦吃（stick one's neck out）並因此而丟人（lose face）！

Unit 6

天上飛的、地上走的、土裡長的

ANIMALS, BIRDS, PLANTS & TREES

動物	ANIMALS
棲息地	DWELLINGS
單位	GROUPINGS
幼獸	YOUNG ANIMALS
鳥類	BIRDS
片語慣用語	IDIOMS AND EXPRESSIONS
拈花惹草	PLANTS AND TREES
片語慣用語	IDIOMS AND EXPRESSIONS
中文英文大不同	A WORLD APART

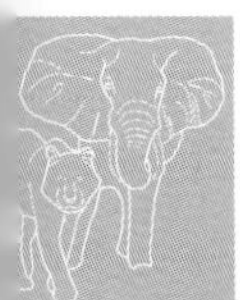

ANIMALS
動物

齧齒類（Rodents）

中文	英文
天竺鼠	guinea pig
沙鼠	gerbil
（野）兔	rabbit
松鼠	squirrel
倉鼠	hamster
草原土撥鼠	prairie dog
野兔	hare
鼠	mouse, rat
蝙蝠	bat

家畜（Domestic Animals）

中文	英文
山羊	goat
牛	ox
母牛	cow
狗	dog
美洲駝（無峰）	llama

ANIMALS
動物

中文	英文
馬	horse
矮種馬，小馬	pony
綿羊	sheep
豬	pig
貓	cat
騾	mule
驢	donkey

野生動物（Wild Animals）

中文	英文
土[郊]狼	coyote
（北美產）山貓	bobcat
山貓	lynx
山貓，野貓	wildcat
水獺	otter
狐狸	fox
花栗鼠	chipmunk

ANIMALS

中文	英文
美洲獅	cougar, mountain lion
負鼠	possum
海[河]狸	beaver
海牛[象]	sea cow
海豚	dolphin
狼	wolf
臭鼬	skunk
浣熊	raccoon
鹿	deer
鼠海豚	porpoise
熊	bear
豪豬	porcupine
駝鹿	elk
麋	moose
鯨魚	whale
獾	badger

ANIMALS
動物

爬蟲及兩棲類（Reptiles and Amphibia）

中文	英文
青蛙	frog
海龜	turtle
蛇	snake
陸龜	tortoise
蜥蜴	lizard
蝌蚪	tadpole
蟾蜍	toad
蠑螈	newt (salamander)

魚類（Fish）

中文	英文
大翻車魚	bluegill
太陽魚	sunfish
古比魚	guppy
河鱸	perch
狗魚	pike

ANIMALS
動物

▸ 中文	▸ 英文
金魚	goldfish
鮟鱇	monk fish
鯊魚	shark
鯰魚	catfish
鯡魚	herring
鰻魚	eel
鱈魚	cod
鱒魚	trout
鱘魚	sturgeon
鱸魚	bass

甲魚甲殼類（Shellfish and Crustaceans）

▸ 中文	▸ 英文
扇貝	scallop
海星	starfish
海膽	sea urchin
蚌，蛤蜊	clam

ANIMALS
動物

▸ 中文	▸ 英文
貽貝，淡菜	mussel
蝦	shrimp
蝸牛	snail
龍蝦	lobster
蟹	crab
蠔	oyster

昆蟲（Insects）

▸ 中文	▸ 英文
毛蟲	caterpillar
白蟻	termite
合掌蟑螂	praying mantis
蚜蟲	aphid
蛀蟲；蠕蟲；寄生蟲	worm
蜈蚣	centipede
蜜蜂	bee
蜻蜓	dragonfly

ANIMALS
動物

▸ 中文	▸ 英文
蜘蛛	spider
蝴蝶	butterfly
蝗蟲，蚱蜢	grasshopper
瓢蟲	lady bug
螞蟻	ant
蟑螂	cockroach
蟋蟀	cricket
蟲子	bug
蠍子	scorpion

動物園中飼養的動物（Zoo Animals）

▸ 中文	▸ 英文
土狼	hyena
大猩猩	gorilla
大象	elephant
水牛	buffalo
老虎	tiger

ANIMALS 動物

▸ 中文	▸ 英文
河馬	hippopotamus (hippo)
長頸鹿	giraffe
美洲豹	leopard
斑馬	zebra
犀牛	rhinoceros (rhino)
猴子	monkey
短吻鱷	alligator
獅子	lion
熊	bear
鱷魚	crocodile

DWELLINGS
棲息地

▸ 中文	▸ 英文
洞穴（狐狸、兔子）	burrow
洞窟	cave
畜欄，畜圈	pen
草地，放牧場	pasture
巢，窩，穴	nest
鳥籠，獸籠	cage
穀倉，糧倉	barn
箱，罐，櫃	tank
養魚缸，水族槽	aquarium
（飼養小動物的）籠子	hutch
（捕捉動物的）籠子	trap

GROUPINGS 單位

▸ 中文	▸ 英文
一大群（小昆蟲）	cloud (of gnats)
一小群（例：鯨魚）	pod (of whales)
一組（例：鳥）	team (of horses)
一群（例：大猩猩）	band (of gorilla)
一群（例：螞蟻）	colony (of ants)
一群（例：鳥）	flock (of birds）
一群（例：鵝）	gaggle (of geese)
一群（例：大象；馬）	herd (of elephants, horses)
一群（例：狗）	pack (of dogs)
一群（例：獅子）	pride (of lions)
一群（例：魚）	school (of fish)
一群（例：猴子）	troop (of monkeys)
一群，一批（例：蜜蜂）	swarm (of bees)
一對（例：牛）	yoke (of oxen)
一窩（例：母雞）	brood (of hens)

GROUPINGS 單位

▸ 中文	▸ 英文
一窩（例：蛇）	nest (of snakes)
一幫，一夥，一族（例：山羊）	tribe (of goats)
苗床（例：蛤蜊）	bed (of clams)

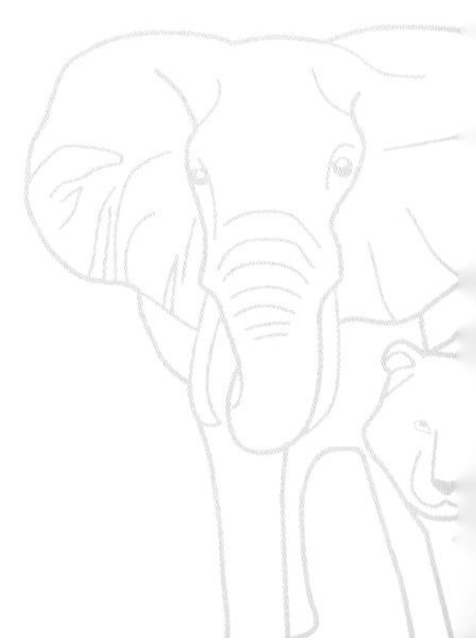

YOUNG ANIMALS
幼獸

中文	英文
山羊，人	kid (goat, man)
天鵝	cygnet (swan)
牛，大象，鯨魚	calf (cattle, elephant, whale)
老鷹	eaglet (eagle)
兔子	bunny (rabbit)
狗	puppy (dog)
狐狸，熊，獅子，鯨魚	colt (fox, bear, lion, whale)
青蛙	polliwog, tadpole (frog)
馬，斑馬	foal (horse, zebra)
野雁	gosling (goose)
魚	fingerling (fish)
魚	fry (fish)
鳥	fledgling (birds)
鹿	dawn (deer)

YOUNG ANIMALS
幼獸

▸ 中文	▸ 英文
綿羊	lamb (sheep)
雌馬	filly (horse)
豬	piglet (pig)
貓	kitten (cat)
鴨子	duckling (duck)
雞，其他飛禽	chick (chicken, other fowl)

BIRDS
鳥類

▸ 中文	▸ 英文
八哥；畫眉	blackbird
兀鷹	condor
山雀	chickadee
山雀	titmouse
天鵝	swan
孔雀	peacock
火雞	turkey
北美夜鷹	whippoorwill
北美紅雀	cardinal
白鷺	egret
企鵝	penguin
杜鵑，布穀鳥	cuckoo
沙錐，鷸	snipe
禿鷹	vulture
走鵑	roadrunner
夜鷹	nighthawk

BIRDS
鳥類

▸ 中文	▸ 英文
知更鳥	robin
金翅雀	goldfinch
松雀；蠟嘴鳥	grosbeak
松鴉	jay
信天翁	albatross
紅鶴	flamingo
軍艦鳥	frigate bird
食火雞	emu
食蜂鶲	kingbird
海鷗	gull
烏鴉	crow
啄木鳥	woodpecker
野雲雀	meadowlark
魚狗，翠鳥	kingfisher
麻雀	sparrow
喜鵲	magpie

BIRDS 鳥類

▸ 中文	▸ 英文
渡鴉	raven
善知鳥	puffin
雲雀	lark
黃鸝，金鶯	oriole
蜂鳥	hummingbird
雉，野雞	pheasant
蒼鷺	heron
鳴禽	warbler
歐掠鳥	starling
潛鳥	loon
燕八哥	cowbird
燕子	swallow
燕雀	phoebe
燕鷗	tern
貓頭鷹	owl
貓鵲	catbird

BIRDS
鳥類

▸ 中文	▸ 英文
鴕鳥	ostrich
鴨子	duck
鴿子	pigeon
獵鷹	falcon
藍知更鳥	bluebird
雞	chicken
（雌）鵝	goose
鵜鶘	pelican
鶉的一種	bobwhite
鵪鶉	quail
鶚	osprey
鶴	crane
鶲	flycatcher
鷓鴣	partridge
鷸	sandpiper
鷸鴕	kiwi

BIRDS 鳥類

▸ 中文	▸ 英文
鷹	eagle
鷹，隼	hawk
鸕鶿	cormorant
鸚鵡	parrot
鸛	stork

鳥類各部器官（Parts of Birds）

▸ 中文	▸ 英文
爪	claw
爪	talon
羽毛	feather
尾巴	tail
冠	crest
翅	wing
胸	breast
啄	peck
蛋	egg

BIRDS
鳥類

▸ 中文	▸ 英文
鳥嘴，喙	beak
殼	shell
群	flock

Idioms and Expressions

片語慣用語

▸ 中文	▸ 英文
一丘之貉	birds of a feather flock together
一鳥在手勝過二鳥在林（到手才是可靠的）	bird in the hand is worth two in the bush
一箭雙鵰，一舉兩得	to kill two birds with one stone
大而無當的東西	white elephant
及早做事的人	early bird
死前的最後演出	swan song
自毀前程	to cook one's goose
吹噓打屁	to throw the bull
完全是另外一回事	horse of another color
快樂（的青鳥）	the bluebird of happiness
每下愈況	to go to the dogs
使用最後一招	to shoot fish in a barrel
取捷徑，走直路	to make a beeline for

Idioms and Expressions

片語慣用語

中文	英文
坦白地說	to talk turkey
披著羊皮外衣的狼	wolf in sheep's clothing
押錯寶	to back the wrong horse
股市上漲	bull session
很難受的	to eat crow
洩露祕密	to let the cat out of the bag
看不見的危險	snake in the grass
胡搞 (v.)	to monkey around
胡鬧 (n.)	monkey business
胡鬧 (v.)	to horse around
值得驕傲的事物	feather in one's cap
剛愎自用的	pig-headed
害群之馬	black sheep
徒勞之舉	wild goose chase

IDIOMS AND EXPRESSIONS

片語慣用語

▸ 中文	▸ 英文
荒誕無稽的故事	cock and bull story
假慈悲	crocodile tears
莽撞的駕駛	road hog
陷入困境	in the doghouse
無主見的人，仿冒者	copycat
發假警報	cry wolf
稍安勿躁	to hold one's horses
絕對可靠的	straight from the horse's mouth
黑馬；不被看好但勝利的人	dark horse
愚弄他人使出醜	to make a monkey out of
當作耳邊風	water off a duck's back
當機立斷	to take the bull by the horn
裝睡裝死	to play possum

IDIOMS AND EXPRESSIONS

片語慣用語

▸ 中文	▸ 英文
對禮品吹毛求疵	to look at a gift horse in the mouth
養老金，緊急準備金	nest egg
激起某人怒氣	to get one's goat
錯誤或不可靠的消息	bum steer
膽怯的	chicken
醜小鴨	ugly duckling
懷才不遇，有志難伸	fish out of the water
覺得事有問題	to smell a rat

地點（Places）

▸ 中文	▸ 英文
公園；遊樂場；停車場	park
果樹林，果樹園	orchard
花園，菜園，果園，庭園	garden
原野，田野；牧場	field
荒野，荒漠	wilderness
喬木	arbor
矮樹叢，灌木	shrub
森林	forest
森林，樹林	woods
樹叢，小樹林	grove
樹籬；籬笆	hedge
灌木（叢）	bush

PLANTS AND TREES
拈花惹草

種類（Types）

中文	英文
小白花，薄雪草	edelweiss
山毛櫸	beech
山茶花	camellia
山茱萸，水木	dogwood
勿忘我	forget-me-not
月見草	evening primrose
月桂樹	bay tree
木蘭	magnolia
仙人掌	cactus
冬青	holly
白楊	abele
白楊木	poplar tree
白樺	birch
白蠟樹，梣	ash
石榴花	pomegranate flower
向日葵	sunflower

PLANTS AND TREES
拈花惹草

中文	英文
百合	lily
竹子	bamboo
西洋杉	cedar
冷衫，樅	fir
杏花	apricot blossom
杜鵑花	azalea
牡丹	poeny
夜來香	tuberose
松樹	pine tree
玫瑰花	rose
金盞花	adonis
長青樹	evergreen
柚樹	shadlock
柳樹	willow
相思樹，洋槐；刺槐	acacia
秋海棠	begonia

PLANTS AND TREES
拈花惹草

▸ 中文	▸ 英文
紅杉	redwood
美人蕉	canna
胡桃木	walnut
茉莉花	jasmine
風信子	hyacinth
風鈴草	bellflower
桂花	osmanthus
栗樹	chestnut
桑樹	mulberry
海棗樹，棗椰樹	date
常春藤	poison ivy
康乃馨	carnation
梧桐	firmiana
梧桐樹	sycamore
梅花	plum blossom
梔子花	gardenia

PLANTS AND TREES
拈花惹草

▸ 中文	▸ 英文
牽牛花	morning glory
雪蓮花	snowdrop
喇叭花	trumpet flower
棕櫚樹	palm tree
紫丁香	lilac
紫羅蘭	violet
菊花	chrysanthemum
雲杉	spruce
黃水仙	daffodil
楓樹	maple
榆樹	elm
葡萄藤	grapevine
睡蓮	water lily
蒲公英	dandelion
鳶尾花	iris
鳳仙花	balsam

PLANTS AND TREES 拈花惹草

中文	英文
劍蘭	gladiolus
樟樹	camphor tree
蓮花	lotus
蝴蝶蘭	phalaenopsis
曇花	epiphyllum
橄欖樹	olive tree
橡膠樹	rubber tree
橡樹	oak tree
雛菊	daisy
罌粟花	poppy
蘭花	orchid
鬱金香	tulip

樹的細部名稱（Tree Parts）

中文	英文
松果	pine cone
根	root

PLANTS AND TREES
拈花惹草

中文	英文
針葉	needle
細枝	twig
殘幹，樹樁	stump
嫩枝	graft
種子	seed
樹皮	bark
樹枝	branch
樹芽；花蕾	bud
樹液	sap
樹幹	trunk
樹葉	leaf
樹輪	ring
橡子[實]	acorn

花的細部名稱（Flower Parts）

中文	英文
子房	ovary

PLANTS AND TREES
拈花惹草

中文	英文
花柱	style
花粉	pollen
花瓣	petal
花藥	anther
柱頭；眼節	stigma
莖，幹，柄	stem
雄蕊	stamen
種子	seed
雌蕊	pistil

IDIOMS AND EXPRESSIONS

片語慣用語

▸ 中文	▸ 英文
上床睡覺	to hit the hay
自陷困境中	out on a limb
年輕時過得縱情逸樂的生活	to sow one's wild oats
沒有舞伴而孤坐著的女人；壁花	wallflower
依賴往日雄風	to rest on one's laurels
祕密來源	grapevine
最後一擊	the last straw
喉結	Adams' apple
開啟新頁	to turn over a new leaf
極好的哪	that's just peachy
違反意願	against the gran
種瓜得瓜，種豆得豆	to reap what one sows
稱心如意的境遇	bed of roses
蓋括地說	in a nutshell

IDIOMS AND EXPRESSIONS

片語慣用語

▸ 中文	▸ 英文
轉彎抹角地說話	to beat around the bush

A World Apart
中文英文大不同

英文表達中常會用動物的一些天性本能來打譬喻：

如大象一樣重　as heavy as an elephant
如小貓般好玩　as playful as a kitten
如天鵝般優雅　as graceful as a swan
如孔雀般高傲　as proud as a peacock
如老鼠般安靜　as quiet as a mouse
如兔子般小膽　as timid as a rabbit
如狐狸般狡猾　as cunning as a fox
如鹿一樣快速　as fast as a deer
如猴子般敏捷　as agaile as a monkey
如猩猩般多毛　as hairy as a gorilla
如雲雀般快樂　as happy as a lark
如獅子般勇敢　as brave as a lion
如綿羊[鴿子]般溫和　as gentle as a lamb [dove]
如蝸牛一樣慢　as slow as a snail
如蝙蝠般視盲　as blind as a bat
如豬一樣胖　as fat as a pig
如貓頭鷹般有智慧　as wise as an owl

如鰻魚一樣滑溜　as slippery as an eel
喝得像魚一樣醉　as drunk as a fish

這些譬喻言簡意賅，是說話或寫文章時相當有用的修辭工具。

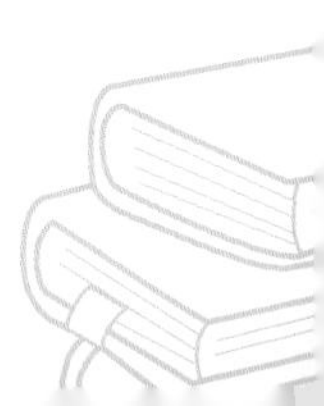

Unit 7

七情六慾

EMOTIONS

相關名詞	NOUNS
相關動詞	VERBS
相關形容詞	ADJECTIVES
片語慣用語	IDIOMS AND EXPRESSIONS
中文英文大不同	A WORLD APART

NOUNS
相關名詞

▸ 中文	▸ 英文
心情不好，喜怒無常	mood
失望	disappointment
好戰，好鬥	belligerence
冷漠，不關心	indifference
困乏，消沉，厭倦	weariness
困窘，難為情	embarrassment
坐立不安，心神不定	restlessness
妒忌，猜忌	jealous
希望	hope
忌妒	envy
快活	joviality
快樂，歡欣	glee
狂怒，盛怒	rage
性情，脾氣	temper
欣喜，愉快	delight
沮喪，灰心，洩氣	dejection
沮喪，意志消沉	depression

NOUNS 相關名詞

中文	英文
勇氣	courage
勇敢	bravery
哀傷	sorrow
苦味	bitterness
恐怖，驚駭	terror
恐怖	horror
恐懼	fear
疲勞，倦怠	tiredness
疲勞，勞累	fatigue
疼痛，痛苦	pain
笑，笑聲	laughter
高興，滿足	pleasure
高興	gladness
偏見，成見	prejudice
眼淚，淚珠	tears
貪婪	greed

NOUNS
相關名詞

▸ 中文	▸ 英文
惡化，加劇	aggravation
悲哀	sadness
焦慮，掛念	anxiety
焦躁，神經質	nervousness
無聊，厭倦	boredom
痛苦，苦惱	anguish
感覺，感受	felling
愛	love
敬畏，畏怯	awe
極樂，至喜	bliss
煩惱，惱怒	annoyance
煩惱，憂慮	trouble
瘋狂	craziness
憐憫，同情	pity
憤怒，生氣	anger
樂趣，興味	amusement

NOUNS 相關名詞

中文	英文
熱心，熱情，熱忱	enthusiasm
熱心，熱情	zest
熱情，激情	passion
熱情	affection
遺憾	regret
歡呼，喝采	cheer
歡樂，高興	joy
驕傲	pride
驚嚇，恐怖	fright

VERBS 相關動詞

▸ 中文	▸ 英文
作嘔	disgust
低泣	weep
冷靜，平息	calm
欣喜，高興	rejoice
沮喪，心灰意冷	depress
哀悼	lament
哀痛，哀悼	mourn
怒氣沖沖	fume
恨	hate
哭	cry
迷惑，難倒	bewilder
發抖，顫震	tremble
煩擾，打攪	bother
厭惡，憎惡	abhor, detest
對抗，敵對	antagonize
憂鬱，鬱悶	mope

VERBS 相關動詞

中文	英文
撫慰，慰問	console
激動，焦慮	agitate
激動，煽動；喚醒	stir
激動，興奮	excite
（因羞澀、尷尬而）臉紅	blush

ADJECTIVES
相關形容詞

▸ 中文	▸ 英文
可惡的	abhorrent
色情的	amorous
快活的，高興的	jolly
快樂的；放蕩的；豔麗的	gay
狂暴的，狂怒的	berserk
性感的	sexy
沮喪的，氣餒的	dejected
苦惱的，不適的	upset
害怕的	afraid
疲倦的，疲勞的	weary
高興的，快樂的	delighted
悽苦的，難堪的，糟透的	abject
羞澀的，靦覥的	shy
被遺棄的，孤獨的	forlorn
焦慮的，掛念的	anxious

ADJECTIVES 相關形容詞

▸中文	▸英文
痛苦的	painful
愛抱怨的	grouchy
煩惱的，煩躁的	irritated
瘋狂的，精神錯亂的	insane
憂慮的，恐懼地	apprehensive
憂鬱的，哀傷地	disconsolate
憂鬱的	melancholy
熱情的	passionate
激動不安的，慌張的	flustered
興高采烈的，情緒好的	cheerful
興高采烈的，輕快的	merry
膽小的，易受驚的	timid

IDIOMS AND EXPRESSIONS
片語慣用語

▸ 中文	▸ 英文
大吵大鬧	to make a scene
大動肝火，勃然大怒	to blow one's top
不安的局勢	troubled waters
不知所措的	at wit's end
不知所措，猶豫的	in a dither
因某事感到激動、擔憂	hot and bothered
有情人終成眷屬	love will find a way
使人傷心的人事物	a heart breaker
非常困擾，極端憤怒	fit to be tied
笑得合不攏嘴；快樂的	happy as a clam
高傲的	standoffish
智窮力竭	at the end of one's rope
精神不爽的	out of sorts
賺人眼淚的電影戲劇或節目	tear jerker

IDIOMS AND EXPRESSIONS
片語慣用語

▸ 中文	▸ 英文
雖瘋狂仍有條理的	method in one's madness
變成碎片	to go to pieces

英文英語中最難搞懂的就是介系詞；「compare with」和「compare to」有何不同？「tired of」和「tired with」又有甚麼不同？列舉出些常和固定字詞連用的介系詞供大家參考：

1. 常與「for」連用的形容詞：possible, impossible, important, necessary, essential, convenient difficult, hard, easy, useful, ...。
2. 常與「of」連用的形容詞：nice, kind, wise, good, polite, clever, bad, wrong, cruel, stupid, foolish, ...。
3. 常與「to」連用的形容詞：able, angry, eager, fit, fortunate, considerate, ready, rude, slow, willing, wrong, ...。
4. 常與「to」連用的動詞（適用於s + v + o/i（間接受詞）+ o/d（直接受詞的句型））：pay give, lend, show, offer, tell, teach, write, bring, deliver, ...。
5. 常與「for」連用的動詞：buy, choose, make, leave, get, order, ...。
6. 常與「of」連用的動詞：ask。
7. 常與「on」連用的動詞：play。

例如：

Jack offered Mary his help.

= Jack offered his help to Mary.

The woman made her husband a cake.

= The woman made a cake for her husband.

Can I ask you a question?

= Can I ask a question of you?

The boy played his friend a trick.

=The boy played trick on his friend.

NOTE 筆記頁

Unit 8

做甚麼哪裡做

WHAT TO DO AND WHERE TO DO IT

JOBS AND WORK
工作

▸ 中文	▸ 英文
人權擁護者；調查員	ombudsman
口譯員，通譯員	interpreter
土木工程師	civil engineer
女管家	housekeeper
工友，小弟	office boy
工程師，技師	engineer
工廠作業員	factory worker
（旅館）內部偵探	house detective
公車司機，巴士駕駛	bus driver
公寓或學校照管房屋的看門人	janitor
化驗員	lab technician
心理學者	psychologist
木工[匠]	carpenter
水手	sailor
水管工	plumber
牙科保健員，牙醫助理	dental hygienist

JOBS AND WORK 工作

▸ 中文	▸ 英文
牙醫	dentist
主廚，大師傅	chef
以花言巧語騙人的騙子	con artist
出版商，發行者，報紙業主，報刊發行人	publisher
出納（員）	cashier
加油站員工	service station attendant
卡[貨]車駕駛	trucker, truck driver
外交人員[官]	diplomat
外科醫生	surgeon
打字員	typist
民意測驗專家	pollster
石匠，泥水匠	mason
立法者，立法委員，國會議員	legislator
交通指揮員	crossing guard

JOBS AND WORK
工作

▸ 中文	▸ 英文
印刷工	printer
收垃圾的人	rubbish collector
收垃圾的工人	garbage collector
肉販	butcher
行李管理員	baggage handler
作家	writer
志願人員	volunteer
（水、電表）抄表員	meter reader
技師	technician
汽車工程師	automobile engineer
男[女]按摩師	masseur; masseuse
足科醫生	podiatrist
官僚（尤指墨守成規，食古不化者）	bureaucrat
店員	store clerk
房地產經紀人	real estate agent

JOBS AND WORK 工作

▸ 中文	▸ 英文
（飯店等）房間部的女服務生	chambermaid
放高利貸者	loan shark
服務生；女服務生	waiter; waitress
法官	judge
油漆工	(house) painter
牧師，神父（猶太教祭司，福音傳播者，修女，伊斯蘭教領袖或學者）	priest, minister (rabbi, evangelist, nun, imam)
（女）牧童[牛仔]	cowboy; cowgirl
空服員	flight attendant
保姆	babysitter
保險代理人	insurance agent
保險索賠審核員	insurance claims adjustor
保險調查員	insurance investigator
宣傳[公關]人員	publicist

JOBS AND WORK
工作

▸ 中文	▸ 英文
室內設計師	interior decorator
室內裝潢商	upholsterer
建築工人	construction worker
建築承包商	building contractor
律師	lawyer
政治人物，政客	politician
洗衣工人	laundry worker
洗車工人	car washer
洗窗工人	window washer
洗碗工人	dishwasher
（女）看門人，（女）門房	doorman [-woman]
科學家	scientist
美容師	beautician
計程車駕駛	taxi driver
軍人	soldier
音樂家，樂師	musician

JOBS AND WORK 工作

▸ 中文	▸ 英文
飛機駕駛	pilot
食物處理員	food handler
（女）修理工	repairman [-woman]
家庭主婦[夫]	housewife [-husband]
旅行社職員	travel agent
旅行推銷員	traveling salesman
旅館[汽車旅館]員工	hotel [motel] clerk
珠寶商，寶石匠	jeweler
祕書	secretary
能做多種工作的人；雜而不精的人	jack of all trades
脊椎指壓治療者	chiropractor
送信人，使者，信差	messenger
送貨人員	delivery person
送遞急件或外交文件的信差	courier
停車場服務員	parking lot attendant

JOBS AND WORK
工作

▸ 中文	▸ 英文
偵探	detective
動物園管理員	zoo keeper
動物標本剝製師	taxidermist
（女）商人，實業家	businessman [-woman]
商船船員	merchant mariner
商業藝術家	commercial artist
售貨員，營業員	sales clerk
接待員	receptionist
掃街工人	street cleaner
排字工人	typesetter
（女）救火員	fireman [-woman], fire-fighter
救生員	life guard
教師，教授	teacher, professor
（女）清潔工	cleaning man [woman]
理髮師	barber

JOBS AND WORK
工作

▸ 中文	▸ 英文
眼鏡商，配眼鏡的人	optician
處理受損樹木的人	tree surgeon
速記員	stenographer
造園技師，環境美化設計師	landscape architect
陶工，陶藝家	potter
（球）場地整[管理員]	groundskeeper
就業服務人員	employment officer
插畫家	illustrator
游泳池包商	swimming pool contractor
稅務顧問	tax consultant
裁縫	tailor
郵差	mail carrier
間諜	spy
園丁	gardener

JOBS AND WORK
工作

▸ 中文	▸ 英文
幹農活的人	field hand
搬家工人	mover
新聞工作者[記者]	journalist
新聞記者[播報員]	news reporter
新聞發言人	press spokesman
暖氣承包商	heating contractor
（註冊）會計師	(Certified Public) Accountant (CPA)
業務顧問	business consultant
照明承包商	lightening contractor
經理	manager
補[製]鞋匠	cobbler
裝玻璃工人	glazier
裝配線工人	assembly line worker
農夫	farmer
農場工人	farmhand
運務員	shipping clerk

JOBS AND WORK 工作

▸ 中文	▸ 英文
遊說通過議案者，陳情者	lobbyist
電工，電氣技師	electrician
電氣[機]工程師	electrical engineer
電梯操作員	elevator operator
（女）電視[收音機]修理工人	TV [radio] repairman [-woman]
電腦程式設計師	computer programmer
電話架線工	telephone lineman
電話接線生	telephone operator
圖書館員	librarian
漁夫	fisherman
精神科醫師	psychiatrist
維修工	maintenance worker
說故事者，出納員	teller
遛狗者	dog walker
銀行出納員	bank teller

JOBS AND WORK 工作

中文	英文
銀行業者	banker
廢舊品商人	junk dealer
廚子	cook
廣告代理	advertising agent
碼頭[港口]工人	longshoreman
碼頭工，搬運工，馬戲場雜工	roustabout
編輯	editor
調查員，考察者	surveyor
鞋匠，製鞋工人，補鞋工人	shoemaker
學生	student
學校行政管理人員	school administrator
樵夫，伐木工	logger
機械工，修理工，技師	mechanic
機場[車站，碼頭]搬運行李的人	red cap

JOBS AND WORK 工作

▸ 中文	▸ 英文
機器操作員	machine operator
鋼琴調音員	piano tuner
檔案管理員	file clerk
殯葬業者	undertaker
醫生	doctor
獸醫	veterinarian
簿記員，記帳人	bookkeeper
藝術家	artist
藥劑師	pharmacist
警員	police officer
警衛，看守員	guard
警衛	security officer
譯者	translator
麵包[糕點]師	baker
攝影師	photographer
護士	nurse

JOBS AND WORK
工作

▸ 中文	▸ 英文
驅蟲人	pest exterminator
驗光師	optometrist

IDIOMS AND EXPRESSIONS
片語慣用語

中文	英文
13個	a baker's dozen
大人物	a big cheese
大概數字	a ball park figure
司空見慣，輕鬆平常	all in a [the] day's work
未事先約定就打電話推銷	to cold call
收工	to call it a day
收支平衡	to balance the books
收支打平	to break even
死裡逃生，僥倖逃過	a close shave
老闆兼打雜	chief cook and bottle washer
努力工作	to work one's finger to the bone
努力工作	by the sweat of one's brow
努力工作	to sweat blood
沒機會或結果的工作	a dead end job

Idioms and Expressions

片語慣用語

▸ 中文	▸ 英文
底線，最重要的事	the bottom line
金雞母；賺錢的事業或單位	a cash cow
非常忙碌	to be snowed under
威脅他人努力工作	to crack the whip
被開除	to get the sack
被開除	to be fired
責備失職下屬並導致離職	blood on the carpet
會計	a bean-counter
樣樣通樣樣鬆的人	Jack [Jill] of all trades
養家餬口	to bring home the bacon
優渥的離職	a golden handshake

A World Apart

中文英文大不同

在以往，若是努力還有白手起家的可能；所謂的行伍出身（to rise from ranks and files）也有飛黃騰達的一天；但隨著競爭日益激烈（cut-throat competition），想要嶄露頭角（to outshine）真是越來越難！也因為想要能讓日子好過些（to make the ends meet），多少人都把退休年齡往後移，而年輕人也往往因為求職不易而在家當「**宅男**」（**OTAKU**）、「**腐女**」（**FUJYO; no-life**），或是「**啃老族**」（**boomerang kids, boomerangers**），或是「**尼特族**」（**Neeters, Not in Education, Employment or Training**），或是自由業的「**飛特族**」（**freeters, freearbeiter**）；就算找工作，也要是錢多事少離家近！所以多少人提出警訊：就業市場並沒有萎縮，只不過求職者在現實和想像之間有很大的落差（discrepancy）。以前是此處不留爺自有留爺處（take the job and shovel it），現在則是一個工作不夠還得兼差（moonshine）！

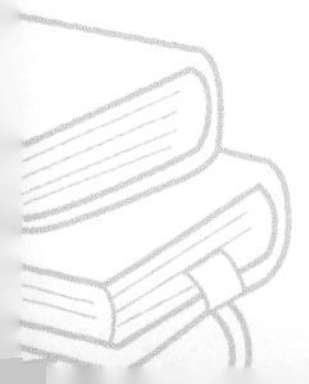

STORES & SHOPS, AGENCIES & SERVICES 各行各業

中文	英文
一元商店；雜貨店	dollar store
大賣場	hypermart
小型便利商店	minimart
不起眼的雜貨店	country store
五金行	hardware store
比薩店	pizza parlor
文具店	stationery store
木工店	carpenter
水電行	plumber
加油站	service station
市[鎮]公所	town [city] office
民間互助會，信用合作社	loan association
印刷行	printing shop
回教寺院，清真寺	mosque
地毯地板店	carpet & flooring store
寺廟	temple

STORES & SHOPS, AGENCIES & SERVICES 各行各業

▸ 中文	▸ 英文
托兒所	day-care center
收音機電視修理店	radio-TV repair
有線電視公司	TV cable company
百貨公司	department store
老人中心	senior citizen's center
自助洗衣店	Laundromat
自助餐館，自助飯館	cafeteria
衣料店	fabric [draperies] store
汽車修理店	auto repair shop
汽車零件店	auto parts store
育樂中心	recreation center
咖啡店	coffee shop
垃圾掩埋場	landfill
垃圾場	dump
房地產公司	real estate agency
服裝店	clothing store

Stores & Shops, Agencies & Services 各行各業

▸ 中文	▸ 英文
武術中心	martial art studio
油漆行	paint store
玩具店	toy store
玩具模型店	hobby shop
股票[證券]經紀人	stockbroker
花店	florist
保險經紀人公司	insurance agency
律師事務所	law firm
洗衣店	dry cleaners
美容院	beauty parlor
美黑[晒黑]沙龍	tanning salon
修理中心；汽車修理店	service center
修鞋店	shoe repair service
家庭計畫中心	Planned Parenthood
旅行社	travel agency
書店	bookstore

STORES & SHOPS, AGENCIES & SERVICES 各行各業

▸ 中文	▸ 英文
書報攤	newsstand
消防隊	fire department
珠寶店	jewelry store
租車公司	auto rental agency
古董店	antique shop
健康中心	health center
健康食品店	healthfood store
汽車商	car dealership
國稅局	Internal Revenue Service
教堂	church
焊接行	welding shop
理髮店	barber shop
眼鏡行	optician
貨運中心	shipping center
連鎖速食店	fast-food chain
家具店	furniture store

Stores & Shops, Agencies & Services 各行各業

中文	英文
報社	newspaper office
就業中心	employment agency
猶太教堂	synagogue
畫廊	art gallery
菸草店，菸店	tobacconist
超級市場	supermarket
郵局	post office
郵購中心	mail-order
募兵站	military recruiting office
廉價商店	discount store
慈善事業	charities
慈善二手商店	thrift shop
搬家公司	moving company
會計師公司	certified public accountant office
照相機店	camera shop
照相館	photography store

STORES & SHOPS, AGENCIES & SERVICES 各行各業

中文	英文
資源回收中心	recycling center
路邊小攤	roadside vendor
跳蚤市場	flea market
農夫市集	farmers' market
運動器材店	sporting goods store
遊民收容所	homeless shelter
電子產品店	electronics store
電腦店	computer store
電話公司營業所	telephone company business office
電器行[維修店]	appliance store [repair]
零食店；販賣部	snack bar
暢貨中心	outlet store
福利救濟中心	welfare office
舞蹈中心	dance studio
銀行	bank

STORES & SHOPS, AGENCIES & SERVICES 各行各業

中文	英文
廣告公司	advertising agency
影印行	copy center
樂器行	music store
熟食店	delicatessen (deli)
鞋店	shoe store
機具修理店	fix-it shop
糖果店	candy store
諮商顧問公司	counseling office
餐廳	restaurant
儲物倉庫	storage warehouse
縫衣機店	sewing center
購物中心	shopping mall
殯儀館	funeral parlor
禮品店	gift shop
二手家具[衣物，車]行	used furniture clothing, car store
醫院	hospital

STORES & SHOPS, AGENCIES & SERVICES 各行各業

▸ 中文	▸ 英文
雜貨店	grocery store
寵物店	pet shop
藝品店	arts and crafts store
藥房	drug store, pharmacy
警察局	police department
麵包店	bakery
體育館	gym

「All walks of life」（各行各業）；人上一百，形形色色，想要嶄露頭角（rist to the occasion）何其容易！近日的林來瘋（Linsanity），林書豪就是一例。「Linderella」（林灰姑娘）；「Linsation」（林轟動）；「Lincredible」（林不可思議）…；不論球迷、媒體如何稱呼，豪帥若非在日常就已經做好準備工作，又怎能在時機來臨時應運而生？

知名財經雜誌富比世（Forbes）針對林來瘋狂熱「mania」提出十件值得我們注意的事「Ten Lessons Jeremy Lin Can Teach Us」：

1. Believe in yourself when no one else does. 對自己深信不疑。
2. Seize the opportunity when it comes up. 把握機會。
3. Your family will always be there for you， so be there for them. 家庭的重要。
4. Find the system that works for your style.
   天下沒有不是的老闆。

5. Don't overlook talent that might exist around you today on your team. 團隊至上。
6. People will love you being an original, not trying to be someone else. 切莫畫虎不成反類犬。
7. Stay humble. 謙虛，謙和。
8. When you make others around you look good, they will love you forever. 有福同享有難同當。
9. Never forget about the importance of luck or fate in life. 天命不可違！
10. Work your butt off. 努力再努力！

NOTE 筆記頁

Unit 9

醫藥保健

MEDICINE AND HEALTH

地點處所	PLACES & AREAS
設備	EQUIPMENT
醫事人員	PEOPLE
治療過程	PROCESSES
藥品	MEDICINE
醫療問題	PROBLEMS
疾病和狀況	DISEASE AND CONDITIONS
片語慣用語	IDIOMS AND EXPRESSIONS
中文英文大不同	A WORLD APART

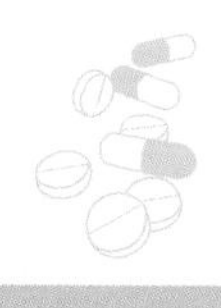
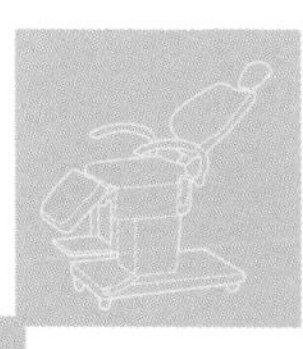
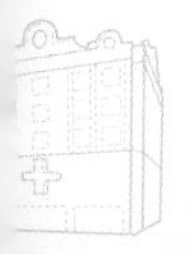
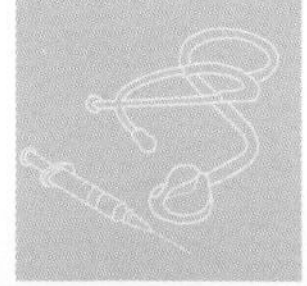

PLACES & AREAS 地點處所

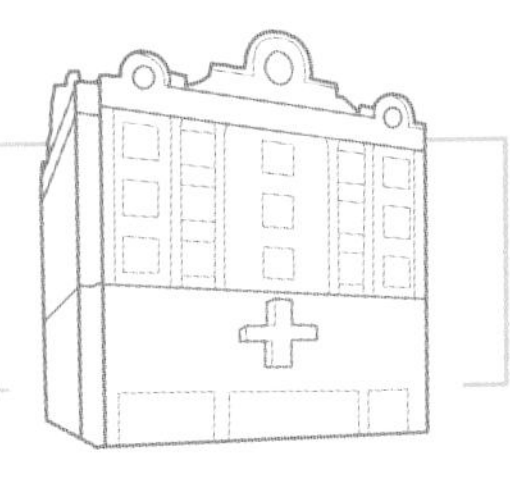

▸ 中文	▸ 英文
小兒科病房	pediatric ward
分娩室，產房	birthing [delivery] room
手術室	operating room
加護病房	ICU (intensive care unit)
私人房間[空間]	private room
門診病人診所	out-patient clinic
待產房	labor room
急診室	emergency room
病房	ward
健保組織	HMO (health maintenance organization)
救護車	ambulance
產房	delivery room
產科病房	maternity ward
復原室	recovery room
等候室，候診間	waiting room

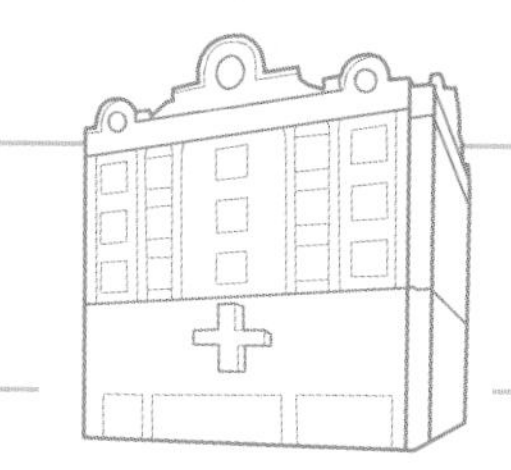

PLACES & AREAS 地點處所

▶ 中文	▶ 英文
診所，門診所	clinic
進入；住院	admitting
實驗室，研究室	laboratory
精神病院	insane asylum, mental hospital
（私立）療養院	nursing home
療養院，休養所	sanitarium
醫院	hospital

EQUIPMENT 設備

▸中文	▸英文
OK繃	band-aid
X光機	x-ray machine
丁型[腋下]拐杖	crutches
公共廁所	sanitary
手術臺	operating table
固定用敷料，石膏	cast
拐杖	cane
便盆	bedpan
氧氣帳，氧氣罩	oxygen tent
病床	bed
紗布	gauze
棉花棒	Q-tip (swab)
（口腔[直腸]）溫度計	(oral [rectal]) thermometer
解剖刀	scalpel
噴霧器，蒸餾器	vaporizer
熱水袋[瓶]	hot water bottle

EQUIPMENT
設備

中文	英文
熱敷墊	heating pad
膠布	adhesive tape
衛生棉（美）；尿布（英）	napkins
輪椅	wheelchair
學步車，助步車	walker
壓板	depressor
繃帶	bandage
聽診器	stethoscope
鑷子，小鉗子	tweezers

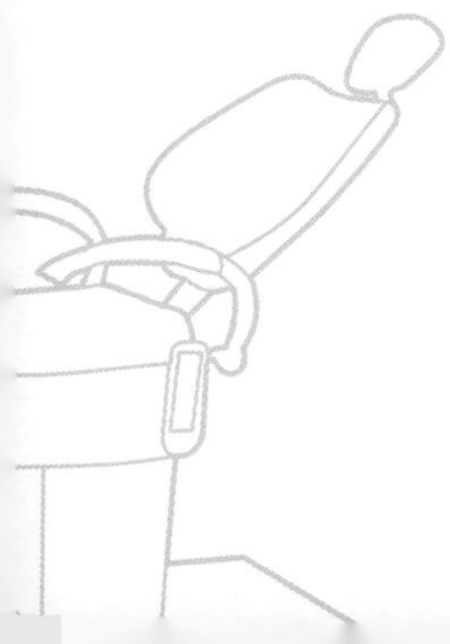

PEOPLE
醫事人員

▸ 中文	▸ 英文
小兒科醫生	pediatrician
皮膚科醫生	dermatologist
全科醫生	general practitioner (G.P.)
有執照[正式]護士	registered nurse (R.N.)
沒有學歷但有經驗的護士	practical nurse
足科醫生	podiatrist
放射線研究家	radiologist
泌尿科醫生	urologist
病理學家	pathologist
神經科醫生	neurologist
脊椎指壓治療師	chiropractor
婦科醫生	gynecologist
專家；專科醫生	specialist
接待員	receptionist

PEOPLE
醫事人員

▸ 中文	▸ 英文
產科醫生	obstetrician
眼科醫生	ophthalmologist
麻醉師	anesthetist
葬儀業者	undertaker
實驗室技師	lab technician
精神[心理]分析學家	psychoanalyst
精神病醫生	psychiatrist
矯形外科醫生	orthopedic surgeon
職業護理師（通常指獲得碩士或博士學位的護理人員）	nurse practitioner (N.P.)
（內科）醫生	physician
（外科）醫生	surgeon
醫師，醫生	doctor (M.D.)
醫院護士的年輕志願助手	candy striper
藥劑師	pharmacist
護士	nurse

PROCESSES
治療過程

▸ 中文	▸ 英文
X光	x-ray
人工流產手術	D&C (Dilation & Curettage)
子宮切除術	hysterectomy
心跳	heart beat
心電圖	EKG (electrocardiogram)
手術	surgery
加重護理	intensive care
打針	shot
生產	delivery (of a baby)
用來化驗的樣品	specimen
血壓	blood pressure
注射	injection
盲腸[闌尾]切除手術	appendectomy
扁桃腺切除術	tonsillectomy
看診	examination

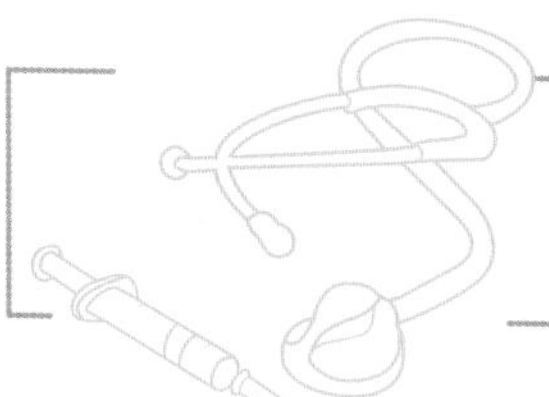

PROCESSES 治療過程

▸ 中文	▸ 英文
剖腹生產	Caesarean section
核磁共振攝影	MRI (Magnetic Resonance Imaging)
脈搏	pulse
接種	vaccination
移植	transplant
診斷	diagnosis
預防接種	inoculation
預後（對日後發展的預測）	prognosis
檢體	sample
體溫	temperature
觀察	observation

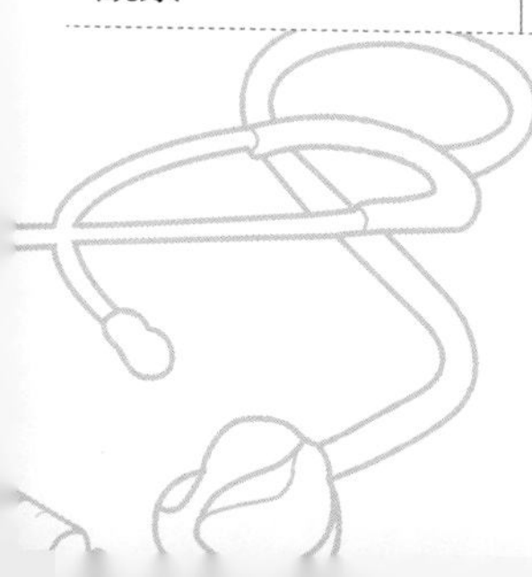

MEDICINE
藥品

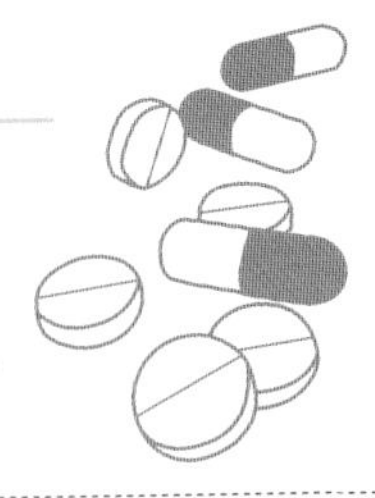

中文	英文
口服避孕藥	the pill
抗組織胺	antihistamine
防腐劑	antiseptic
阿斯匹靈	aspirin
栓劑	suppository
眼藥水	eyedrops
（藥）處方	prescription
解[抗]酸劑	antacid
解充血藥	decongestant
解毒劑	antidote
維他命	vitamins
鼻塞藥	nasal spray
盤尼西林，青黴素[消炎片]	penicillin
膠囊	capsules
避孕劑，避孕用品	contraceptive
瀉藥	laxative

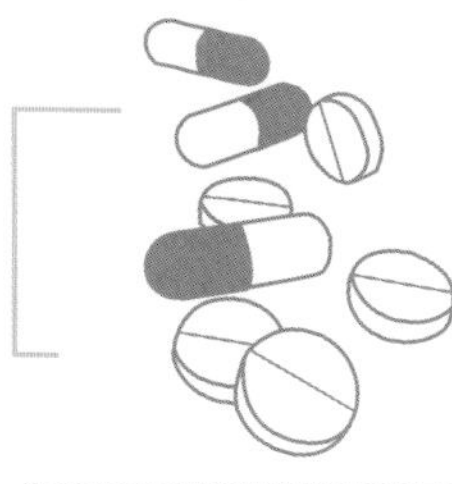

MEDICINE 藥品

▸ 中文	▸ 英文
鎮靜劑	sedative
藥丸	pill
藥片	tablet
藥膏，油膏，軟膏	ointment

PROBLEMS
醫療問題

▸ 中文	▸ 英文
失明	blind
耳聾	deaf
冷顫	chills
扭傷（肌肉）	strain
扭傷（腳踝）	sprain
受傷	injury
便祕	constipation
咳嗽	cough
流感	the flu
流鼻涕	runny nose
紅疹	rash
消化不良	indigestion
浮腫的	swollen
病毒	virus
疼痛	ache
疼痛[發炎]的	sore

PROBLEMS 醫療問題

中文	英文
骨折	fracture
啞的	dumb
痔瘡	hemorrhoids
痛	pain
發炎	inflammation
發燒	fever
筋疲力竭的	exhaustion
傷（口）	wound
意外事件	accident
感冒	cold
感染，傳染	infection
腹瀉	diarrhea
過敏	allergy
嘔吐	vomit
僵硬	stiff
噁心，作嘔	nausea

PROBLEMS
醫療問題

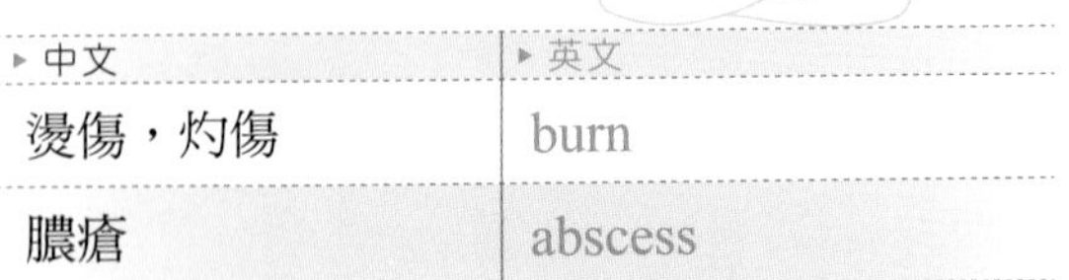

中文	英文
燙傷，灼傷	burn
膿瘡	abscess

DISEASE AND CONDITIONS 疾病和狀況

▸ 中文	▸ 英文
小兒痲痺症	polio
中風	stroke
天花	smallpox
心臟病	heart attack
支氣管炎	bronchitis
水痘	chicken pox
白血病，血癌	leukemia
皮膚癌	skin cancer
多發性硬化	multiple sclerosis
免疫力	immunity
肝炎	hepatitis
孤獨症，自閉症	autism
性病	V.D. (venereal disease)
疝氣，脫腸	hernia
肺炎	pneumonia
肺氣腫	emphysema

DISEASE AND CONDITIONS
疾病和狀況

▸ 中文	▸ 英文
肺結核	tuberculosis (T.B.)
咽喉炎	angina
急性關節風溼症	rheumatic fever
毒品上癮	drug addiction
流行性感冒	influenza (flu)
胎兒酒精症候群	fetal alcohol syndrome
氣喘	asthma
症候群	syndrome
皰疹	herpes
神經官能病	neurosis
高血壓	high blood pressure
偏執狂	paranoia
動脈硬化（症）	arteriosclerosis
梅毒	syphilis
淋病	gonorrhea
酗酒	alcoholism

DISEASE AND CONDITIONS 疾病和狀況

▸ 中文	▸ 英文
痲疹	measles
黏液囊炎	bursitis
智力遲鈍，智能缺陷	mental retardation
猩紅熱	scarlet fever
感染性單核血球病	mononucleosis (mono)
愛滋病毒陽性反應	HIV positive
愛滋病	AIDS (acquired immunodeficiency syndrome)
腮腺炎	mumps
腫瘤	tumor
腹瀉	diarrhea
腦膜炎	meningitis
過敏	allergy
瘧疾	malaria
精神分裂症	schizophrenia

DISEASE AND CONDITIONS
疾病和狀況

▸ 中文	▸ 英文
精神變態，精神病	psychosis
德國麻疹	rubella (German measles)
潰瘍	ulcer
糖尿病	diabetes
霍亂	cholera
癌症	cancer
關節炎	arthritis

Idioms and Expressions

片語慣用語

▸ 中文	▸ 英文
上班[營業]時間	office hours
不希望受到…影響	turn your head and cough
不得不忍受的苦事	a bitter pill to swallow
不情願地交出…	to cough up
以其人之道還治其人之身	to give someone a dose of their own medicine
令人噁心	to turn one's stomach
平安無恙	safe and sound
生在富貴人家	born with a silver spoon in ones' mouth
由於病癒而延年益壽；重新過生活	a new lease on life
休想	over one's dead body
有點阿達，有點瘋	to have a screw loose
死了	to give up the ghost
死亡	to croak
死到臨頭	one foot in the grave

IDIOMS AND EXPRESSIONS

片語慣用語

▸ 中文	▸ 英文
戒酒	on the wagon
沉重的打擊，侮辱	a black eye
走下坡	over the hill
身體不適	under the weather
刺激，鼓勵	a shot in the arm
受應得的懲罰	to take one's medicine
受歡迎的人	a sight for sore eyes
非常健康	in the pink
勃然大怒，精神崩潰	to go off the deep end
待命	on call
毒癮很深；為麻煩的事煩惱	monkey on your back
重聽	hard of hearing
祝福，祝…成功	break a leg
發癮[戒斷]症狀	horrors (withdrawal)
菸不離口的老菸槍	chain smoker
超優的人	a shiner

IDIOMS AND EXPRESSIONS

片語慣用語

▸ 中文	▸ 英文
嗑藥上癮	hooked on drugs
感染	come down with
厭倦極了	sick and tired of
瘋子，怪人；瘋狂的	nuts, nutty as a fruit-cake
僵死了，完全聾了	dead as a doornail
瘦成皮包骨	skin and bones
翹辮子	to kick the bucket

A World Apart

中文英文大不同

上癮（got hooked up with..., be addictictedto...）實在不是件好事；別以為只有藥物酒精才會上癮，只要不使用就會渾身不自在那就是上癮！所以吃維他命丸也會上癮！要戒除（to kick the habit），有的人意志信心堅強（well-determined），所以不需任何理由（to stop drinking [smoking] cold turkey）就能達到目的，但也有人要加入組織（如戒酒協會：AA (Alcohol Asylum)）並在他人的協助下甚至愈要在醫生宣告生死關頭（do or die）時才能痛定思痛下決心！身體健康也是一樣；年輕時不知道到珍惜（cherish），到了有病痛時才著急；或找偏方萬靈丹（panacea）或另類治療（alternative healing），若因此而誤了大事才真是得不償失呢！

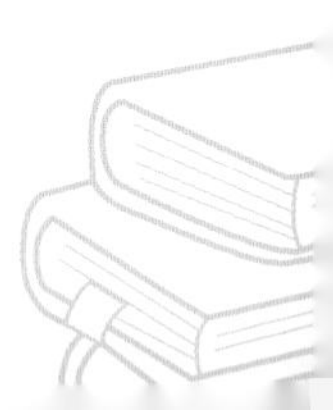

Unit 10

運動比賽

SPORTS AND GAMES

名稱	NAMES
裝備	EQUIPMENT
場所	AREAS
片語慣用語	IDIOMS AND EXPRESSIONS
自娛娛人	AMUSEMENT
片語慣用語	IDIOMS AND EXPRESSIONS
中文英文大不同	A WORLD APART

NAMES
名稱

中文	英文
水球	water polo
可賭錢的落袋撞球戲	pool
打獵	hunting
乒乓球	ping pong
冰上滾石遊戲	curling
回力球；壁球	racquetball
曲棍球	hockey
羽毛球	badminton
自行車	bicycling
足球	soccer
直排輪	roller blade
花式溜冰	figure skating
保齡球	bowling
射箭	archery
徒步旅行，遠足	hiking
徑賽運動	track

NAMES 名稱

中文	英文
拳擊	boxing
馬球	polo
高爾夫球	golf
排球	volleyball
釣魚	fishing
棒球	baseball
游泳	swimming
登山，爬山	mountaineering
跑步	running
（坡道）滑雪	(downhill) skiing
（越野）滑雪	(cross-country) skiing
溜冰，滑冰	skating
馴服野馬	bronco busting
慢跑	jogging
摔角	wrestling
網球	tennis

NAMES 名稱

▸ 中文	▸ 英文
撞球	billiards
潛水；跳水	diving
衝浪	surfing
獨木舟	canoeing
擊劍	fencing
舉重	weight lifting
壘球	softball
騎馬	horseback riding
攀岩	(rock) climbing
競速滑冰	speed skating
籃球	basketball
體操	gymnastic

EQUIPMENT
裝備

中文	英文
弓	bow
平衡木	balance beam
皮製韁繩	reins
乒乓球	ping pong
吊環	flying rings
曲棍球棍	hockey stick
羽毛球	birdie
自行車	bicycle
柱，桿	pole
拳擊[棒球]手套	glove
馬鞍	saddle
高爾夫球	golf ball
高爾夫球桿	golf clubs
球拍	racket, racquet
球座，發球處	tee
（體操用的）瓶狀木棒	Indian clubs

EQUIPMENT 裝備

中文	英文
魚竿	fishing rod
魚餌	fishing lure
滑雪杖	ski pole
滑雪板，滑雪屐	skis
墊子	mat
網子	net
彈簧墊，蹦床	trampoline
撞球桿	puck
槳	paddle
箭	arrow
衝浪板	surfboard
輪式溜冰鞋	skates
（冰上曲棍球用的）橡皮圓盤	puck
獨木舟	canoe
雙槓	parallel bars

AREAS 場所

▸ 中文	▸ 英文
小徑；蹤跡	trail
果嶺	green
馬戲場；拳擊場	ring
（網球等的）場地	court
跑道；徑賽運動	track
跑道；泳道	lane
跑道；場地	course
鄉村俱樂部	country club
溜冰場	rink
運動場，田賽場地	field
運動場	stadium
競技場；比賽場	arena
競技場；體育館	coliseum
體育館，健身房	gymnasium

Idioms and Expressions
片語慣用語

▸ 中文	▸ 英文
一日連賽兩場；行程緊湊	double-header
了解實情	to know what the score is
不費力地贏得	to win hands down
代打	to go to bat for
可以自由參加的競賽	free-for-all
打擊率；表現	batting average
立即，馬上	right off the bat
在緊急狀況下代替	to pinch hit
成功	to make a hit
成功機會渺茫的計畫	long shot
完全地（上癮，著迷）	hook, line, and sinker
延期，暫緩	rain check
故意不用力打；謹慎行動	to pull one's punches
重新	second wind

IDIOMS AND EXPRESSIONS
片語慣用語

▸ 中文	▸ 英文
破紀錄	to break the record
強而有力	to be punchy
捲土重來，東山再起	come-back
處境危險	behind the eight ball
最後階段	last lap
遊戲一部分；非針對個人的	all part of the game
實際接觸	to get on the ball
滿分	to rate a ten
盡忠職守	to have a lot of the ball
鳴槍前偷跑；行動過早	to jump the gun
標準桿以下；不舒服	below par
瞎猜	a shot in the dark
璞玉	in the rough
隨意，漫不經心的	hit or miss
歸勝利者所有	for keeps
讓某事繼續進行	to keep the ball rolling

天籟之音（Music）

中文	英文
女低音，男聲最高部，中音部	alto
女高音	soprano
小節（線）	bar
卡式磁帶	cassette
民歌	folk song
交響樂	symphony
曲調，旋律	tune
作曲	composition
作品，曲，篇	piece
男低音	bass
男高音	tenor
協奏曲	concerto
拍子，小節	measure
拍子，節奏	beat
芭蕾舞	ballad
奏鳴曲	sonata

AMUSEMENT 自娛娛人

▸ 中文	▸ 英文
指揮家	conductor
流行樂團	group
相簿；集郵簿；唱片套冊	album
背誦，朗誦，吟誦	recital
音樂會	concert
唱片，錄音	record
唱片	disc
唱片音樂節目主持人	disc jockey (DJ)
旋律；主調	melody
發行，發表	release
節目單，程序表	program
節奏，韻律	rhythm
聖歌，讚美詩	hymn
雷射唱片	compact disc (CD)
歌手	singer
歌曲	song

中文	英文
歌詞	lyrics
樂隊，樂團	band
調子	note
賣座	hit
獨唱，單飛	solo
錄音[影]帶	tape
爵士樂	jazz
藝術家，美術家，畫家	artist

音樂種類（Types of Music）

中文	英文
巴洛克式的（過分裝飾的）	baroque
古典樂	classical
必波普式爵士樂	bebop
民間音樂	folk
交響樂	symphonic

AMUSEMENT
自娛娛人

▸ 中文	▸ 英文
宗教音樂	religious
室內樂	chamber
流行樂	popular, pop
背景，幕後，雜音	background
重金屬音樂	heavy metal
重搖滾	hard rock
音樂劇	musical
氣氛音樂	mood music
教堂音樂	church
現代音樂	contemporary
現代樂	modern
鄉村西部音樂	country and western
鄉村音樂	bluegrass
搖滾樂	rock and roll
新世紀音樂（以電子樂器為主）	New Age [space]
節奏藍調	rhythm and blues

▸ 中文	▸ 英文
聖歌，靈歌	spirituals
雷鬼音樂	reggae
電子樂	electronic
歌劇	opera
舞曲	dance
輕古典	light classical
輕歌劇	operetta
嘻哈音樂	hip hop
爵士樂	jazz
饒舌音樂	rap
聽覺的，音響的	acoustic
靈魂樂	soul

樂器（Instruments）

中文	英文
大提琴	cello
大號	tuba
大鼓	drums
小喇叭，小號	trumpet
小提琴	fiddle
小提琴	violin
中提琴	viola
五弦琴	banjo
巴松笛	bassoon
吉他	guitar
低音樂器	bass
弦樂器	strings
長號，伸縮喇叭	trombone
音樂合成器	synthesizer
曼陀林	mandolin

中文	英文
單簧管，黑管，豎笛	clarinet
揚琴	dulcimer
短號	cornet
鈸	cymbals
鈴鼓，手鼓	tambourine
電吉他	electric guitar
管風琴	organ
管樂器	horn
豎琴	harp
鋼琴	piano
薩克斯管	saxophone
雙簧管	oboe

攝影（Photography）

中文	英文
一捲底片	roll of film
三腳架	tripod

AMUSEMENT
自娛娛人

▸ 中文	▸ 英文
幻燈片	slide
失焦	out-of-focus
布帶；皮帶；金屬帶	strap
布景	setting
正片	positive
光面紙	matte
光圈	aperture
（全）自動	automatic
快門	shutter
快照	snapshot
投影機	projector
取景器	viewfinder
底片，影片	film
底片	negative
放大	blow up, enlargement
金屬容器	canister

▸ 中文	▸ 英文
附加物品	accessory
相片	portrait
（照）相機	camera
相簿	album
重複曝光	double exposure
特寫鏡頭	mug shot
送件者	mailer
閃光燈	flash
捲（底片）	rewind
清晰度	definition
盒子，容器	case
連續變焦或調距的鏡頭	zoom lens
減淡加深	dodge and burn
測光錶	light meter
焦距	focal length
畫面，鏡頭	frame

AMUSEMENT 自娛娛人

中文	英文
畫素	pixel
間歇式拍攝	time lapse
傻瓜相機	instamatic
感光速率	speed
暗房	darkroom
滑面的	glossy
裝軟片	load
解析度	rez (resolution)
電池	battery
構圖	composition
廣角鏡頭	wide-angle lens
數位的	digital
膠捲，卡帶	cartridge
複製	duplicate
調焦，聚焦	focus
螢幕	screen

AMUSEMENT
自娛娛人

▸中文	▸英文
褪色的	washed out
縮小	reduce
擺姿勢	pose
濾光鏡	filter
曝光	exposure
曝光不足	under-exposed
曝光過度	over-exposed
鏡頭	lens
攝遠鏡頭，遠攝照片	telephoto
攝影室，照相館	studio
晒印照片	print
顯像，沖洗照片	process
顯像	come out
顯影劑	developer
（電視）觀眾	viewer

AMUSEMENT
自娛娛人

電影（Movies）

中文	英文
女演員	actress
小說原著	based on a novel
內景	interiors
日場，午後的演出	matinee
片長	running time
片頭	leader
主演	starring
主題曲	theme song
以…主演	feature
外景	exteriors
全景	full scene
合演	co-star
字幕	subtitle
快轉	fast forward
快鏡	fast motion
改編	adapted

AMUSEMENT
自娛娛人

▸ 中文	▸ 英文
男[女]配角	supporting actor [actress]
男演員	actor
角色，人物	character
放映日期	playing date
放映室	projection booth
長景	long shot
客串	guest star
星探	scout
重來	N.G. (No Good)
重拍	retake
首映	premier
倒片	rewind
倒述	flashback
原聲帶	sound track
海報	poster
特效	special effect

AMUSEMENT
自娛娛人

中文	英文
特寫	close-up
配音（同步）	synchronize
配音	dubbed
配景	entourage
剪接	editing
推拉鏡頭	dolly shot
排名	billing
排演	rehearsal
殺青	crank up
淡入，漸顯	fade-in
淡出，漸隱	fade-out
現場	location
場面大綱	scene plot
提名	nomination
替身	stunt
發行	release

中文	英文
評論	critic
搖鏡	panorama shot
跟鏡	follow up
預告片	trailer
對白	dialogue
歌詞	lyrics
演員表	cast
製片	producer
劇本大綱	synopsis
劇情	story
編劇	playwright
諧星	comedian
龍套演員，臨時演員	extra (player)
隱藏式字幕（供聽力障礙人士閱讀）	close-captioned
攝影棚	studio

電影種類（Types of Movies）

▸中文	▸英文
武俠片	martial art
冒險片	adventure
科幻片	sci-fi (science-fiction)
紀錄片	documentary
音樂片	musical
家庭片	family
恐怖片	horror
浪漫片	romance
神祕[神蹟]片	mystery
動作片	action
動畫片	animation
喜劇片	comedy
悲劇片	tragedy
新潮片	nouvelle vague
劇情片	melo-drama

▸ 中文	▸ 英文
暴力片	violent
戰爭片	war
賺人熱淚片	tear-jerker
懸疑片	suspense
驚悚片	thriller

電影分級（Movie Rating）

▸ 中文	▸ 英文
保護級	PG 13 (Parental Guidance 13)
限制級	R (Restricted)
普遍級	G (General)
輔導級	PG (Parental Guidance)

IDIOMS AND EXPRESSIONS
片語慣用語

▸ 中文	▸ 英文
不惹人注意	to soft-pedal
令某人覺得悅耳	music to one's ear
自吹自擂	to blow your own horn
沉默	to pipe down
居次要位置	to play second fiddle
沮喪	the blues
非常便宜的	for a song
胡言亂語	song and dance
面對困難	to face the music
做分內的事情	to sing for one's supper
感到困窘而亂撥弄…	to fiddle around with
精力充沛的	to beat the band

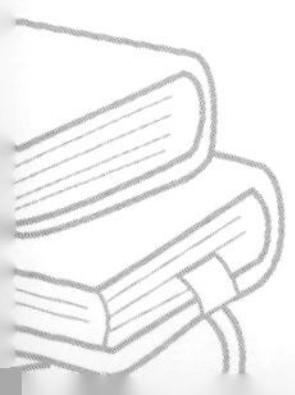

A World Apart
中文英文大不同

運動在歐美文化中一直扮演著重要的角色，否則為何在美式足球的季節中，家庭主婦都會自稱足球寡婦（football windows）呢？語言中與運動相關的用法更是不勝枚舉：

1. 開始：to kick off（美式足球用語）；to tip off（籃球用語）；to tee off（高爾夫球用語）。
2. 處理：to tackle（美式足球用語）。
3. 恰到好處：right on the money（美式足球用語）。
4. 一語中的：to hit home（棒球用語）。
5. 事後諸葛：Monday morning quarterback（美式足球用語）。

看來要真正地說出一口道地的美語還得先把運動弄懂？！

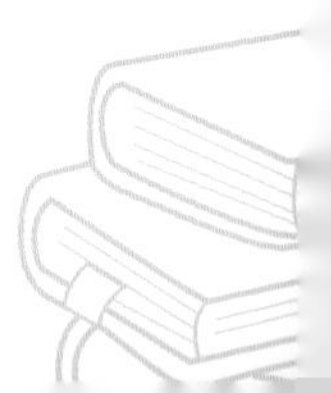

Unit 11

人算不如天算

MAN PROPOSES, GOD DISPOSES

DISASTERS 天災人禍

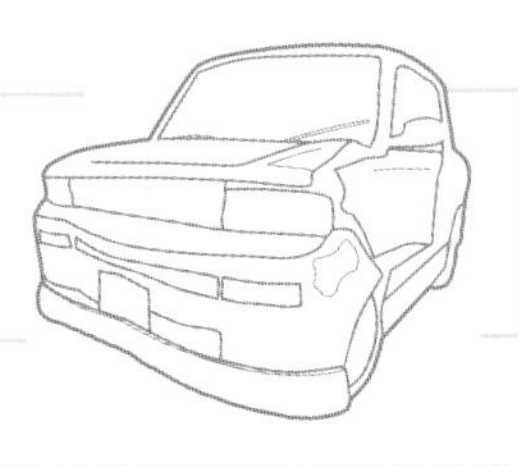

▸中文	▸英文
大火災	conflagration
大災難	catastrophe
大風雪，暴風雪	blizzard
大屠殺	carnage
內戰	civil war
火山爆發，熔岩噴出	eruption
火災	fire
全球暖化	global warming
因地震所引起的海嘯	tsunami
因如空襲所造成的火海而引起的風暴	fire storm
因意外事件的死亡，死亡事故	fatality
地震	earthquake
死亡	death, loss of life
汙染	pollution
坍方山崩，土石流	mud slide

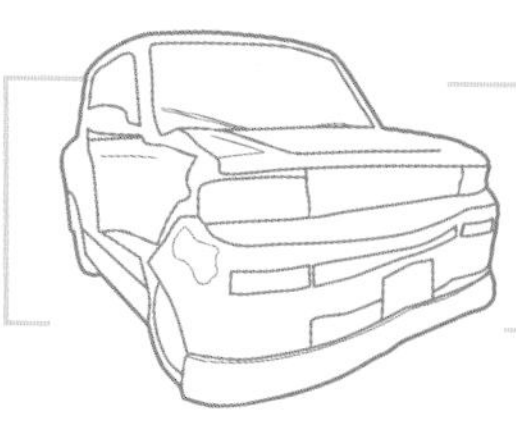

DISASTERS
天災人禍

▸ 中文	▸ 英文
沙漠化	desertification
沉沒	sinking
事故，災禍	accident
受傷	injury
油輪漏油	oil spill
芮氏地震分級標準	Richter scale
急救	first aid
洪水	flood
炸彈	bomb
砍伐森林	deforestation
突然的水災	flash flood
飛機墜毀	airplane crash
原[核子]災禍	atomocitc [nuclear] disaster
恐怖主義	terrorism
核熔毀	nuclear meltdown
海面石油汙染	oil slick

DISASTERS
天災人禍

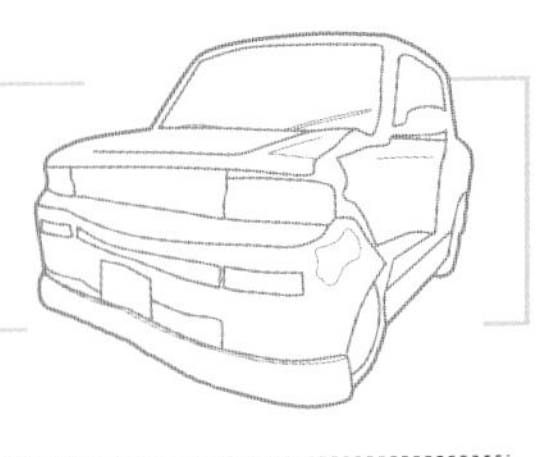

中文	英文
海嘯；滿潮	tidal wave
飢荒	famine
飢餓；餓死	starvation
乾旱，旱災	drought
救援	rescue
救濟（物品；金）	relief
救護車	ambulance
旋風	twister
船隻的失事；失事船隻或飛機的殘骸	wreckage
船難；船舶的遺骸	shipwreck
野火	wild fire
雪崩，山崩	avalanche
惡性傳染病	pestulence
傳染[流行]病	epidemic
碰撞，相撞	collision
撤離，疏散	evacuation

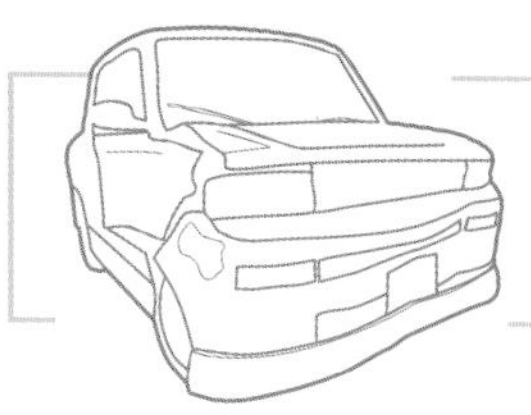

DISASTERS 天災人禍

▸ 中文	▸ 英文
種族淨化	ethnic cleansing
種族滅絕	genocide
緊急狀態	state of emergency
緊急情況，突發事件	emergency
賑災	disaster relief
颱風	typhoon
暴風，龍捲風	cyclone
暴風雨	storm
暴動，暴亂	riot
熱帶風暴	tropical storm
（如鼠疫等的）瘟疫	plague
餘震	aftershock
戰爭	war
蹂躪，荒廢	devastation
龍捲風，旋風；颶風	tornado
環境毀滅	environmental destruction

DISASTERS
天災人禍

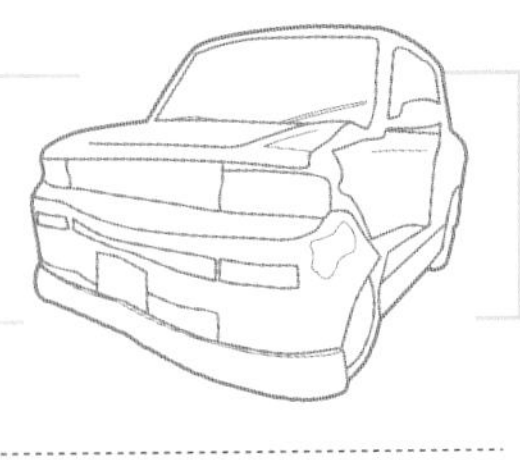

▸ 中文	▸ 英文
避難所	shelter
颶風，暴風雨	hurricane
爆炸	explosion
犧牲者，遇難者	victim

Idioms and Expressions

片語慣用語

▸ 中文	▸ 英文
天災	an act of God
避風港；聊勝於無	any port in a storm
防患未然	better safe than sorry
暴風雨前的寧靜	clam before the storm
死亡數	death toll

A World Apart

中文英文大不同

律師（lawyer, barrister, solicitor, counsel）是個地位崇高的職業；就如同醫生一般，這兩種職業的執行業務還非得用不同於其他職業的說法：「to practice law [medicine]」，但在實際生活中，興訴似乎總會帶來些負面的意義（with some negative tones）！所以英文中常用「ambulance chaser」（追救護車的人），來形容律師。而以律師為主題的笑話或腦筋急轉彎也不少：

What a lawyer usually names his [her] daughter?
Sue.
律師通常用哪個名字來命名他[她]的女兒？
蘇（又同「控訴」）。

看來想要變成高級專業人員（professionals）還是要付出些代價的（Nothing comes cheap）！

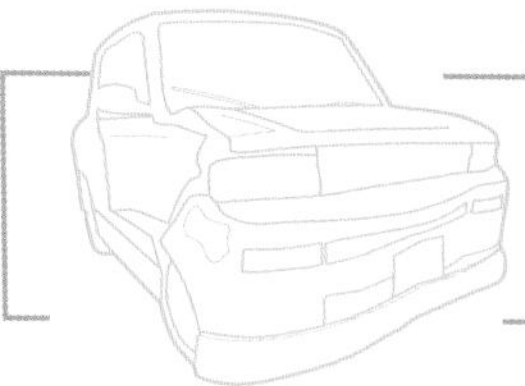

ENERGY AND ENVIRONMENT 能源環境

▸中文	▸英文
一桶油	barrel of oil
乙醇，酒精	ethanol
大眾運輸	mass transit
不可靠的操作員	wildcat operator
公用事業（水、電、瓦斯）	utilities
（核）分裂	fission
（如煤、石油、天然氣等的）化石燃料	fossil fuel
天然氣	natural gas
太陽能	solar power
引擎	engine
水力發電	hydro-electric power
水壩	dam
丙烷	propane
加油口	gas pump
可更新的資源	renewable resources

ENERGY AND ENVIRONMENT 能源環境

▸ 中文	▸ 英文
可供消費的資源	consumable resources
石油	oil
石油生產	oil production
石油挖掘	oil drilling
回收	recycling
汽車	motor
汽油	gasoline (gas) (美) petroleum (英)
來源，出處	source
垃圾掩埋場	landfill
油井	oil well
油田	oil field
油管	pipeline
保護，保存	conservation
洗滌器，刷子	scrubbers
風力	wind power
風車	windmill

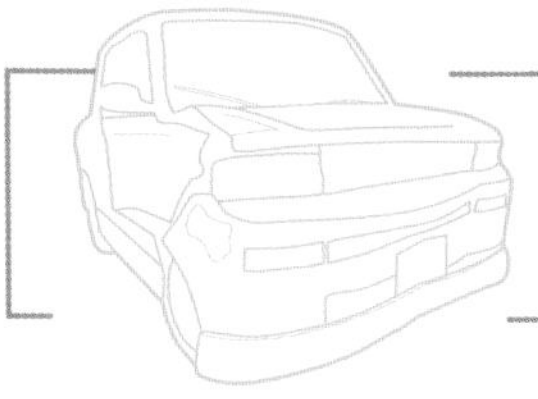

▸ 中文	▸ 英文
核子反應器	nuclear reactor
核能	nuclear power
核廢料	atomic waste
消耗，用盡	depletion
消費，使用	consumption
海底鑽油設備	oil rig
海嘯	tidal wave, tsunami
海潮	tidal
能源成本	energy costs
能源效率	emergency efficiency
能源稅	emergency tax
能源損失	emergency loss
臭氧（臭氧層）	ozone (ozone layer)
動能	kinetic
渦輪（機）	turbine
發電機	generator

ENERGY AND ENVIRONMENT
能源環境

▸ 中文	▸ 英文
絕種，滅絕的	extinct
絕緣（體）	insulation
超導體	super conductors
溶解；融合	fusion
煙霧	smog
煤	coal
煉油廠	refinery
電力	electricity
電池，電瓶	battery
對能源的（不）依賴	emergency (in) dependence
蒸氣	steam
酸雨	acid rain
熱度，溫度；高溫，暑熱	heat
燃料	fuel
燃燒	combustion

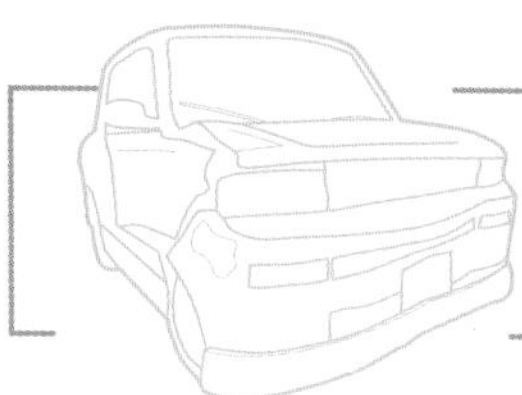

ENERGY AND ENVIRONMENT 能源環境

▸ 中文	▸ 英文
環保分子	environmentalist
環保政策	environmental policy
環保科學	environmental science
環境法	environmental law
環境清理	environmental cleanup
濾器	filter
瀕臨絕種的動植物	endangered species
觸媒轉化器	catalytic converter
鑿岩機	drilling rig

A World Apart

中文英文大不同

3Rs（re-duce, re-use, re-cycle）一直是環保中重要的環節；現在也有人提倡 4Rs（re-duce, re-use, re-cycle, re-produce）；不管是 3 或 4，珍惜資源、保護環境是現在最熱門的議題。雖然全球暖化（global warming）究竟是真是假，地球資源是否已經被人類消耗殆盡等爭議依然未定（up in the air），但人類的未來日子會一天比一天難過（with a gloomy picture）則是不爭的事實。

老實說，只要每個人少用或不用（use not, waste not），我們今天所遭遇到的問題和未來所有的隱憂都會消失。不用任何對環境造成傷害的物品，多用本地產品而不是來自於遙遠他鄉的進口貨，因而減少運輸時所造成的汙染，拒絕不必要的消費；對所有人而言，這些做法都只不過是舉手之勞。

與其絞盡腦汁想新對策，我們只要在日常生活中多注意一下，永續的生活（LOHAS, Lifestyle of Health and Sustainability）絕不是夢想。

A WORLD APART
中文英文大不同

如在本書開始所說的，其中收集編篡的字彙絕不代表英文字彙既如此，所列舉出項目也絕非是唯一的；就如在最後單元中所引用的「林來瘋」例證，只有不斷地常保對知識的好奇和飢渴「stay foolish, stay hungry」不斷在日常生活工作中找尋自己感興趣或是能力有所不足的領域和挑戰，英語文學習才能不斷提升，不斷精進！

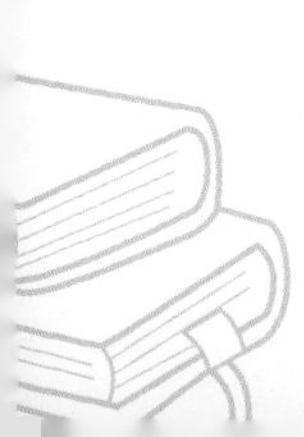

NOTE 筆記頁

Unit 12

大江東去，淘盡多少風雲字

DO YOU KNOW THAT WORDS COME AND WORDS GO!

「林來瘋」（Linsanity）這個字已經正式的為「國際語言觀察」（Global Language Monitor）機構認可並列為公認的字彙！倒底「林書豪熱」（mania, zest, fad, ...）還會續燒多久？豪帥能否真的能在尼克隊隻手撐天，扭轉乾坤（a 180-degree turnaround）？林灰姑娘（Linderella）是否又是資本主義下遭剝削的廉價勞工「over-worked and under-paid」？…太多太多的疑問可能還要一段時間方能有解，但從「林來瘋」這個新字彙的出現中，我們可以知道任何語言中的字彙會因為某社會中現象的產生而出現，也會因為某種現象的消失而死亡；語言是個有機體，能生會死而非單純且無生命的符號又再一次得到證明！

下列所列舉出的是21世紀第一個十年所選出各年度風雲字；各位讀者知道嗎？而這些字中有多少在今日仍為我們所記得及採用的呢?

21世紀第一個十年風雲字：「9/11」，「Google」，「Chinglish」（在如新加坡、日本等國家將本身語言和英語文結合後所產生出的發音獨特且字彙、語意不同於傳統用法的新語言），「bailout」（紓困），和「Tsunami」（海嘯）等字緊接其後。

2011

風雲字：「occupy」（占領）（華爾街運動）；當1%的人掌握了90%的財富時，改革是勢在必行！

金融危機使得「deficit」（赤字）這個字也成為2011年度大字；（地球村）「global village」的事實使得天涯若比鄰，但「butterfly effects」（蝴蝶效應）卻也使得世界上所有國家息息相關、唇亡齒寒！

年度最佳詞句：「Arab Spring」（阿拉伯之春）所及之處使得多少獨裁者下臺，也使得民主在最不可能發生的地方生根發芽！

「Steve Jobs」蘋果電腦的（賈伯斯）則成為年度風雲姓名。

2010

風雲字：「Spillcam」（即時漏油轉播）；英國石油公司（BP, British Petroleum）流年不利（having a bad year），連續在美國南部沿海及波斯灣因油輪漏油而造成全球生態大變；「Snowmagedden, Snowpocalpse」「snow +apocalypse, armageddon」因在美國東部及歐洲突如其來的「大風雪」而將雪與世界末日連結而成；

「3-D」（Three-dimensional）電影成為主流娛樂也將這個字推上年度風雲榜。

2009

「Twitter」（推特）在本年度獨領風騷；「H1N1」（流感病毒）也緊追在後；因「Thrill」（顫慄）一歌而成為搖滾樂傳奇人物的Michael

Jackson 也在本年度乘鶴歸去，「King of Pop」（流行樂之王）因而成年度風雲詞句。

2008

美國現任總統（歐巴馬）在本年度成功當選，成為年度風雲字實在是當之無愧，而「Yes, we can」（我們能改變）也成為年度風雲詞句。

2007

「Hybrid」（汽電車）成為該年度人人矚目的字；或許是因為早先不知惜福，所以造成「global warming」（全球暖化），現在突然，覺悟想為地球盡份心力使然？！同時，「climate change」（氣候改變）也成為當年度風雲詞句。

2006

樂活觀念中的「Sustainable」（永續經營）是2006的年度風雲字；而「Stay on Course」（永不改變）則是風雲詞句。

2005

風雲字：「Katrina」颶風侵襲美國南部各州及「Tsunami」在東南亞造成千上萬人喪命或妻離子散，流離失所的（大海嘯）；地方不同但所有損失傷害卻是相同！

風雲詞句：「Outside the Mainstream」（離開主流文化）；「creativity」（創意力）和

「originality」（原創性）成為個人的「trade-mark」（標記）始能營造出多元氣息。

2004

戰亂和「racial cleansing」（種族屠殺）使得「Incivility」（= in Civil War）（內戰中）成為當年代表字；美國政治上民主黨和共和黨的對立也讓政治立場明顯的各州「Blue States」（藍州，泛指共和黨）和「Red States」（紅州，泛指民主黨）因對立而成為風雲詞句。

2003

電腦軟體霸主「微軟」自文字處理系統後又再一次把所有電腦使用者綁架；「Embedded」（微軟式嵌入系統）之成為風雲字就很明顯地告訴我們想要跳出」Microsoft」（微軟）的掌握還真是不容易啊！當年度的第二次波斯灣戰爭也使「Shock and Awe」（震攝戰術）成為風雲詞句。

2002

風雲字：「Misunderestimate」（錯估）

風雲詞句：「Threat Fatigue」；喊（狼來了）太多次，最後大家都麻木了。

2001

9/11時近四千條人命因少數一些宗教狂熱分子，脅迫三架飛機分別撞入美國財經重鎮大樓

和國防部；「Ground Zero」飛機碰撞的（中心點），這個字將會長存你我心中！

而機上乘客因了解自己無法存活而一擁而上，想將劫機者制伏時所喊出「Let's Roll！」（我們上）這句話也成為本年度的風雲詞句。

2000

美國小布希總統因為選舉時，選票是否為廢票而以微不足道的票數當選；投票時在選票上「Chad」（打孔）是否正確就決定了誰能主政，進駐白宮8年！

「Dot.com」（達康）則是人人朗朗上口的風雲詞句。

另外有兩個網站連結：

Urban Dictionary
Cyber Translator

雖然未必是為大家所公認的字彙，但這兩個網站每日提供給讀者反映社會現狀的最新表達。對喜歡了解英語文用法的學習者而言，只要登錄且不必花一分錢，就能掌握英文脈動（heartbeat），實在是不可多得的助力！

13個 / 023, 175
MP3播放器 / 058
OK繃 / 192
T恤 / 048
X光 / 196
X光機 / 192

一 畫

一人吃兩人補；懷孕 / 023
一大群 / 121
一小群 / 121
一元商店 / 178
一文不值 / 023
一日連賽兩場；行程緊湊 / 218
一丘之貉 / 131
一行人 / 078
一時想不起來 / 107
一動也不動 / 107
一捲底片 / 226
一桶油 / 247
一組 / 121
一鳥在手勝過二鳥在林 / 131
一群 / 121
一群，一批 / 121
一夥人 / 078
一對 / 121
一窩 / 121, 122
一箭雙鵰 / 023

一箭雙鵰，一舉兩得 / 131
一幫，一夥，一族 / 122

二 畫

乙醇，酒精 / 247
丁型[腋下]拐杖 / 192
丁香 / 014
九層塔 / 014
了解實情 / 218
二手家具[衣物，車]行 / 184
人 / 123
人工流產手術 / 196
人多手雜 / 023
人字拖 / 053
人物 / 232
人要衣裝 / 055
人們 / 077
人群恐懼症 / 099
人權擁護者 / 162
八哥 / 125
十歲以前的孩童 / 081

三 畫

三角褲 / 048
三腳架 / 226
丈夫 / 074
上床睡覺 / 044, 143
上流社會 / 023

上班[營業]時間　/ 207
上漿的正式襯衫　/ 048
兀鷹　/ 125
口服避孕藥　/ 198
口紅　/ 068
（口腔[直腸]）溫度計　/ 192
口碑　/ 107
口譯員　/ 162
土[郊]狼　/ 113
土木工程師　/ 162
土司　/ 007
土狼　/ 118
土間　/ 030
（大）白菜　/ 002
（大）哥[姊]　/ 075
大[小]腸　/ 094
大[核心]家庭　/ 088
大人物　/ 175
大比目魚　/ 010
大火災　/ 240
大而無當的東西　/ 131
大衣　/ 048
大吵大鬧　/ 156
大災難　/ 240
大拇指　/ 094
大風雪，暴風雪　/ 240
大師傅　/ 163
大動肝火，勃然大怒　/ 156

大屠殺 / 240
大淺盤 / 017
大眾運輸 / 247
大提琴 / 225
大湯匙 / 017
大猩猩 / 118
大象 / 118, 123
大廈 / 028
大概數字 / 175
大碗 / 017, 019
大肆整頓 / 044
大號 / 225
大鼓 / 225
大腿 / 094
大蒜 / 014
大鳴不平 / 044
大樓 / 028
大盤 / 017
大賣場 / 178
大頭針 / 059
大聲的 / 083
大膽的，莽撞的 / 083
大翻車魚 / 115
（女）牧童[牛仔] / 165
（女）門房 / 166
（女）看門人 / 166
（女）修理工 / 167
（女）商人，實業家 / 168

（女）救火員 / 168
（女）清潔工 / 168
（女）電視[收音機]修理工人 / 171
女用內褲 / 048
女用手提袋 / 062
女用胸針 / 058
女用襯衫 / 048
女低音 / 220
女兒 / 074
女性友人 / 078
女服務生 / 165
女朋友 / 078
女高音 / 220
女演員 / 231
女管家 / 162
子房 / 141
子宮切除術 / 196
小刀 / 059
小心提防 / 107
小本經營 / 055
小白花 / 136
（小）白菜 / 002
小耳朵 / 041
小弟 / 162
（小）弟[妹] / 074
小兒科師生 / 194
小兒科病房 / 190
小兒麻痺症 / 203

小物包 / 058
小型便利商店 / 178
小孩 / 081
小徑 / 217
小書房 / 030
小烤箱 / 034
小茴香 / 014
小茶几 / 032
小喇叭 / 225
小提琴 / 225
小節 / 220
小節（線） / 220
小號 / 225
小鉗子 / 193
小零錢包 / 058
小夥子 / 071
小腿肚 / 094
小說原著 / 231
小蝦 / 010
小樹林 / 135
小鬍子 / 098
山中小木屋 / 028
山毛櫸 / 136
山羊 / 112, 123
山羊鬍 / 098
山茶花 / 136
山茱萸 / 136
山崩 / 242

山雀 / 125
山貓 / 113
山藥 / 002
工友 / 162
工作室 / 030
工具儲藏室 / 040
工程師 / 162
工廠作業員 / 162
弓 / 215

四 畫

不可靠的操作員 / 247
不安的局勢 / 156
不自然的，扭捏的 / 083
不含阿斯匹靈的止痛藥 / 106
不含酒精的飲料 / 016
不希望受到…影響 / 207
不周詳的計畫 / 044
不知所措，猶豫的 / 156
不知所措的 / 156
不待強求 / 088
不氣餒，堅持下去 / 088
不起眼的雜貨店 / 178
不得不忍受的苦事 / 207
不情願地交出… / 207
不費力地贏得 / 218
不惹人注意 / 237
中年人 / 081

中要害的，中肯的 / 044
中音部 / 220
中風 / 203
中提琴 / 225
中暑 / 099
丹麥麵包 / 007
五斗櫃 / 033
五弦琴 / 225
五金行 / 178
仁慈的 / 083
內衣襯衣 / 048
（內科）醫生 / 195
內景 / 231
內戰 / 240
內褲 / 048
公公 / 075
公用事業 / 247
公共廁所 / 192
公車司機 / 162
公事包 / 058
公寓 / 028
公寓或學校照管房屋的看門人 / 162
公園 / 135
分戶出售的公寓 / 028
分娩室，產房 / 190
切 / 021
切丁 / 021
切片 / 021

切柳 / 021
切絲 / 021
勿忘我 / 136
化妝 / 066
化妝品 / 066
化驗員 / 162
午後的演出 / 231
友人 / 078
友善的 / 083
及早做事的人 / 131
及膝襪子 / 053
天井 / 030
天生的 / 107
天災 / 245
天竺鼠 / 112
天花 / 203
天花板 / 032
天然氣 / 247
天鵝 / 123, 125
太陽穴 / 094
太陽能 / 247
太陽魚 / 115
孔雀 / 125
少了溫馨，房子不是家 / 044
巴士駕駛 / 162
巴松笛 / 225
巴洛克式的 / 222
幻燈片 / 227

引擎 / 247
心不在焉 / 023
心情不好，喜怒無常 / 148
心理學者 / 162
心裡緊張 / 107
心跳 / 196
心電圖 / 196
心臟 / 094
心臟病 / 099, 203
手 / 094
手[拐]杖 / 058
手[腕]錶 / 058
手用乳液 / 066
手肘 / 094
手帕 / 058
手拙 / 107
手持式個人電腦 / 058
手指 / 094
手指甲 / 094
手套 / 048
手挽斜背袋 / 058
手術 / 196
手術室 / 190
手術臺 / 192
手部清潔劑 / 066
手掌 / 094
手提或膝上型電腦 / 058
手提袋 / 058

手機 / 058
手臂 / 094
手鐲 / 058
支氣管炎 / 203
支票簿 / 058
文火慢烤 / 021
文火慢煮 / 021
文具店 / 178
斗篷 / 048
方頭巾 / 058
方頭鞋 / 053
日場 / 231
月見草 / 136
月桂葉 / 014
月桂樹 / 136
木工[匠] / 162
木工店 / 178
木瓜 / 005
木屋 / 028
木屐 / 053
木蘭 / 136
止咳片 / 106
比賽場 / 217
比薩店 / 178
毛巾架 / 036
毛衣 / 048
毛線褲 / 048
毛蟲 / 117

水（礦泉水） / 016
（水、電表）抄表員 / 164
水力發電 / 247
水手 / 162
水手刀 / 059
水木 / 136
水牛 / 118
水泡 / 099
水族槽 / 120
水球 / 212
水壺 / 017
水煮 / 021
水痘 / 099, 203
水電行 / 178
水管工 / 162
水槽 / 034
水龍頭 / 034
水獺 / 113
水壩 / 247
火山爆發，熔岩噴出 / 240
火災 / 240
火柴 / 059
火腿 / 010
火雞 / 010, 125
爪 / 129
父[母] / 088
父系的 / 074
父親 / 074

父親的 / 074
片長 / 231
片頭 / 231
牙刷 / 066
牙科保健員 / 162
牙粉 / 066
牙痛 / 099
牙膏 / 066
牙線 / 066
牙醫 / 163
牙醫助理 / 162
牛 / 112, 123
牛仔馬[短]靴 / 053
牛仔褲 / 048
牛奶奶油混合乳 / 012
牛肉 / 010
牛角麵包 / 007
丙烷 / 247
世代相傳 / 088
主人 / 078
主演 / 231
主廚 / 163
主調 / 221
主題曲 / 231
以…主演 / 231
以其人之道還治其人之身 / 207
以花言巧語騙人的騙子 / 163

五畫

代打 / 218
令人愉快的，舒適的 / 083
令人噁心 / 207
令某人覺得悅耳 / 237
仙人掌 / 136
充實的一餐 / 023
兄弟 / 074
兄弟姊妹鬩牆 / 088
冬瓜 / 002
冬青 / 136
冬蔥 / 002
出血 / 099
出版商 / 163
出疹子 / 099
出納（員） / 163
出納員 / 171
加入 / 021
加油口 / 247
加油站 / 178
加油站員工 / 163
加重護理 / 196
加強 / 023
加護病房 / 190
包心菜 / 002
包皮 / 094
包紮傷口 / 104

包腳鞋 / 053
（北美印第安人穿的）鹿皮軟鞋 / 054
北美夜鷹 / 125
北美紅雀 / 125
（北美產）山貓 / 113
卡[貨]車駕駛 / 163
卡式磁帶 / 220
卡帶 / 229
去角質 / 066
可以自由參加的競賽 / 218
可可 / 014
可更新的資源 / 247
可供消費的資源 / 248
可惡的 / 154
可愛的 / 083
可疑 / 023
可樂 / 016
可賭錢的落袋撞球戲 / 212
古比魚 / 115
古典樂 / 222
古怪的男人 / 078
古董店 / 181
古龍香水 / 066
司空見慣，輕鬆平常 / 175
只對家人公開 / 088
四角[平口]內褲 / 048
四肢發達頭腦簡單的人 / 078
（外）孫子女 / 075

（外）祖父 / 076
（外）祖父[母] / 076
（外）祖母 / 076
（外）曾孫子[女] / 076
（外）曾祖父[母] / 076
外交人員[官] / 163
（外科）醫生 / 195
外科醫生 / 163
外景 / 231
外甥 / 075
失去知覺 / 099
失言 / 107
失事船隻或飛機的殘骸 / 242
失明 / 200
失望 / 148
失焦 / 227
奶油 / 012
奶油[喝咖啡用的奶精]壺 / 017
奶油乳酪 / 012
奶油碟 / 017
奶精 / 007, 012
奶頭 / 094
孕婦裝 / 048
尼特族 / 081
尼龍襪子 / 048
市[鎮]公所 / 178
市鑰 / 064
布丁 / 013

布朗尼 / 013
布帶 / 227
布景 / 227
布穀鳥 / 125
平安無恙 / 207
平底鞋 / 053
平底鍋 / 019
平淡無奇的 / 083
平衡木 / 215
幼兒 / 081
幼稚 / 081
必波普式爵士樂 / 222
打火機 / 059
打字員 / 163
打扮漂亮 / 055
打破；折斷 / 021
打針 / 196
打蛋器 / 019
打麻醉藥 / 104
打飽嗝 / 099
打嗝 / 099
打噴嚏 / 099
打擊率；表現 / 218
打獵 / 212
打蠟 / 042
扒 / 021
未成年的人 / 081
未成年者 / 081

未事先約定就打電話推銷　/ 175
未婚夫[妻]　/ 074, 078
正片　/ 227
正式外套　/ 049
母牛　/ 112
母系的　/ 074
母親　/ 074
母親的　/ 074
民間互助會　/ 178
民間音樂　/ 222
民意測驗專家　/ 163
民歌　/ 220
玄關　/ 030
玉米　/ 002
玉米麵包　/ 007
甘[番]薯　/ 002
生在富貴人家　/ 207
生理痛　/ 100
生產　/ 196
用功的　/ 083
用來化驗的樣品　/ 196
田野　/ 135
田賽場地　/ 217
由於病癒而延年益壽；重新過生活　/ 207
白米　/ 008
白血病　/ 203
白灼　/ 021
白楊　/ 136

白楊木 / 136
白樺 / 136
白蟻 / 117
白蘭地 / 016
白蠟樹 / 136
白鷺 / 125
皮夾 / 059
皮夾子 / 059
皮夾克 / 049
皮帶 / 049, 227
皮帶扣環 / 049
皮製韁繩 / 215
皮膚 / 095
皮膚科醫生 / 194
皮膚癌 / 203
石匠 / 163
石油 / 248
石油生產 / 248
石油挖掘 / 248
石榴花 / 136
石膏 / 192
穴 / 120
立即，馬上 / 218
立法委員 / 163
立法者 / 163
立燈，落地燈 / 032

六畫

乒乓球　/ 212, 215
交通指揮員　/ 163
交響樂　/ 220, 222
仿晒油　/ 066
伐木工　/ 172
休閒西裝外套　/ 049
休閒襯衫　/ 049
休想　/ 207
休養所　/ 191
企鵝　/ 125
光面紙　/ 227
光圈　/ 227
（全）自動　/ 227
全科醫生　/ 194
全球暖化　/ 240
全景　/ 231
共同生活　/ 088
再多再好也不要　/ 023
（冰上曲棍球用的）橡皮圓盤　/ 216
冰上滾石遊戲　/ 212
冰屋　/ 028
冰淇淋　/ 012
冰箱　/ 034
印刷工　/ 164
印刷行　/ 178
吉他　/ 225

同父異母 / 074
同父異母[同母異父]的兄弟姊妹 / 074
同母異父 / 074
同行 / 078
同伴 / 078
同志 / 078
同事 / 078
吊褲[襪]帶 / 049
吊環 / 215
向日葵 / 136
名片夾 / 059
合作的 / 083
合掌蟑螂 / 117
合演 / 231
吃的很少 / 023
吃相難看 / 023
因地震所引起的海嘯 / 240
因如空襲所造成的火海而引起的風暴 / 240
因某事感到激動、擔憂 / 156
（因羞澀、尷尬而）臉紅 / 153
因意外事件的死亡，死亡事故 / 240
回力球 / 212
回收 / 248
回教寺院 / 178
地下室 / 030
地毯地板店 / 178
地窖 / 030
地震 / 240

在人背後 / 107
在緊急狀況下代替 / 218
多發性硬化 / 203
好朋友 / 079
好戰，好鬥 / 148
如坐針氈 / 055
（如煤、石油、天然氣等的）化石燃料 / 247
（如鼠疫等的）瘟疫 / 243
字幕 / 231
存不住錢 / 055
安靜的，輕聲地，沉默的 / 083
寺廟 / 178
尖頭鞋 / 053
帆布運動鞋 / 053
年長者，輩分高的人 / 081
年輕人 / 081
年輕時過得縱情逸樂的生活 / 143
成人 / 081
成功 / 218
成功機會渺茫的計畫 / 218
托兒所 / 179
托盤 / 017
收工 / 175
收支平衡 / 175
收支打平 / 175
收垃圾的人 / 164
收垃圾的工人 / 164
收音機電視修理店 / 179

曲 / 220
曲棍球 / 212
曲棍球棍 / 215
曲調，旋律 / 220
有才智的，有理性的 / 083
有支架的拐杖 / 059
有決心的 / 083
有使…心服的能力 / 107
有所保留的 / 083
有很多…，很忙 / 107
有玻璃天花板的室內空間 / 030
有執照[正式]護士 / 194
有情人終成眷屬 / 156
有帽沿的帽子 / 049
有蓋的罐子 / 034
有線電視公司 / 179
有幫助的 / 083
有點阿達，有點瘋 / 207
有禮貌的 / 083
有藝術技巧[鑑賞力]的 / 084
死了 / 207
死亡 / 207, 240
死亡數 / 245
死到臨頭 / 207
死前的最後演出 / 131
死巷子；沒結果的事 / 044
死裡逃生，僥倖逃過 / 175
汗衫貼身內衣 / 049

汙染 / 240
百合 / 137
百貨公司 / 179
百葉窗 / 032
竹子 / 137
竹筍 / 002
羊肉 / 010
羽毛 / 129
羽毛背心 / 049
羽毛球 / 212, 215
羽絨外套 / 049
老人中心 / 179
老年人 / 081
老虎 / 118
老處女 / 078
老闆兼打雜 / 175
老鷹 / 123
考察者 / 172
耳朵 / 095
耳朵發炎 / 099
耳痛 / 099
耳罩 / 049
耳環 / 059
耳聾 / 200
肉丸子 / 010
肉桂 / 014
肉桂[果醬，蛋糕]捲 / 013
肉販 / 164

肌肉 / 095
自行車 / 212, 215
自助洗衣店 / 179
自助飯館 / 179
自助餐館 / 179
自吹自擂 / 237
自私的 / 084
自來水筆 / 060
自制自律的 / 084
自負的，驕傲自滿的 / 084
自閉症 / 203
自陷困境中 / 143
自毀前程 / 131
色情的 / 154
血肉之軀 / 107
血緣 / 077
血濃於水 / 088
血壓 / 196
血癌 / 203
行李管理員 / 164
行為漂亮才漂亮 / 071
行為端莊的，文雅的 / 084
衣料店 / 179
衣櫥 / 030
西瓜 / 005
西洋杉 / 137
西裝上衣 / 049

七畫

住院 / 191
伴侶 / 078
伸縮喇叭 / 225
作曲 / 220
作品 / 220
作家 / 164
作嘔 / 152
伯[叔]母 / 075
伯[叔]祖 / 074
伯[叔]祖母 / 074
低泣 / 152
低音樂器 / 225
低脂牛奶 / 012
免疫力 / 203
冷衫 / 137
冷凍庫 / 034
冷漠，不關心 / 148
冷漠不關心的 / 084
冷酷[冷淡，不友善]的 / 084
冷靜，平息 / 152
冷霜 / 066
冷顫 / 200
別針 / 059
別針型領帶夾 / 059
別墅 / 028
刨絲 / 021

助步車 / 193
努力工作 / 175
吹風機 / 036
吹嘘打屁 / 131
吸引人注意的，迷人的 / 084
吸塵 / 042
吸鼻煙 / 059
吵來吵去自相殘殺 / 107
吟誦 / 221
困乏，消沉，厭倦 / 148
困窘，難為情 / 148
坍方山崩，土石流 / 240
坐立不安，心神不定 / 148
妒忌，猜忌 / 148
完全地（上癮，著迷） / 218
完全是另外一回事 / 131
屁股 / 095, 098
尿布 / 193
尿布桶 / 038
尾巴 / 129
希望 / 148
床 / 033
床架 / 033
床單 / 033
床罩 / 033
床墊 / 033
床頭板 / 033
床頭櫃 / 033

弄清楚 / 064
忌妒 / 148
志得意滿的 / 084
志願人員 / 164
忍氣吞聲 / 023
快門 / 227
快活 / 148
快活的，高興的 / 154
快照 / 227
快樂（的青鳥） / 131
快樂，歡欣 / 148
快樂的；放蕩的；豔麗的 / 154
快轉 / 231
快鏡 / 231
戒酒 / 208
抗組織胺 / 198
技師 / 162, 164, 172
扶手椅 / 032
扭傷 / 099
扭傷（肌肉） / 200
扭傷（腳踝） / 200
折疊式嬰兒推車 / 038
投影機 / 227
抓住 / 055
抓傷 / 099
改編 / 231
束腰 / 049
李子 / 005

杏子 / 005
杏花 / 137
杜鵑 / 125
杜鵑花 / 137
每下愈況 / 131
沙拉碗 / 017
沙拉醬 / 009
沙發 / 032
沙鼠 / 112
沙漠化 / 241
沙錐 / 125
沉沒 / 241
沉重的打擊，侮辱 / 208
沉默 / 237
沐浴油 / 066
沖洗照片 / 230
沒有舞伴而孤坐著的女人；壁花 / 143
沒有學歷但有經驗的護士 / 194
沒問題！ / 107
沒機會或結果的工作 / 175
汽水 / 016
汽車 / 248
汽車工程師 / 164
汽車修理店 / 179, 180
汽車商 / 181
汽車零件店 / 179
汽油 / 248
灼傷 / 202

災難的前兆 / 044
牢不可分的夥伴 / 088
牡丹 / 137
狂怒，盛怒 / 148
狂暴的，狂怒的 / 154
男[女]按摩師 / 164
男[女]配角 / 232
男低音 / 220
男性友人 / 078
男朋友 / 078
男高音 / 220
男演員 / 232
男聲最高部 / 220
私人房間[空間] / 190
（私立）療養院 / 191
私室 / 030
私家車道 / 040
禿鷹 / 125
肝炎 / 203
肝臟 / 095
育樂中心 / 179
育嬰房 / 030
芒果 / 005
芋頭 / 002
角色 / 232
豆 / 002
豆芽 / 002
走下坡 / 208

走鵑 / 125
足科醫生 / 164, 194
足球 / 212
身分手掛牌 / 059
身分證 / 059
身體不適 / 208
身體乳液 / 066
車庫 / 030, 040
辛勤工作的 / 084
防水衣 / 049
防晒乳 / 066
防晒油 / 066
防狼噴霧器 / 059
防患未然 / 245
防滑墊 / 036
防腐劑 / 198

八畫

乳房 / 095
乳酪 / 012
乳瑪琳 / 012
事事往光明方向看 / 064
事故，災禍 / 241
依賴往日雄風 / 143
依賴某人過日子；寄生蟲 / 088
使人傷心的人事物 / 156
使用最後一招 / 131
使者 / 167

來源，出處 / 248
兔子 / 123
兒子 / 074
刻意迴避的 / 084
刷子 / 248
刺槐 / 137
刺激，鼓勵 / 208
刮鬍膏 / 066
刮鬍鬚後用乳液 / 067
制酸劑 / 106
剁碎 / 021
協奏曲 / 220
卑鄙的 / 084
卸甲液 / 067
取捷徑，走直路 / 131
取景器 / 227
叔[舅，伯，姨]公 / 075
叔[舅，伯，姨]婆 / 075
受母親或妻子的操縱 / 055
受傷 / 200, 241
受應得的懲罰 / 208
受歡迎的人 / 208
咖哩 / 014
咖啡 / 016
咖啡店 / 179
咖啡壺 / 017
咖啡機 / 034
咀嚼式菸草 / 059

咀嚼式菸草袋 / 060
和左鄰右舍較量 / 044
固定用敷料 / 192
垃圾掩埋場 / 179, 248
垃圾桶 / 034
垃圾場 / 179
垃圾壓縮機 / 034
垃圾輾碎機 / 034
（坡道）滑雪 / 213
坦白地說 / 132
夜來香 / 137
夜燈 / 038
夜鷹 / 125
奇異果 / 005
妻子 / 075
姑[姨]婆 / 074
姑公 / 074
姑嬸 / 075
姊妹 / 075
孤兒 / 075
孤獨症 / 203
宗教音樂 / 223
宗譜 / 076
官僚 / 164
居次要位置 / 237
岳父 / 075
岳母 / 075
店員 / 164

底片 / 227
底線，最重要的事 / 176
延期，暫緩 / 218
弦樂器 / 225
怪傑 / 079
性急地問問題 / 024
性格軟弱的人 / 079
性病 / 203
性情，脾氣 / 148
性感的 / 084, 154
房地產公司 / 179
房地產經紀人 / 164
抹布 / 034
披肩 / 049
披著羊皮外衣的狼 / 132
拔毛鉗 / 067
拔毛器 / 060
拔絲 / 021
拋硬幣決定 / 064
抽血 / 104
抽風機 / 036
抽筋 / 100
押錯寶 / 132
拐杖 / 060, 192
拍子 / 220
拍子 / 220
拖地 / 042
拖車式房屋 / 028

拖鞋 / 053
放大 / 227
放牧場 / 120
放映日期 / 232
放映室 / 232
放射線研究家 / 194
放高利貸者 / 165
昆蟲叮咬 / 100
明蝦 / 010
服務生 / 165
服裝店 / 179
服藥過量 / 100
朋友 / 078, 079
枕頭 / 033
枕頭套 / 033
果汁 / 016
果園 / 135
果樹林 / 135
果樹園 / 135
果嶺 / 217
杯子蛋糕 / 013
松果 / 140
松雀 / 126
松鼠 / 112
松鴉 / 126
松樹 / 137
欣喜，高興 / 152
欣喜，愉快 / 148

欣喜若狂 / 108
武俠片 / 235
武術中心 / 180
注射 / 196
泳衣 / 050
泳道 / 217
泌尿科醫生 / 194
泥水匠 / 163
河馬 / 119
河鱸 / 115
法式捲餅 / 013
法官 / 165
油井 / 248
油田 / 248
油桃 / 005
油腔滑調的 / 071
油漆工 / 165
油漆行 / 180
油管 / 248
油膏 / 069, 199
油輪漏油 / 241
油頭粉面的人 / 071
沮喪 / 237
沮喪，心灰意冷 / 152
沮喪，灰心，洩氣 / 148
沮喪，意志消沉 / 148
沮喪的，氣餒的 / 154
泡沫澡 / 067

泡芙 / 013
炒 / 021
爬山 / 213
爸爸 / 075
牧師 / 165
牧場 / 135
牧場莊園 / 028
狀況良好 / 064
狗 / 112, 123
狗魚 / 115
狐狸 / 113, 123
狐臭 / 071
玩具店 / 180
玩具模型店 / 180
玩具箱 / 038
玫瑰花 / 137
疝氣 / 203
盲腸 / 095
盲腸[闌尾]切除手術 / 196
直排輪 / 212
知更鳥 / 126
知道了解內幕或祕密 / 108
空服員 / 165
空氣芳香劑 / 036
空巢期 / 081
空談不如實證 / 024
肺炎 / 203
肺氣腫 / 203

肺結核 / 100, 204
肺臟 / 095
肥皂 / 067
肥皂盒 / 036
肥胖症 / 100
股市上漲 / 132
股票[證券]經紀人 / 180
肩[側背]背包 / 060
肩膀 / 095
臥室 / 030
芭蕾舞 / 220
芽甘藍 / 002
芹菜 / 002
花式溜冰 / 212
花店 / 180
花柱 / 142
花栗鼠 / 113
花粉 / 142
花園 / 135
花椰菜 / 003
花蕾 / 141
花瓣 / 142
花藥 / 142
花露水 / 067
芥末 / 014
芥末醬 / 009
表示歡迎 / 108
表面裝出…的動作 / 088

近[遠]親 / 089
金瓜 / 003
金翅雀 / 126
金魚 / 116
金盞花 / 137
金雞母；賺錢的事業或單位 / 176
金屬容器 / 227
金屬帶 / 227
金鶯 / 127
長披肩 / 050
長青樹 / 137
長袖運動衫 / 050
長景 / 232
長號 / 225
長褲 / 050
長頸鹿 / 119
門把 / 040
門徒 / 079
門廊 / 030
門診所 / 191
門診病人診所 / 190
門鈴 / 040
阿斯匹靈 / 106, 198
附加物品 / 228
雨衣 / 049, 050
雨傘 / 060
雨鞋 / 050
青少年 / 081, 082

青花菜 / 003
青椒 / 003
青蛙 / 115, 123
青蔥 / 003
青黴素[消炎片] / 198
非常忙碌 / 176
非常困擾，極端憤怒 / 156
非常便宜的 / 237
非常健康 / 208
侄[外甥]女 / 075
侄子 / 075
芮氏地震分級標準 / 241

九 畫

信口開河 / 055
信天翁 / 126
信用卡夾 / 060
信用合作社 / 178
信差 / 167
信徒 / 079
信箱 / 040
便盆 / 192
便祕 / 200
便褲 / 050
保存 / 248
保姆 / 165
保持冷靜 / 055
保險代理人 / 165

保險索賠審核員 / 165
保險經紀人公司 / 180
保險調查員 / 165
保齡球 / 212
保護 / 248
保護級 / 236
冒生命危險 / 108
冒險片 / 235
冠 / 129
剃刀 / 067
削皮 / 022
削皮器 / 019
削鉛筆刀 / 060
削鉛筆器 / 060
前門 / 040
前背式嬰兒背帶 / 038
前面一層後面兩層的房子 / 028
（前胸雙排鈕扣）對襟毛衣 / 052
前廊 / 040
前廊臺階 / 040
前臂 / 095
勇氣 / 149
勇敢 / 149
勇敢的 / 084
勃然大怒，精神崩潰 / 208
南瓜 / 003
厚底鞋 / 053
（厚重）外套 / 048

哀悼 / 152
哀痛，哀悼 / 152
哀傷 / 149
咳嗽 / 100, 200
咳嗽糖漿 / 106
咽喉炎 / 100, 204
哈密瓜 / 005
哈蜜瓜 / 005
城鎮宅邸 / 028
奏鳴曲 / 220
姨公 / 074
娃娃鞋 / 053
威士忌 / 016
威脅他人努力工作 / 176
姻親 / 075
孩童時代 / 082
宣傳[公關]人員 / 165
室內設計師 / 166
室內裝潢商 / 166
室內樂 / 223
室友 / 079
客人 / 079
客主易位，扭轉局勢 / 044
客串 / 232
客廳 / 030
屋頂 / 040
幽閉恐懼症 / 100
幽默的 / 084

建築工人 / 166
建築承包商 / 166
很多 / 071
很容易 / 024
很難受的 / 132
待命 / 208
待產房 / 190
律師 / 166
律師事務所 / 180
後母 / 089
後門 / 040
後背式嬰兒背帶 / 038
後跟勾帶鞋 / 053
怒氣沖沖 / 152
思考反省的事 / 024
急性關節風溼症 / 204
急救 / 241
急診室 / 190
恨 / 152
扁桃腺切除術 / 196
拜把兄弟 / 089
按壓式肥皂 / 036
拮据的，經濟狀況不佳的 / 085
指甲刀 / 060
指甲刀[剪] / 067
指甲油 / 067
指甲砂銼 / 067
指甲銼 / 067

指揮家 / 221
指關節 / 095
挑嘴的人 / 024
政治人物 / 166
政治寵兒 / 089
政客 / 166
故意不用力打；謹慎行動 / 218
施口惠；只說不做 / 108
星探 / 232
染髮劑 / 067
柱 / 215
柱頭 / 142
架子 / 036
柄 / 142
柚樹 / 137
柳橙 / 005
柳樹 / 137
毒品上癮 / 204
毒癮很深；為麻煩的事煩惱 / 208
洋香瓜 / 005
洋香菜 / 014
洋裝 / 050
洋槐 / 137
洪水 / 241
流行性感冒 / 204
流行樂 / 223
流行樂團 / 221
流感 / 200

流鼻涕 / 200
洞穴 / 120
洞窟 / 120
洗手肥皂 / 067
洗耳恭聽 / 108
洗衣工人 / 166
洗衣店 / 180
洗衣服 / 042
洗衣間 / 030
洗衣籃 / 036
洗車工人 / 166
洗面乳 / 067
洗眼劑 / 068
洗窗工人 / 166
洗窗戶 / 042
洗碗工人 / 166
洗碗專用洗滌劑 / 034
洗碗精 / 034
洗碗盤 / 042
洗碗機 / 034
洗滌器 / 248
洗髮精 / 068
洗臉肥皂 / 068
（活動式）百葉窗 / 040
活動房屋 / 028
派 / 013
洩露祕密 / 024, 132
為人老實重義氣的人 / 079

為已發生的事難過 / 024
炸 / 022
炸彈 / 241
（珍珠）洋蔥 / 003
畏寒 / 100
疣 / 100
皇宮 / 028
省省吧 / 108
相片 / 228
相思樹 / 137
相親 / 089
相簿 / 221, 228
眉筆 / 068
看不見的危險 / 132
看守員 / 173
看診 / 196
研究室 / 191
砍伐森林 / 241
科幻片 / 235
科學家 / 166
秋海棠 / 137
秋葵 / 003
突然的水災 / 241
紅杉 / 138
紅洋蔥 / 003
紅疹 / 200
紅椒粉 / 014
紅蔥頭 / 002

紅燒 / 022
紅鶴 / 126
紀錄片 / 235
約會記事簿 / 060
約會對象 / 079
美乃滋 / 009
美人蕉 / 138
美洲豹 / 119
美洲獅 / 114
美洲駝（無峰） / 112
美容乳液 / 068
美容師 / 166
美容院 / 180
美容霜 / 068
美術家 / 222
美黑[晒黑]沙龍 / 180
美貌只是一層皮；沒內涵的外表 / 071
美麗的 / 085
耍大牌 / 108
胃痛 / 100
背心 / 050
背部 / 095
背景 / 223
背痛 / 100
背誦 / 221
胡言亂語 / 237
胡桃木 / 138
胡椒 / 009

胡椒瓶 / 017
胡搞 / 132
胡鬧 / 132
胡蘿蔔 / 003
胎兒酒精症候群 / 204
茅屋 / 028
茅草房屋 / 028
苦瓜 / 003
苦味 / 149
苦惱的，不適的 / 154
茄子 / 003
茉莉花 / 138
苗床 / 122
英俊的；慷慨的 / 085
計程車駕駛 / 166
計算機 / 060
訂婚[學校，圖章，結婚]戒指 / 060
負鼠 / 114
軍人 / 166
軍艦鳥 / 126
重來 / 232
重拍 / 232
重金屬音樂 / 223
重搖滾 / 223
重新 / 218
重複曝光 / 228
重聽 / 208
限制級 / 236

面紙 / 068
面對困難 / 237
面膜 / 068
韭菜 / 003
音樂片 / 235
音樂合成器 / 225
音樂家 / 166
音樂會 / 221
音樂劇 / 223
音響的 / 224
風力 / 248
風衣外套 / 050
風車 / 248
風信子 / 138
風鈴草 / 138
飛行恐懼症 / 100
飛機墜毀 / 241
飛機駕駛 / 167
食火雞 / 126
食物保溫箱 / 038
食物處理員 / 167
食物處理機 / 019
食品儲藏室 / 031
食蜂鶲 / 126
食譜 / 019
首映 / 232
首領 / 089
香水 / 068

香瓜　/ 005
香料植物　/ 014
香菸　/ 060
香菜　/ 014
香菇　/ 003
香蕉　/ 005

十畫

乘坐帚柄；無遠弗及　/ 044
倖免於難　/ 071
值得信賴的　/ 085
值得信賴的，可靠的　/ 085
值得疼愛的　/ 085
值得驕傲的事物　/ 132
倒　/ 022
倒片　/ 232
倒垃圾（垃圾桶）　/ 042
倒述　/ 232
候診間　/ 190
修理工　/ 172
修理中心　/ 180
修鞋店　/ 180
倉鼠　/ 112
凍傷　/ 100
剖腹生產　/ 197
剛愎自用的　/ 132
原[核子]災禍　/ 241
原子筆　/ 060

原野　/ 135
原聲帶　/ 232
哥們　/ 079
哭　/ 152
唇膏　/ 068
夏被　/ 033
套房公寓　/ 029
套裙　/ 050
套裝　/ 050
套鞋　/ 053
害怕的　/ 154
害群之馬　/ 132
家人在廚房進餐時的角落　/ 030
家犬　/ 075
家具店　/ 181
家庭仇隙　/ 089
家庭片　/ 235
家庭主婦[夫]　/ 167
家庭室　/ 031
家庭計畫中心　/ 180
家族　/ 075
家譜　/ 076, 089
家屬　/ 077
容易上當受騙的人　/ 089
容易受騙的　/ 085
容器　/ 228
射箭　/ 212
庭園　/ 135

徒步旅行 / 212
徒勞之舉 / 132
徑賽運動 / 212, 217
恐水症 / 100
恐怖 / 149
恐怖，驚駭 / 149
恐怖片 / 235
恐怖主義 / 241
恐懼 / 149
扇貝 / 010, 116
拳 / 095
拳擊 / 213
拳擊[棒球]手套 / 215
拳擊場 / 217
（捕捉動物的）籠子 / 120
料理油 / 009
旅行社 / 180
旅行社職員 / 167
旅行推銷員 / 167
（旅館）內部偵探 / 162
旅館[汽車旅館]員工 / 167
晒印照片 / 230
晒衣服 / 043
晒傷 / 100
書呆子；書蟲 / 079
書店 / 180
書房 / 031
書架 / 032

書報攤 / 181
書櫃 / 032
朗誦 / 221
（核）分裂 / 247
核子反應器 / 249
核能 / 249
核熔毀 / 241
核磁共振攝影 / 197
核廢料 / 249
根 / 140
桂花 / 138
梳子 / 061, 068
梳妝臺 / 033
栗樹 / 138
桌布 / 017
桑樹 / 138
桃子 / 005
栓劑 / 198
氣氛音樂 / 223
氣喘 / 101, 204
氣喘所發出的聲音 / 101
氣管 / 095
氧氣帳 / 192
氧氣罩 / 192
浪費時間 / 108
浪漫片 / 235
浪漫的 / 085
消化不良 / 200

消防隊 / 181
消耗，用盡 / 249
消費，使用 / 249
海[河]狸 / 114
海牛[象] / 114
海底撈針，徒勞無功 / 055
海底鑽油設備 / 249
海星 / 116
海面石油汙染 / 241
海豚 / 114
海報 / 232
海棗樹 / 138
海綿 / 036
海嘯 / 242, 249
海潮 / 249
海龜 / 115
海膽 / 116
海鷗 / 126
浮腫，腫脹 / 101
浮腫的 / 200
浴用鹽 / 068
浴室 / 031
浴室梳妝臺 / 036
浴室擦腳墊 / 036
浴缸 / 036
浴香粉 / 068
浴袍 / 050
烘培 / 022

烤 / 022
烤肉用具 / 019
烤肉架 / 040
烤盤 / 019
烤箱 / 019
烤麵包（片） / 007
烤麵包機 / 034
烈酒 / 016
烏鴉 / 126
特效 / 232
特寫 / 233
特寫鏡頭 / 228
狼 / 114
狼吞虎嚥地吃 / 024
狼狽為奸 / 108
班 / 080
（珠子）項鍊 / 061
珠光唇膏 / 068
珠寶店 / 181
珠寶商 / 167
畜圈 / 120
畜欄 / 120
病床 / 192
病房 / 190
病毒 / 200
病理學家 / 194
症候群 / 204
疲倦的，疲勞的 / 154

疲勞，倦怠 / 149
疲勞，勞累 / 149
疼痛 / 200
疼痛，受傷 / 101
疼痛，痛苦 / 149
疼痛[發炎]的 / 200
皰疹 / 204
砧板 / 019
破紀錄 / 219
祕書 / 167
祕密來源 / 143
神父 / 165
神氣十足的小人物 / 055
神氣活現的 / 085
神祕[神蹟]片 / 235
神智正常，頭腦清楚的 / 085
神經 / 095
神經官能病 / 204
神經科醫生 / 194
祝福，祝…成功 / 208
租車公司 / 181
笑，笑聲 / 149
笑得合不攏嘴；快樂的 / 156
紗布 / 192
紗門 / 040
紗窗 / 040
（紙）餐巾 / 017
紙巾 / 061, 068

紙巾架 / 034
缺乏禮貌的 / 085
翅 / 129
耗損 / 055
胰臟 / 095
胭脂 / 068
胸 / 096, 129
胸痛 / 101
胸腔 / 096
胸罩 / 050
脈搏 / 197
能做多種工作的人；雜而不精的人 / 167
能源成本 / 249
能源效率 / 249
能源稅 / 249
能源損失 / 249
脊柱 / 096
脊椎指壓治療者 / 167
脊椎指壓治療師 / 194
脊椎神經 / 096
臭氧（臭氧層） / 249
臭鼬 / 114
荒野 / 135
荒漠 / 135
荒誕無稽的故事 / 133
草地 / 120
草坪 / 031, 040
草原土撥鼠 / 112

草莓 / 005
草藥 / 014
茶 / 016
茶几 / 032
茶杯托盤 / 017
茶匙 / 017
茶壺 / 018, 035
蚌 / 116
蚜蟲 / 117
記載祕密的小冊子；愛情黑名單 / 064
送件者 / 228
送信人 / 167
送貨人員 / 167
送遞急件或外交文件的信差 / 167
迷你磁碟隨身聽 / 061
迷迭香 / 014
迷惑，難倒 / 152
退休人員 / 082
追隨者 / 079
酒會外套（非全正式） / 050
酒窩 / 096
配音 / 233
配偶 / 076
配偶互相稱呼 / 089
配眼鏡的人 / 169
配景 / 233
針葉 / 141
閃光燈 / 228

院子 / 031
飢荒 / 242
飢餓 / 242
馬 / 113, 123
馬甲 / 050
馬克杯 / 018
馬芬 / 007
馬桶 / 036
馬球 / 213
馬鈴薯 / 003
馬鞍 / 215
馬戲場 / 217
馬戲場雜工 / 172
骨折 / 101, 201
骨盆 / 096
骨頭 / 096
高血壓 / 101, 204
高級頂樓公寓 / 029
高筒球鞋 / 053
高筒橡皮套鞋 / 053
高傲的 / 156
高腳椅 / 038
高跟鞋 / 054
高爾夫球 / 213, 215
高爾夫球桿 / 215
高領毛衣 / 050
高樓 / 029
高興 / 149

高興，滿足 / 149
高興的，快樂的 / 154
鬼扯騙人，一派胡言 / 024
浣熊 / 114

十一畫

乾旱，旱災 / 242
停車場 / 135
停車場服務員 / 167
假慈悲 / 133
假髮 / 051
做分內的事情 / 237
健身房 / 217
健保組織 / 190
健康中心 / 181
健康食品店 / 181
偵探 / 168
側門 / 041
偏見，成見 / 149
偏執狂 / 204
剪接 / 233
動作片 / 235
動物園管理員 / 168
動物標本剝製師 / 168
動脈 / 096
動脈硬化（症） / 204
動能 / 249
動畫片 / 235

曼陀林　/ 225
商船船員　/ 168
商業藝術家　/ 168
啄　/ 129
啄木鳥　/ 126
啞的　/ 201
啃老族　/ 082
唱片　/ 221
唱片音樂節目主持人　/ 221
唱片套冊　/ 221
啤酒　/ 016
售貨員　/ 168
國稅局　/ 181
國會議員　/ 163
堂[表]兄弟姊妹　/ 076
婦女　/ 089
婦科醫生　/ 194
婆婆　/ 075
寄生蟲　/ 117
密友　/ 079
專科醫生　/ 194
專家　/ 194
巢　/ 120
常春藤　/ 138
帳篷　/ 029
帷　/ 032
康乃馨　/ 138
張三李四　/ 089

強而有力 / 219
強行留人長談 / 055
強烈的，強健的 / 085
得理饒人 / 055
悽苦的，難堪的，糟透的 / 154
情人眼裡出西施 / 071
情有獨鍾 / 108
情勢已經轉過來 / 056
捲（底片） / 228
捲土重來，東山再起 / 219
捲餅 / 013
接待員 / 168, 194
接種 / 197
掃街工人 / 168
掃興[煞風景]者 / 044
掛在浴室的用品袋 / 061
掛式旋轉玩具 / 038
推拉鏡頭 / 233
排水孔 / 036
排名 / 233
排字工人 / 168
排行中間的孩子；個性較冷漠的孩子 / 076
排球 / 213
排演 / 233
救生員 / 168
救援 / 242
救濟 / 242
救護車 / 190, 242

教父[母] / 076
教師，教授 / 168
教堂 / 181
教堂音樂 / 223
敏感的 / 085
旋律 / 221
旋風 / 242, 243
晚禮服 / 051
桿 / 215
桿麵棍 / 019
梧桐 / 138
梧桐樹 / 138
梅花 / 138
梅毒 / 204
梔子花 / 138
梨子 / 005
殺青 / 233
殺銳氣，讓某人栽跟頭 / 089
毫不保留地告訴他人你的想法 / 089
涼鞋 / 054
淡入，漸顯 / 233
淡出，漸隱 / 233
淺口便鞋 / 053
清洗牙齒 / 104
清真寺 / 178
清掃浴室 / 042
清晰度 / 228
清新的 / 085

清潔傷口 / 104
淋病 / 204
淚珠 / 149
烹煮 / 022
烹飪用書 / 019
焊接行 / 181
牽牛花 / 139
（球）場地整[管理員] / 169
球拍 / 215
球座 / 215
理髮店 / 181
理髮師 / 168
現代音樂 / 223
現代樂 / 223
現場 / 233
瓠瓜 / 003
瓷器櫥櫃 / 018
甜甜圈 / 007
甜椒 / 004
甜菜 / 004
產房 / 190
產科病房 / 190
產科醫生 / 195
痔瘡 / 201
盒子 / 228
盛裝 / 056
眼科醫生 / 195
眼淚 / 149

眼睛 / 096
眼節 / 142
眼影 / 068
眼線筆 / 068
眼藥水 / 069, 106,198
眼鏡行 / 181
眼鏡商 / 169
眼鏡盒 / 061
移植 / 197
笨的，愚蠢的 / 085
第一任先生[太太] / 076
粗棉布的工作服 / 051
粗魯的，沒禮貌的 / 086
細枝 / 141
組 / 080
羞怯的，侷促不安的 / 086
羞澀的 / 086
羞澀的，靦覥的 / 154
脖子 / 096
脖子僵硬 / 101
脫毛藥 / 069
脫臼 / 101
脫腸 / 203
船屋 / 029
船隻的失事 / 242
船舶的遺骸 / 242
船難 / 242
莎莎醬 / 009

莖 / 142
莽撞的駕駛 / 133
莊園 / 029
荷蘭芹 / 014
處理受損樹木的人 / 169
處境危險 / 219
蛇 / 115
蛀牙 / 101
蛀蟲 / 117
蛋 / 129
蛋糕 / 013
蛋糕粉 / 007
被子 / 033
被開除 / 176
被遺棄的，孤獨的 / 154
袖扣 / 061
袖珍本書 / 061
袋子 / 061
許終身，論及婚嫁的伴侶 / 090
設身處地，將心比心 / 056
販賣部 / 183
責備失職下屬並導致離職 / 176
貨運中心 / 181
貪多必失 / 024
貪食症 / 101
貪婪 / 149
貪婪的 / 086
軟膏 / 069

軟膏 / 199
通心粉 / 008
通訊簿 / 061
通譯員 / 162
連身衣 / 051
連身衣褲 / 051
連指手套 / 051
連帽毛外套 / 051
連鎖速食店 / 181
連鏡小粉盒 / 069
連續變焦或調距的鏡頭 / 228
速記員 / 169
造園技師 / 169
酗酒 / 204
（野）兔 / 112
野火 / 242
野兔 / 112
野雁 / 123
野雲雀 / 126
野貓 / 113
野雞 / 127
釣魚 / 213
陳舊[陳腐]的 / 024
陸龜 / 115
陶工 / 169
陶藝家 / 169
陷入困境 / 133
雪花膏 / 066

雪茄 / 061
雪崩 / 242
雪蓮花 / 139
魚 / 123
魚和熊掌兼得 / 024
魚狗 / 126
魚竿 / 216
魚餌 / 216
鳥 / 123
鳥嘴 / 130
鳥籠 / 120
鹿 / 114, 123
麥片 / 007
麥克筆 / 061
麥酒 / 016
麻疹 / 101, 205
麻雀 / 126
麻煩的人或事 / 108
麻醉師 / 195
桲 / 136
脛 / 096
荳蔻 / 014

十二畫

最後一擊 / 143
最後階段 / 219
割傷 / 101
喜劇片 / 235

喜鵲 / 126
喜歡嗎？（你）好好考慮 / 064
喇叭花 / 139
單戶住宅 / 029
單飛 / 222
單簧管 / 226
喬木 / 135
喉片 / 106
喉結 / 143
喉嚨痛 / 101
喙 / 130
圍巾 / 051
場地 / 217
場面大綱 / 233
報刊發行人 / 163
報社 / 182
報紙業主 / 163
壺 / 019
就業中心 / 182
就業服務人員 / 169
廁所 / 031
復原室 / 190
惡化，加劇 / 150
惡性傳染病 / 242
悲哀 / 150
悲劇片 / 235
（掌上）電子助理[萬用手冊] / 062
插畫家 / 169

提名 / 233
換尿布檯 / 038
換床單 / 042
揚琴 / 226
斑馬 / 119, 123
普遍級 / 236
智力遲鈍，智能缺陷 / 205
智窮力竭 / 156
替身 / 233
朝鮮薊 / 004
棕櫚樹 / 139
棗子 / 005
棗椰樹 / 138
森林 / 135
棒球 / 213
植物[人造]奶油 / 012
棉花球 / 069
棉花棒 / 192
殘幹，樹樁 / 141
殘酷的 / 086
殼 / 130
毯子 / 033
游泳 / 213
游泳池包商 / 169
渡假村 / 028
渡鴉 / 127
減淡加深 / 228
渦輪（機） / 249

測光錶 / 228
焙果 / 007
焦距 / 228
焦慮，掛念 / 150
焦慮的，掛念的 / 154
焦躁，神經質 / 150
無主見的人，仿冒者 / 133
無咖啡因的咖啡 / 016
無花果 / 006
無恥，厚臉皮的 / 086
無情的，殘忍的 / 086
無理的 / 086
無聊，厭倦 / 150
無袖背心 / 051
無袖連身裙 / 051
無邊帽 / 051
犀牛 / 119
猶太教堂 / 182
猴子 / 119
猩紅熱 / 205
畫眉 / 125
畫面 / 228
畫家 / 222
畫素 / 229
畫廊 / 182
番茄 / 004
番茄醬 / 009
痛 / 201

痛苦，苦惱 / 150
痛苦的 / 155
痙攣 / 100
登山 / 213
發行 / 233
發行，發表 / 221
發行者 / 163
發抖，顫震 / 152
發牢騷 / 024
發炎 / 201
發假警報 / 133
發球處 / 215
發電機 / 249
發燒 / 101, 201
發燒友 / 079
發癢 / 102
發癮[戒斷]症狀 / 208
短吻鱷 / 119
短號 / 226
短褲 / 051
硬幣 / 061
稍安勿躁 / 133
程序表 / 221
稅務顧問 / 169
窗戶 / 032
窗簾 / 032
等待最後結果 / 056
等候室 / 190

筆記型電腦 / 061
筆記簿 / 061
筋疲力竭 / 102
筋疲力竭的 / 201
絨布寬鬆外套 / 051
絕交，斷交 / 090
絕對可靠的 / 133
絕種，滅絕的 / 250
絕緣（體） / 250
紫丁香 / 139
紫羅蘭 / 139
紫蘇 / 014
絲襪 / 054
善知鳥 / 127
腋窩 / 096
腎臟 / 096
脹氣 / 102
菸不離口的老菸槍 / 208
菸斗 / 061
菸草店，菸店 / 182
菠菜 / 004
萊姆 / 006
菊花 / 139
菜園 / 135
虛弱無力 / 102
蛤蜊 / 010, 116
裁縫 / 169
（註冊）會計師 / 170

評論 / 234
診所 / 191
診斷 / 197
貽貝，淡菜 / 117
（越野）滑雪 / 213
超級市場 / 182
超導體 / 250
超優的人 / 208
跑步 / 213
跑道 / 217
進入 / 191
郵局 / 182
郵差 / 169
郵購中心 / 182
鄉村西部音樂 / 223
鄉村音樂 / 223
鄉村俱樂部 / 217
鄉村起司 / 012
鄉間宅邸 / 029
量血壓 / 104
量杯 / 019
量體溫 / 104
開啟新頁 / 143
開誠布公 / 108
開罐[瓶器] / 019
間歇式拍攝 / 229
間諜 / 169
隊友 / 079

陽具，陰莖 / 096
陽臺 / 030
雄蕊 / 142
集中風險 / 025
集郵簿 / 221
雲杉 / 139
雲雀 / 127
項鍊 / 062
（飯店等）房間部的女服務生 / 165
飯廳 / 031
黃水仙 / 139
黃瓜 / 004
黃鸝 / 127
黑馬；不被看好但勝利的人 / 133

十三畫

韮黃 / 004
黑管 / 226
傳呼器 / 062
傳染[流行]病 / 242
傷（口） / 201
傻瓜相機 / 229
募兵站 / 182
勤勉的 / 086
嗑藥上癮 / 209
嗅到麻煩 / 071
園丁 / 169
圓麵包 / 007

塗了脂粉的女人　/ 071
填牙　/ 104
奧勒岡・牛至　/ 014
嫉妒的　/ 086
嫌隙怨恨　/ 108
媽媽（暱稱）　/ 076
幹　/ 142
幹農活的人　/ 170
廉價商店　/ 182
微波爐　/ 035
愚弄他人使出醜　/ 133
愚笨的；不願說話的　/ 086
愚蠢不堪　/ 109
愚蠢的　/ 086
意外事件　/ 201
慈善二手商店　/ 182
慈善事業　/ 182
感光速率　/ 229
感到困窘而亂撥弄…　/ 237
感冒　/ 102, 201
感冒藥片　/ 106
感染　/ 102, 209
感染，傳染　/ 201
感染性單核血球病　/ 205
感情豐富的　/ 086
感覺，感受　/ 150
愛　/ 150
愛人　/ 079

愛好清潔是僅次於敬神的美德 / 071
愛抱怨的 / 155
愛炫耀的人 / 025
愛滋病 / 102, 205
愛滋病毒陽性反應 / 205
搭檔 / 079
搬家工人 / 170
搬家公司 / 182
搬運工 / 172
搶婦女錢包的人 / 064
搖滾樂 / 223
搖鏡 / 234
搖籃 / 038
搗成糊狀 / 022
敬畏，畏怯 / 150
新世紀音樂（以電子樂器為主） / 223
新官上任三把火 / 044
新郎 / 076
新娘 / 076
新聞工作者[記者] / 170
新聞記者[播報員] / 170
新聞發言人 / 170
新潮片 / 235
暗中傷人 / 056
暗房 / 229
暖氣承包商 / 170
會計 / 176
會計師公司 / 182

業務顧問 / 170
極好的哪 / 143
極為悲痛 / 109
極樂，至喜 / 150
椰子 / 006
楓樹 / 139
榆樹 / 139
溶解；融合 / 250
溫和地 / 056
滑面的 / 229
滑雪外套 / 051
滑雪杖 / 216
滑雪屐 / 216
滑稽的 / 086
溜冰，滑冰 / 213
溜冰場 / 217
煎鍋 / 019
煙囪 / 041
煙燻肉 / 010
煙霧 / 250
煩惱，惱怒 / 150
煩惱，憂慮 / 150
煩惱的，煩躁的 / 155
煩擾，打攪 / 152
煤 / 250
煉油廠 / 250
（照）相機 / 228
照明承包商 / 170

照相機店 / 182
照相館 / 182
照相館 / 230
照胸部X光 / 104
照顧的無微不至的，衣著入時的 / 064
獅子 / 119, 123
當作耳邊風 / 133
當機立斷 / 133
瘀血，瘀傷 / 102
痴心妄想，白日夢 / 064
睫毛膏 / 069
矮種馬，小馬 / 113
矮樹叢，灌木 / 135
碰撞，相撞 / 242
碗盤瀝水架 / 035
禁果 / 025
節目單 / 221
節奏 / 220, 221
節奏藍調 / 223
節食 / 025
經理 / 170
義大利麵條 / 008
義父[母] / 076
群 / 130
群眾 / 079
聖代 / 013
聖歌 / 221, 224
腰部 / 096

腮紅 / 069
腮腺炎 / 102, 205
腳 / 096
腳底 / 097
腳後跟 / 097
腳趾 / 097
腳趾甲 / 097
腫瘤 / 205
腹部 / 097
腹瀉 / 102, 201, 205
腦 / 097
腦膜炎 / 205
舅公 / 074
舅婆 / 074
葬儀業者 / 195
萵苣 / 004
葡萄 / 006
葡萄柚 / 006
葡萄酒 / 016
葡萄乾 / 006
葡萄藤 / 139
蜈蚣 / 117
蜂鳥 / 127
蜂蜜 / 015
裙子 / 051
補[製]鞋匠 / 170
補鞋工人 / 172
裝刮鬍膏的杯子 / 069

裝玻璃工人 / 170
裝配線工人 / 170
裝軟片 / 229
裝睡裝死 / 133
解[抗]酸劑 / 198
解充血藥 / 198
解析度 / 229
解毒劑 / 198
解剖刀 / 192
詢問病史 / 104
資源回收中心 / 183
跟鏡 / 234
路燈（柱） / 041
路邊小攤 / 183
跳水 / 214
跳蚤市場 / 183
農夫 / 170
農夫市集 / 183
農舍 / 029
農場工人 / 170
運務員 / 170
運動場 / 217
運動短褲 / 051
運動鞋 / 054
運動器材店 / 183
遊民收容所 / 183
遊伴 / 079
遊伴，玩伴 / 080

遊說通過議案者，陳情者 / 171
遊樂場 / 135
遊戲一部分；非針對個人的 / 219
遊戲床 / 038
遊戲間 / 031
違反意願 / 143
遇難者 / 244
過敏 / 201
過敏 / 205
過敏反應 / 102
酪梨 / 006
鈸 / 226
鉛筆 / 062
鈴鼓，手鼓 / 226
隔熱墊 / 035
隔離霜 / 069
雉 / 127
雷射唱片 / 221
雷鬼音樂 / 224
電力 / 250
電子記事簿 / 062
電子產品店 / 183
電子樂 / 224
電工 / 171
電吉他 / 226
電池 / 229
電池，電瓶 / 250
電氣[機]工程師 / 171

電氣技師 / 171
（電動）牙刷 / 036
（電動）開罐器 / 035
電動刮鬍刀 / 069
電梯操作員 / 171
電毯 / 033
（電視）觀眾 / 230
電視天線 / 041
電腦店 / 183
電腦恐懼症 / 102
電腦程式設計師 / 171
電話公司營業所 / 183
電話架線工 / 171
電話接線生 / 171
電器行[維修店] / 183
零食店 / 183
零錢包 / 062
預告片 / 234
預防接種 / 197
預後 / 197
（飼養小動物的）籠子 / 120
馴服野馬 / 213
鼠 / 112
鼠尾草 / 015
鼠海豚 / 114
像，與…類似 / 090
厭食症 / 102
厭倦極了 / 209

厭惡，憎惡 / 152
嘔吐 / 102, 201
圖書館員 / 171
墊子 / 216
夥伴 / 078
夥伴，好友 / 080
夥伴，拍檔 / 080
嫩枝 / 141
嫩煎 / 022
寡婦 / 076
實際接觸 / 219
實驗室 / 191
實驗室技師 / 195
對 / 080
對白 / 234
對抗，敵對 / 152
對某位異性著迷 / 090
對能源的（不）依賴 / 250
對禮品吹毛求疵 / 134

十四畫

幕後 / 223
幔 / 032
慢跑 / 213
慢跑鞋 / 054
摔角 / 213
撤離，疏散 / 242
摺衣服 / 043

暢貨中心 / 183
構圖 / 229
歌手 / 221
歌曲 / 221
歌詞 / 222, 234
歌劇 / 224
演員表 / 234
漏匙 / 020
漂亮的 / 086
漢堡肉 / 010
滿分 / 219
滿潮 / 242
漱口水 / 069
漱口杯 / 037
漁夫 / 171
熊 / 114, 119
熊 / 123
瘧疾 / 205
瘋子，怪人；瘋狂的 / 209
瘋狂 / 150
瘋狂的 / 086
瘋狂的，精神錯亂的 / 155
盡忠職守 / 219
監護人 / 077
睡衣 / 052
睡袍 / 052
睡蓮 / 139
福利救濟中心 / 183

種子 / 141, 142
種瓜得瓜，種豆得豆 / 143
種族淨化 / 243
種族滅絕 / 243
稱心如意的境遇 / 143
窩 / 120
管風琴 / 226
管樂器 / 226
精力充沛的 / 237
精神[心理]分析學家 / 195
精神不爽的 / 156
精神分裂症 / 205
精神科醫師 / 171
精神病 / 206
精神病院 / 191
精神病醫生 / 195
精神變態 / 206
精華 / 025
綜合果汁酒 / 016
緊身運動衣 / 052
緊身褲 / 052
緊急狀態 / 243
緊急情況，突發事件 / 243
網子 / 216
網球 / 213
（網球等的）場地 / 217
網球鞋 / 054
綿羊 / 113, 124

維他命 / 106, 198
維修工 / 171
翠鳥 / 126
聚焦 / 229
膀胱 / 097
舞曲 / 224
舞蹈中心 / 183
蒲公英 / 139
蓋子 / 020
蓋括地說 / 143
蒸 / 022
蒸氣 / 250
蒸餾器 / 192
蒼鷺 / 127
蜜棗 / 006
蜜蜂 / 117
蜻蜓 / 117
蜥蜴 / 115
蜘蛛 / 118
製片 / 234
製鞋工人 / 172
說故事者 / 171
豪豬 / 114
賑災 / 243
輔導級 / 236
輕古典 / 224
輕歌劇 / 224
輕鬆不受拘束 / 090

辣椒　/ 015
遠足　/ 212
遠攝照片　/ 230
遛狗者　/ 171
酸奶（油）　/ 012
酸雨　/ 250
酸葡萄　/ 025
酷肖[像]父母者　/ 090
銀行　/ 183
銀行出納員　/ 171
銀行業者　/ 172
銀髮族　/ 082
閣樓　/ 031
（雌）鵝　/ 128
雌馬　/ 124
雌蕊　/ 142
領帶　/ 052
領帶夾　/ 062
領袖，指揮者　/ 080
領結　/ 052
颱風　/ 243
餅乾　/ 007, 008
鳴禽　/ 127
鳴槍前偷跑；行動過早　/ 219
鳶尾花　/ 139
鳳仙花　/ 139
鳳梨　/ 006
鼻子　/ 097

鼻血 / 102
鼻塞 / 103
鼻塞噴劑 / 106
鼻塞藥 / 198
緋聞 / 090
蒔蘿 / 015

十五畫

僵死了，完全聾了 / 209
僵硬 / 201
劇本大綱 / 234
劇情 / 234
劇情片 / 235
劍蘭 / 140
嘻哈音樂 / 224
嘴 / 097
噴霧器 / 192
寬大的工作服 / 052
廢紙簍 / 037
廢舊品商人 / 172
廚子 / 172
廚房 / 031
廣告公司 / 184
廣告代理 / 172
廣角鏡頭 / 229
彈簧墊 / 216
影片 / 227
影印行 / 184

德國麻疹 / 206
憂慮的，恐懼地 / 155
憂鬱，鬱悶 / 152
憂鬱的 / 155
憂鬱的，哀傷地 / 155
憂鬱症 / 103
慫恿 / 025
憐憫，同情 / 150
憤怒，生氣 / 150
摩天大樓 / 029
撞球 / 214
撞球桿 / 216
撲克牌 / 062
撲粉；化妝用粉 / 069
撫慰，慰問 / 153
撫養親屬 / 077
敵人 / 080
敵手，對手 / 080
數位的 / 229
暴力片 / 236
暴民，烏合之眾 / 080
暴風，龍捲風 / 243
暴風雨 / 243, 244
暴風雨前的寧靜 / 245
暴動，暴亂 / 243
樣樣通樣樣鬆的人 / 176
樟樹 / 140
標準桿以下；不舒服 / 219

樓中樓；雙層公寓 / 029
槳 / 216
樂師 / 166
樂隊，樂團 / 222
樂趣，興味 / 150
樂器行 / 184
樅 / 137
歐掠鳥 / 127
潛水 / 214
潛鳥 / 127
潰瘍 / 206
潤絲精 / 069
潤膚膏[霜，露] / 069
潤膚霜 / 069
熟食店 / 184
熱心，熱情 / 151
熱心，熱情，熱忱 / 151
熱水袋[瓶] / 192
熱狗 / 010
熱度，溫度；高溫，暑熱 / 250
熱帶風暴 / 243
熱情 / 151
熱情，激情 / 151
熱情的 / 155
熱敷墊 / 193
瘦成皮包骨 / 209
盤尼西林 / 198
瞎猜 / 219

磅秤 / 037
碼頭[港口]工人 / 172
碼頭工 / 172
穀倉 / 120
穀類 / 007
穀類食品 / 008
箭 / 216
箱 / 120
篇 / 220
編劇 / 234
編輯 / 172
膝 / 097
膠布 / 193
膠捲 / 229
膠囊 / 198
蓮花 / 140
蓮蓬頭 / 037
蓮藕 / 004
蔓越莓 / 006
蝴蝶 / 118
蝴蝶蘭 / 140
蝶魚片 / 011
蝦 / 117
蝸牛 / 117
蝙蝠 / 112
蝗蟲，蚱蜢 / 118
蝌蚪 / 115
衛生棉 / 193

衛星接收器　/ 041
衝浪　/ 214
衝浪板　/ 216
複製　/ 229
調子　/ 222
調味罐架　/ 035
調查員　/ 162, 172
調焦　/ 229
豌豆　/ 004
豎笛　/ 226
豎琴　/ 226
豬　/ 113, 124
豬肉　/ 011
賣座　/ 222
踝　/ 097
輪式溜冰鞋　/ 216
輪椅　/ 193
醋　/ 009
醃漬類開胃食品　/ 009
鋪床　/ 043
鞋子　/ 054
鞋匠　/ 172
鞋店　/ 184
鞋帶　/ 054
養子[女]　/ 077
養父[母]　/ 074, 077
養老金，緊急準備金　/ 134
養家活口　/ 025

養家餬口 / 176
養魚缸 / 120
餓死 / 242
餘震 / 243
駝鹿 / 114
髮夾 / 062
髮刷 / 069
髮梳 / 062
齒齦 / 097
噁心，作噁 / 201
噁心想吐 / 103
撣書架上的灰塵 / 043

十 六 畫

凝膠牙膏 / 070
壁球 / 212
壁櫥 / 032
壁爐 / 032
學生 / 172
學步車 / 038, 193
學步的小孩 / 082
學校行政管理人員 / 172
戰爭 / 243
戰爭片 / 236
擁護者 / 079
整潔的 / 045
曇花 / 140
橘子 / 006

樹皮 / 141
樹枝 / 141
樹林 / 135
樹芽 / 141
樹屋 / 029
樹液 / 141
樹幹 / 141
樹葉 / 141
樹輪 / 141
樹叢 / 135
樹籬 / 135
橄欖油 / 009
橄欖樹 / 140
橡子[實] / 141
橡皮套鞋 / 054
橡膠樹 / 140
橡樹 / 140
樵夫 / 172
機具修理店 / 184
機械工 / 172
機場[車站，碼頭]搬運行李的人 / 172
機器操作員 / 173
激起某人怒氣 / 134
激動，焦慮 / 153
激動，煽動；喚醒 / 153
激動，興奮 / 153
激動不安的，慌張的 / 155
燉 / 022

燉鍋 / 020
燒烤 / 022
燈 / 032
燈筆 / 062
燕八哥 / 127
燕子 / 127
燕尾服 / 052
燕雀 / 127
燕鷗 / 127
燙衣服 / 043
燙傷 / 103, 202
燃料 / 250
燃燒 / 250
獨木舟 / 214, 216
獨唱 / 222
璞玉 / 219
瓢蟲 / 118
糖 / 015
糖尿病 / 103, 206
糖果店 / 184
糖漿 / 015
糖罐 / 018
興高采烈的，心情好的 / 087
興高采烈的，情緒好的 / 155
興高采烈的，輕快的 / 155
蕪菁 / 004
螞蟻 / 118
螢幕 / 229

褪色的　/ 230
褲裝　/ 052
褲襪　/ 052
親兄弟姊妹　/ 077
親生父母　/ 077
親戚　/ 075, 080
親屬　/ 077
親屬關係　/ 077
諧星　/ 234
諮商顧問公司　/ 184
貓　/ 113, 124
貓頭鷹　/ 127
貓鵲　/ 127
蹂躪，荒廢　/ 243
輸光　/ 056
遺憾　/ 151
錯誤或不可靠的消息　/ 134
錢包　/ 062
鋼琴　/ 226
鋼琴調音員　/ 173
錄音　/ 221
錄音[影]帶　/ 222
隨身行李　/ 058
隨身聽　/ 062
隨意，漫不經心的　/ 219
隨意的　/ 109
霍亂　/ 206
靜脈　/ 097

頸鍊 / 062
頭 / 097
頭骨 / 098
頭痛 / 103
頭暈目眩 / 103
頭髮 / 098
餐刀 / 018
餐叉 / 018
餐具室 / 031
餐桌 / 018, 035
餐桌墊 / 035
餐椅 / 018, 035
餐盤 / 018
餐廳 / 184
鬍 / 098
鴕鳥 / 128
鴨子 / 124, 128
鴨肉 / 011
龍套演員 / 234
龍捲風 / 243
龍蝦 / 011, 117

十七畫

優格 / 012
優渥的離職 / 176
儲物倉庫 / 184
儲藏室 / 031
壓力鍋 / 020

壓板 / 193
嬰兒 / 081
嬰兒 / 082
嬰兒用洗髮精 / 070
嬰兒床 / 038
嬰兒汽車安全椅 / 038
嬰兒馬桶 / 038
嬰兒專用墊高椅 / 039
嬰兒推車 / 039
嬰兒提籃 / 039
嬰兒無線監測器[對講機] / 039
嬰兒搖鈴 / 039
擊劍 / 214
擦亮 / 056
擦亮家具 / 043
擦傷 / 103
擦碗布 / 035
檔案管理員 / 173
檢查… / 104
檢體 / 197
營業員 / 168
燦爛的，美麗的 / 087
爵士樂 / 222, 224
環保分子 / 251
環保政策 / 251
環保科學 / 251
環境法 / 251
環境美化設計師 / 169

環境清理 / 251
環境毀滅 / 243
療養院 / 191
癌症 / 103, 206
矯形外科醫生 / 195
縮小 / 230
繃帶 / 193
縫合傷口 / 104
縫衣機店 / 184
聲音沙啞說不出話 / 109
聯合起來對付某人 / 090
臀部 / 098
膿瘡 / 202
膽小的，易受驚的 / 155
膽怯的 / 087, 134
膽囊 / 098
臉 / 098
臉部泥膜 / 070
臉頰 / 098
臨時演員 / 234
舉重 / 214
薄脆餅乾 / 008
薄雪草 / 136
薄煎餅 / 007
薑 / 015
蟑螂 / 118
蟋蟀 / 118
賺人眼淚的電影戲劇或節目 / 156

賺人熱淚片 / 236
購物中心 / 184
避孕用品 / 198
避孕劑 / 198
避風港；聊勝於無 / 245
避難所 / 244
醜小鴨 / 134
醜陋的 / 087
鍋 / 019
鍋鏟 / 020
闌尾 / 095
隱形眼鏡 / 062
隱瞞掩飾過失或缺點 / 045
隱藏式字幕 / 234
雖瘋狂仍有條理的 / 157
颶風 / 243, 244
鮭魚 / 011
鮟鱇 / 116
鴿子 / 128
麋 / 114
黏液囊炎 / 205

十八畫

壘球 / 214
擺姿勢 / 230
擺設餐桌 / 043
櫃 / 120
檸檬 / 006

檸檬水 / 016
歸巢族 / 082
歸勝利者所有 / 219
殯葬業者 / 173
殯儀館 / 184
瀉藥 / 198
濾光鏡 / 230
濾網 / 020
濾器 / 251
獵鷹 / 128
禮品店 / 184
簡直一模一樣的人 / 090
糧倉 / 120
翹辮子 / 209
職業護理師 / 195
舊識 / 078
薩克斯管 / 226
藍知更鳥 / 128
藍莓 / 006
蟲子 / 118
覆盆子 / 006
蹦床 / 216
蹤跡 / 217
轉彎抹角地說話 / 144
醫生 / 173, 195
醫師 / 195
醫院 / 184, 191
醫院護士的年輕志願助手 / 195

醬油 / 009
鎮靜劑 / 199
雜音 / 223
雜貨店 / 178, 185
雜誌架 / 032
雙人座沙發 / 032
雙焦距[太陽，老花]眼鏡 / 063
雙槓 / 216
雙親 / 077
雙簧管 / 226
雛菊 / 140
雞 / 124, 128
雞肉 / 011
雞蛋餅 / 007
額頭 / 098
顎 / 098
騎馬 / 214
鬆餅 / 007
鯊魚 / 116
鵜鶘 / 128

十九畫

壞人 / 025
壞蛋；可憐蟲；倒楣的人 / 090
寵物店 / 185
懷才不遇，有志難伸 / 134
懷恨的，惡意的 / 087
懶惰的 / 087

攀岩 / 214
曝光 / 230
曝光不足 / 230
曝光過度 / 230
櫥櫃 / 035
瀕臨絕種的動植物 / 251
爆炸 / 244
獸醫 / 173
獸籠 / 120
簿記員，記帳人 / 173
繫帶牛津鞋 / 054
羅勒 / 014
藝品店 / 185
藝術家 / 173, 222
（藥）處方 / 198
藥丸 / 199
藥片 / 199
藥房 / 185
藥盒 / 063
藥膏 / 199
藥劑師 / 173, 195
藥櫃 / 037
蠍子 / 118
蟹 / 011, 117
蟾蜍 / 115
鏡子 / 037
鏡頭 / 228, 230
關係密切 / 025

關係親密的人 / 090
關節炎 / 206
韻律 / 221
鬍渣 / 071
鬍鬚 / 098
鯨魚 / 114, 123
鶉的一種 / 128
鵪鶉 / 128
鯰魚 / 011, 116
嚴肅正經的 / 087
嚴厲的懲罰 / 071

二十畫

寶石匠 / 167
（懸於項鍊下的）紀念品小盒子 / 060
懸疑片 / 236
爐子 / 020
競技場 / 217
競速滑冰 / 214
籃球 / 214
罌粟花 / 140
蘆筍 / 004
蘋果 / 006
蠔 / 117
蠕蟲 / 117
覺得事有問題 / 134
觸媒轉化器 / 251
警員 / 173

警察局 / 185
警衛 / 173
譯者 / 173
饒舌音樂 / 224
麵包 / 007
麵包[糕點]師 / 173
麵包店 / 185
麵包捲 / 007
麵包模 / 020
麵條 / 008
黨派 / 079
蠑螈 / 115
鰈魚，比目魚 / 011
鶚 / 128

二十一畫

懼高症 / 103
攝遠鏡頭 / 230
攝影室 / 230
攝影師 / 173
攝影棚 / 234
攜帶式嬰兒床 / 039
攜帶型傳呼器 / 063
櫻桃 / 006
櫻桃[迷你]蘿蔔 / 004
灌木（叢） / 135
犧牲者 / 244
蘭花 / 140

蠟嘴鳥 / 126
襪子 / 054
襪帶 / 052
護士 / 173, 195
護手霜 / 070
護唇膏 / 070
護膚霜 / 070
露天平臺 / 041
露臺 / 030, 041
顧問，參事 / 080
驅蟲人 / 174
騾 / 113
鰥夫 / 077
鶴 / 128
獾 / 114
鷂 / 128

二十二畫

歡呼，喝采 / 151
歡樂，高興 / 151
聽診心臟 / 105
聽診器 / 193
聽覺的 / 224
襯褲 / 048
驕傲 / 151
鰻魚 / 116
鷓鴣 / 128
鱈魚 / 011, 116

攪和器，果汁機 / 020
攪拌 / 022
攪拌器 / 020
蘿蔔（大根） / 004
變成碎片 / 157
變更住址或職業 / 045
顯像 / 230
顯影劑 / 230
驚悚片 / 236
驚嚇，恐怖 / 151
驗光師 / 174
體育館 / 185, 217
體香劑 / 070
體溫 / 197
體操 / 214
（體操用的）瓶狀木棒 / 215

二十三畫

鱒魚 / 011, 116
鱘魚 / 116
鷸 / 125, 128
鷸鴕 / 128

二十四畫

罐 / 120
蠶豆 / 002
讓某事繼續進行 / 219
靈歌 / 224
靈魂樂 / 224

鬢角 / 094, 098
鷹 / 129
鷹，隼 / 129
鹽 / 009
鹽瓶 / 018

二十五畫

廳 / 031
籬笆 / 041, 135
觀察 / 197
鑰匙圈 / 063
鑰匙鍊 / 063

二十六畫

讚美詩 / 221
鑷子 / 193
驢 / 113

二十七畫

鑽蛀牙 / 105
鱷魚 / 119
鱸魚 / 116
鸕鶿 / 129
鑿岩機 / 251
鸚鵡 / 129

二十九畫

鬱金香 / 140
鸛 / 129

NOTE 筆記頁

A

a baker's dozen / 175
a ball park figure / 175
a bean-counter / 176
a big cheese / 175
a bitter pill to swallow / 207
a black eye / 208
a cash cow / 176
a close shave / 071, 175
a dead end job / 175
a golden handshake / 176
a greaser / 071
a heart breaker / 156
a house is not a home / 044
a house of cards / 044
a little shaver / 071
a new broom sweeps clean / 044
a new lease on life / 207
a pain in the neck / 108
a painted woman / 071
a picky eater / 024
a shiner / 208
a shot in the arm / 208
a shot in the dark / 219
a sight for sore eyes / 208
a slip of tongue / 107
abdomen / 097

abele / 136
abhor / 152
abhorrent / 154
abject / 154
abscess / 202
acacia / 137
accessory / 228
accident / 201, 241
ache / 200
acid rain / 250
acorn / 141
acorn squash / 003
acoustic / 224
acquaintance / 078
acrophobia / 103
action / 235
actor / 232
actress / 231
Adams' apple / 143
adapted / 231
add / 021
address book / 061
adhesive tape / 193
admitting / 191
adolescent / 081
adonis / 137
adopted [foster] child / 077
adoptive parent / 074

adventure / 235
advertising agency / 184
advertising agent / 172
aeruophobia / 100
affection / 151
afraid / 154
after one's heart / 109
after-shaving lotion / 067
aftershock / 243
against the gran / 143
aged / 081
aggravation / 150
agitate / 153
AIDS / 102, 205
air freshener / 036
airplane crash / 241
albatross / 126
album / 221, 228
alcoholism / 204
ale / 016
all dress up / 056
all ears / 108
all in a [the] day's work / 175
all in the family / 088
all part of the game / 219
all thumbs / 107
allergic reaction / 102
allergy / 201, 205

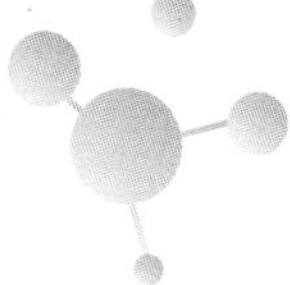

alligator / 119
aloof / 084
alto / 220
ambulance / 190, 242
amorous / 154
amusement / 150
an act of God / 245
aneroxia / 102
anesthetist / 195
anger / 150
angina / 204
anguish / 150
animation / 235
ankle / 097
annoyance / 150
ant / 118
antacid / 198
antacid tablets / 106
antagonist / 080
antagonize / 152
anther / 142
antidote / 198
antihistamine / 198
antique shop / 181
antiseptic / 198
anxiety / 150
anxious / 154
any port in a storm / 245

apartment / 028
aperture / 227
aphid / 117
appendectomy / 196
appendix / 095
apple / 006
apple of one's eye / 108
appliance store [repair] / 183
apprehensive / 155
apricot / 005
apricot blossom / 137
aquarium / 120
arbor / 135
archery / 212
arena / 217
arm / 094
armchair / 032
armpit / 096
arrow / 216
art gallery / 182
arteries / 096
arteriosclerosis / 204
arthritis / 206
artichoke / 004
artist / 173, 222
artistic / 084
arts and crafts store / 185
as easy as apple pie / 024

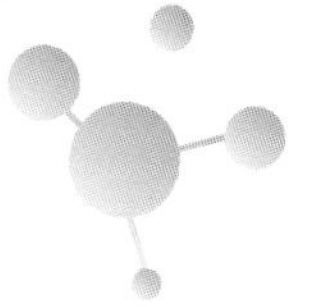

ash / 136
ask your some questions about your health history / 104
asparagus / 004
aspirin / 106, 198
assembly line worker / 170
associate / 078
asthma / 204
asthma, shortness of breath / 101
at each other's throat / 107
at the end of one's rope / 156
at wit's end / 156
atomic waste / 249
atomocitc [nuclear] / 241
attic / 031
attractive / 084
aunt / 075
autism / 203
auto parts store / 179
auto rental agency / 181
auto repair shop / 179
automatic / 227
automobile engineer / 164
avalanche / 242
avocado / 006
awe / 150
azalea / 137

B

baby / 082
baby backpack / 038
baby brother [sister] / 074
baby carriage / 039
baby carrier / 039
baby frontpack / 038
baby monitor [intercom] / 039
baby seat / 038
baby shampoo / 070
(baby) Bok choy / 002
babysitter / 165
back / 095
back door / 040
backache / 100
background / 223
bacon / 010
bad blood (between people) / 108
bad egg / 025
badger / 114
badminton / 212
bag / 061
bagel / 007
baggage handler / 164
bake / 022
baker / 173
baker's dozen / 023

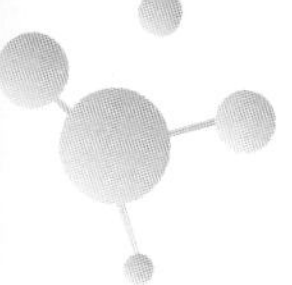

bakery / 185
baking pan / 019
balance beam / 215
ballad / 220
(ball point [fountain]) pen / 060
baloney / 024
balsam / 139
bamboo / 137
bamboo shoot / 002
banana / 005
band / 222
band (of gorilla) / 121
bandage / 193
band-aid / 192
banjo / 225
bank / 183
banker / 172
bank teller / 171
bar / 220
barbeque grill / 040
barber / 168
barber shop / 181
bark / 141
barn / 120
baroque / 222
barrel of oil / 247
barrette / 058
baseball / 213

based on a novel / 231
basement / 030
bashful / 086
basil / 014
basketball / 214
bass / 116, 220, 225
bassoon / 225
bat / 112
bath (room) / 031
bath mat / 036
bath oil / 066
bath salts / 068
bath soap / 067
(bath) tub / 036
bathing suit / 050
bathrobe / 050
battery / 229, 250
batting average / 218
battle gourd / 003
bay leave / 014
bay tree / 136
beads / 061
beak / 130
bean / 002
bean sprout / 002
bear / 114, 119
beard / 098
beat / 022, 220

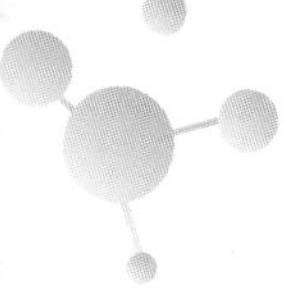

beautician / 166
beautiful / 085
beauty cream / 068
Beauty is in the eye of the beholder. / 071
Beauty is only skin deep. / 071
beauty lotion / 068
beauty parlor / 180
beaver / 114
bebop / 222
bed (of clams) / 122
bed / 033, 192
bed box [frame] / 033
bed of roses / 143
bed spread / 033
bedpan / 192
bedroom / 030
bee / 117
beech / 136
beef / 010
beeper (B.B. Call) / 062
beer / 016
beet / 004
begonia / 137
behind the eight ball / 219
bell pepper / 004
bellflower / 138
belligerence / 148
below par / 219

belt / 049
berserk / 154
better half / 089
better safe than sorry / 245
bewilder / 152
bicycle / 215
bicycling / 212
bifocal [sun, reading] (eye) glasses / 063
(big) brother, sister / 075
billfold / 059
billiards / 214
billing / 233
biological parents / 077
birch / 136
bird in the hand is worth two in the bush / 131
birdie / 215
birds of a feather flock together / 131
birthing [delivery] room / 190
biscuit / 007
bitter gourd / 003
bitterness / 149
black sheep / 132
blackbird / 125
bladder / 097
blanket / 033
blazer / 051
bleed / 099
blender / 020

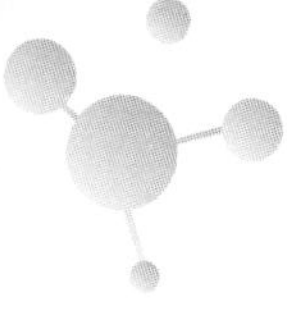

blind / 032, 200
blind alley / 044
blind date / 089
bliss / 150
blister / 099
blizzard / 240
bloated / 102
blood brother / 089
Blood is thicker than water. / 088
blood on the carpet / 176
blood pressure / 196
bloody nose / 102
blouse / 048
blow up, enlargement / 227
blueberry / 006
bluebird / 128
bluegill / 115
(blue) jeans / 048
bluegrass / 223
blush / 069, 153
B.O. (body odor) / 071
bobby pin / 062
bobcat / 113
bobwhite / 128
body cream / 069
body lotion / 066
boil / 021
bold / 083

bomb / 241
bone / 096
bookcase / 032
bookkeeper / 173
bookstore / 180
boomerang / 082
booster seat / 039
boredom / 150
born with a silver spoon in ones' mouth / 207
bother / 152
bow / 215
bow tie / 052
bowl / 019
bowling / 212
boxer shorts / 048
boxing / 213
boyfriend / 078
bra / 050
bracelet / 058
brain / 097
braise / 022
branch / 141
brandy / 016
brave / 084
bravery / 149
brazen / 086
bread / 007
bread pan / 020

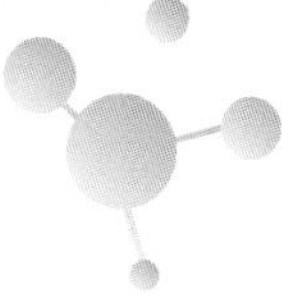

break / 021, 101
break a leg / 208
breast / 095, 129
bride / 076
(bride) groom / 076
briefcase / 058
briefs / 048
broccoli / 003
broil / 022
broiler / 019
bronchitis / 203
bronco busting / 213
brooch / 058
brood (of hens) / 121
brother / 074
brownie / 013
bruise / 102
brussels sprouts / 002
bubble bath / 067
buckle / 049
bud / 141
buddy / 079
buffalo / 118
bug / 118
building / 028
building contractor / 166
bulimia / 101
bull session / 132

bum steer / 134
bunglow / 028
bunny (rabbit) / 123
bureaucrat / 164
burn / 103, 202
burner / 020
burp / 099
burrow / 120
bursitis / 205
bus driver / 162
bush / 135
business consultant / 170
businessman [-woman] / 168
butcher / 164
butter / 012
butter dish / 017
butterfly / 118
butternut squash / 002
buttocks / 095, 098
by the sweat of one's brow / 175
by word of mouth / 107

C

cabbage / 002
cabinet / 035
cactus / 136
Caesarean section / 197
cafeteria / 179

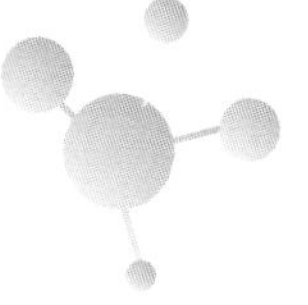

cage / 120
cake / 013
cake mix / 007
calculator / 060
calf / 094, 123
calling [business] card case / 059
calm / 152
camellia / 136
camera / 228
camera shop / 182
camphor tree / 140
can [bottle] opener / 019
cancer / 103, 206
candy store / 184
candy striper / 195
cane / 058, 192
canister / 034, 227
canna / 138
canoe / 216
canoeing / 214
cantaloupe / 005
cap / 051
cape / 049
capsules / 198
car dealership / 181
car washer / 166
caramelize / 021
cardigan / 052

cardinal / 125
carnage / 240
carnation / 138
carpenter / 162, 178
carpet & flooring store / 178
carrot / 003
carry one's own weight / 107
cartridge / 229
case / 228
cashier / 163
cassette / 220
cast / 192, 234
cat / 113
catalytic converter / 251
catastrophe / 240
catbird / 127
caterpillar / 117
catfish / 011, 116
cauliflower / 003
cave / 120
cavity / 101
CD player / 062
cedar / 137
ceiling / 032
celery / 002
cell phone / 058
cellar / 030
cello / 225

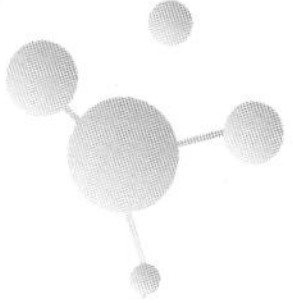

centipede / 117
cereal / 008
certified public accountant office / 182
(Certified Public) Accountant / 170
chain smoker / 208
chalet / 028
chamber / 223
chambermaid / 165
change purse / 062
change the linen [sheets] / 042
changing table / 038
character / 232
charities / 182
check your blood pressure / 104
checkbook / 058
cheek / 098
cheer / 151
cheerful / 087, 155
cheese / 012
chef / 163
cherry / 006
chest / 096
chest pain / 101
chestnut / 138
chest (with drawers) / 033
chewing [smokeless, dipping] tobacco / 059
chick / 124
chickadee / 125

chicken / 011, 128, 134
chicken pox / 203
chickenpox / 099
chief cook and bottle washer / 175
child, kid / 081
childhood / 082
childish / 081
chili pepper (cayenne pepper) / 015
chill / 100
chills / 200
chimney / 041
china cabinet / 018
Chinese cabbage / 002
Chinese chive, leek / 003
Chinese radish/daikon / 004
Chinese yam / 002
chip off the old block / 090
chipmunk / 113
chiropractor / 167, 194
choker / 062
cholera / 206
chop (up) / 021
chopping board / 019
chrysanthemum / 139
church / 181, 223
cigar / 061
cigarette / 060
cinnamon / 014

cinnamon [jelly, des-ser] roll / 013
civil engineer / 162
civil war / 240
clam / 116
clam before the storm / 245
clams / 010
clarinet / 226
classical / 222
claustrophobia / 100
claw / 129
clean one's teeth / 104
clean the bathroom / 042
clean the wound / 104
cleaning man [woman] / 168
Cleanliness is next to Godliness. / 071
clinic / 191
clogs / 053
close [distant] relatives / 089
close the wound / 104
close-captioned / 234
closet / 030
close-up / 233
clothes make the man / 055
clothing store / 179
cloud (of gnats) / 121
clove / 014
coal / 250
coat / 048

cobbler / 170
cock and bull story / 133
cockroach / 118
cocktail jacket / 050
cocoa / 014
coconut / 006
cod / 011, 116
coffee / 016
coffee maker / 034
coffee pot / 017
coffee shop / 179
coffee table / 032
coin / 061
coin purse / 058
coke / 016
cold / 084, 102, 201
cold cream / 066
cold tablets / 106
coliseum / 217
colleague / 078
collision / 242
cologne / 066
colony (of ants) / 121
colt / 123
comb / 061, 068
combustion / 250
come down with / 209
come out / 230

come-back / 219
comedian / 234
comedy / 235
comforter / 033
commercial artist / 168
compact / 069
compact disc (CD) / 221
companion, company / 078
complacent / 084
composition / 220, 229
computer programmer / 171
computer store / 183
comrade / 078
con artist / 163
conceited / 084
concert / 221
concerto / 220
condominium (condo) / 028
condor / 125
conductor / 221
conflagration / 240
congested / 103
conservation / 248
console / 153
constipation / 200
construction worker / 166
consumable resources / 248
consumption / 249

contact lens / 062
contemporary / 223
contraceptive / 198
cook / 022, 172
cookbook / 019
cookie / 008
(cooking) oil / 009
cooperative / 083
copy center / 184
copycat / 133
coriander / 014
cormorant / 129
corn / 002
corn bread / 007
cornet / 226
corny / 024
cosmetic [makeup] base / 069
co-star / 231
cottage / 029
cottage cheese / 012
cotton balls / 069
couch / 032
cougar, mountain lion / 114
cough / 100, 200
cough drops / 106
cough syrup / 106
counseling office / 184
counselor / 080

country and western / 223
country club / 217
country house / 029
country store / 178
courage / 149
courageous / 084
courier / 167
course / 217
court / 217
courteous, polite / 083
cousin / 076
cow / 112
cowardly / 087
cowbird / 127
cowboy / 165
cowboy [dress, riding] boots / 053
cowgirl / 165
coyote / 113
crab / 117
crabs / 011
crackers / 008
cradle / 038
cramp / 100
cranberry / 006
crane / 128
crank up / 233
craziness / 150
crazy / 086

cream / 007, 012
cream cheese / 012
cream of the crop / 025
creamer / 017
credit card case / 060
crepe / 013
crest / 129
crib / 038
cricket / 118
critic / 234
crocodile / 119
crocodile tears / 133
croissant / 007
crony / 079
(cross-country) skiing / 213
crossing guard / 163
crow / 126
crowd / 079
cruel / 086
crutches / 059, 192
cry / 152
cry wolf / 133
cuckoo / 125
cucumber / 004
cufflinks / 061
cumin / 014
cup / 037
cupcake / 013

curling / 212
curry / 014
curtain / 032
cut / 101
cut (up) / 021
cuticle remover / 066
cyberphobia / 102
cyclone / 243
cygnet (swan) / 123
cymbals / 226

D

D&C (Dilation & Curettage) / 196
dad / 075
daddy / 075
daffodil / 139
daisy / 140
dam / 247
dance / 224
dance studio / 183
dandelion / 139
Danish pastry / 007
dark horse / 133
darkroom / 229
date / 005, 079, 138
date book / 060
daughter / 074
dawn (deer) / 123

day-care center / 179
dead as a doornail / 209
dead from the neck up / 109
deaf / 200
death toll / 245
death, loss of life / 240
decaf. (decaffeinated) / 016
deck / 041
decongestant / 198
decongestant spray / 106
deer / 114
definition / 228
deforestation / 241
dejected / 154
dejection / 148
delicatessen (deli) / 184
delight / 148
delighted / 154
delivery (of a baby) / 196
delivery person / 167
delivery room / 190
demophobia / 099
den / 030
dental floss / 066
dental hygienist / 162
dentist / 163
deodorant / 070
department store / 179

dependable / 085
dependent / 077
depilatory / 069
depletion / 249
depress / 152
depression / 103, 148
depressor / 193
dermatologist / 194
desertification / 241
detective / 168
determined / 083
detest / 152
devastation / 243
developer / 230
diabetes / 103, 206
diagnosis / 197
dialogue / 234
diaper pail / 038
diarrhea / 102, 201, 205
dice / 021
digital / 229
diligent / 086
dill / 015
dimple / 096
dining room / 031
(dining room) table, chair / 018
dinner jacket / 049
diplomat / 163

disappointment / 148
disaster / 241
disaster relief / 243
disc / 221
disc jockey (DJ) / 221
disciple / 079
disciplined / 084
disconsolate / 155
discount store / 182
disgust / 152
dish rack / 035
dish towel / 035
dishrag / 034
dishwasher / 034, 166
dishwasher detergent / 034
dishwasher liquid / 034
dislocate / 101
diving / 214
dizzy / 103
do the dishes / 042
do the ironing / 043
do the laundry / 042
doctor / 173
doctor (M.D.) / 195
documentary / 235
dodge and burn / 228
dog / 112
dog walker / 171

dogwood / 136
dollar store / 178
dolled up / 055
dolly shot / 233
dolphin / 114
donkey / 113
door knob / 040
doorbell / 040
doorman [-woman] / 166
double exposure / 228
double-header / 218
doughnut / 007
down jacket / 049
down vest / 049
(downhill) skiing / 213
dragonfly / 117
drain / 036
draining spoon / 020
drapes / 032
draw some blood / 104
dress / 050
dress shirt / 048
dress the wound / 104
dresser, bureau / 033
drilling rig / 251
drill the cavity / 105
drip / 079
driveway / 040

drought / 242
drug addiction / 204
drug store / 185
drums / 225
dry cleaners / 180
dubbed / 233
duck / 011, 128
duckling (duck) / 124
dulcimer / 226
dumb / 086, , 201
dump / 179
dungarees / 051
duplicate / 229
dust the bookshelves / 043

E

eagle / 129
eaglet / 123
ear / 095
earache / 099
ear infection / 099
early bird / 131
earmuffs / 049
earring / 059
earthquake / 240
edelweiss / 136
editing / 233
editor / 172

eel / 116
egg / 129
eggbeater / 019
eggplant / 003
egret / 125
EKG (electrocardiogram) / 196
elbow / 094
elderly / 081
electric blanket / 033
electric guitar / 226
(electric) can opener / 035
(electric) shaver / 069
(electric) toothbrush / 036
electrical engineer / 171
electrician / 171
electricity / 250
electronic / 224
electronics store / 183
elephant / 118
elevator operator / 171
elk / 114
elm / 139
embarrassment / 148
emergency / 243
emergency (in) dependence / 250
emergency efficiency / 249
emergency loss / 249
emergency room / 190

emergency tax / 249
emery board / 067
emphysema / 203
employment agency / 182
employment officer / 169
empty nest(er) / 081
emu / 126
end table / 032
endangered species / 251
enemy / 080
energy costs / 249
engagement [school, signet, wedding] ring / 060
engine / 247
engineer / 162
English muffin / 007
enthusiasm / 151
entourage / 233
environmental cleanup / 251
environmental destruction / 243
environmentalist / 251
environmental policy / 251
environmental science / 251
environmental law / 251
envy / 148
epidemic / 242
epiphyllum / 140
eruption / 240
ethanol / 247

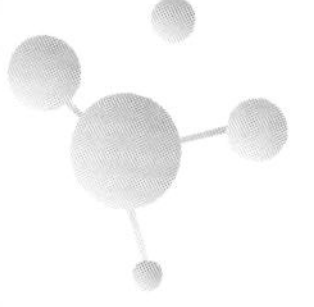

ethnic cleansing / 243
evacuation / 242
(evening) gown / 051
evening primrose / 136
evergreen / 137
every Tom, Dick and Harry / 089
examination / 196
examine one's eyes [ears, nose, throat, teeth] / 104
excite / 153
exhausted / 102
exhaustion / 201
explosion / 244
exposure / 230
extende [nuclear] family / 088
exteriors / 231
extinct / 250
extra (player) / 234
eye / 096
eyedrops / 198
eye drops / 069, 106
eyebrow pencil / 068
eye-liner / 068
eye-shadow / 068
eye wash / 068

F

fabric [draperies] store / 179
face / 098

face wash / 067
facial cleanser / 067
facial mask / 068
facial soap / 068
factory worker / 162
fade-in / 233
fade-out / 233
faint / 102
fair sex / 089
falcon / 128
fall-guy / 089
family / 235
family dog / 075
family feud / 089
family room / 031
family tree / 089
famine / 242
fan / 036
farmer / 170
farmers' market / 183
farmhand / 170
fast forward / 231
fast motion / 231
fast-food chain / 181
fatality / 240
father / 074
father-in-law / 075
fatigue / 149

faucet / 034
favorite son / 089
fear / 149
feather / 129
feather in one's cap / 132
feature / 231
felling / 150
female friend / 078
fence / 041
fencing / 214
fetal alcohol syndrome / 204
fever / 101, 201
fiance [fiancee] / 078
fiance(e) / 074
fiddle / 225
field / 135, 217
field hand / 170
fig / 006
figure skating / 212
file clerk / 173
filet of sole / 011
fillet / 021
fill the tooth / 104
filly (horse) / 124
film / 227
filter / 230, 251
finger / 094
fingerling / 123

fingernail / 094
fir / 137
fire / 240
fire department / 181
fire storm / 240
firefighter / 168
fireman [-woman] / 168
fireplace / 032
firmiana / 138
first aid / 241
first husband [wife] / 076
fish out of the water / 134
fisherman / 171
fishing / 213
fishing lure / 216
fishing rod / 216
fission / 247
fist / 095
fit to be tied / 156
five o'clock shadow / 071
fix-it shop / 184
flamingo / 126
flash / 228
flashback / 232
flash flood / 241
flat / 028
flats / 053
flea market / 183

fledgling / 123
flesh and blood / 107
flight attendant / 165
flip-flops / 053
flock / 130
flock (of birds) / 121
flood / 241
floor lamp / 032
florist / 180
flounder / 011
flustered / 155
flycatcher / 128
flying rings / 215
foal / 123
foaming / 067
focal length / 228
focus / 229
fold the laundry / 043
folk / 222
folk song / 220
folks / 077
follow up / 234
follower / 079
food for thought / 024
food handler / 167
food processor / 019
food warmer / 038
foolish / 086

for a song / 237
for keeps / 219
forbidden fruit / 025
forearm / 095
forehead / 098
foreskin / 094
forest / 135
forget-me-not / 136
fork / 018
forlorn / 154
fossil fuel / 247
foster parent / 077
fox / 113
fracture / 201
frame / 228
free-for-all / 218
freezer / 034
fresh / 085
friend / 079
friendly / 083
frigate bird / 126
fright / 151
frog / 115
front door / 040
front porch / 040
front steps / 040
frostbite / 100
(fruit) punch / 016

fry / 022, 123
frying pan / 019
fuel / 250
full scene / 231
fume / 152
funeral parlor / 184
funny / 086
furner / 020
furniture store / 181
fusion / 250
fvied-simmer / 021

G

G (General) / 236
gaggle (of geese) / 121
gallbladder / 098
galoshes / 053
gang / 079
garage / 030, 040
garbage collector / 164
garbage disposal / 034
garbage pail / 034
garden / 135
gardener / 169
gardenia / 138
garlic / 014
garter / 052
gas pump / 247

gasoline (gas) / 248
gauze / 192
gay / 154
geek / 079
geezer / 078
genealogy / 076
general practitioner (G.P.) / 194
generator / 249
genocide / 243
gerbil / 112
get butterfly in one's stomach / 107
gift shop / 184
ginger / 015
giraffe / 119
girdle / 049
girlfriend / 078
give one a shot of anesthetic / 104
gladiolus / 140
gladness / 149
glasses case / 061
glazier / 170
glee / 148
global warming / 240
glossy / 229
glove / 215
gloves / 048
goat / 112
godparent(s) / 076

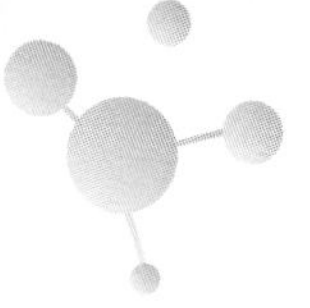

goldfinch / 126
goldfish / 116
golf / 213
golf ball / 215
golf clubs / 215
gonorrhea / 204
goose / 128
gorgeous / 087
gorilla / 118
gosling (goose) / 123
graft / 141
grain / 007
grandaunt / 074
grandchild (ren) / 075
grandma / 076
grandpa / 076
grandparent(s) / 076
granduncle / 074
grape / 006
grapefruit / 006
grapevine / 139, 143
grasshopper / 118
grate / 021
great grandchild(ren) / 076
great grandparent(s) / 076
great uncle [aunt] / 075
greed / 149
greedy / 086

green / 217
green onion / 003
green pepper / 003
grill / 022
grocery store / 185
grosbeak / 126
grouchy / 155
groundskeeper / 169
group / 221
grove / 135
grownup / 081
guard / 173
guardian / 077
guest / 079
guest star / 232
guinea pig / 112
guitar / 225
gull / 126
gullible / 085
gums / 097
guppy / 115
gym / 185
gym shoes / 054
gymnasium / 217
gymnastic / 214
gynecologist / 194

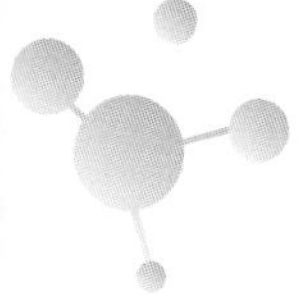

H

hair / 098
hair brush / 062, 069
hair color [dye] / 067
hair dryer / 036
hair pin / 062
hair pull / 060
hair remover / 067
hair rinse / 069
half and half / 012
half-brother [sister] / 074
halibut / 010
hall / 031
ham / 010
(hamburger) bun / 007
hamburger/meat patty / 010
hamper / 036
hamster / 112
hand / 094
hand cleanser / 066
hand cream / 070
hand lotion / 066
hand soap / 067
handbag / 058
handheld PC (HPC) / 058
handkerchief / 058
handsome / 085

Handsome is as handsome does. / 071
handwritings on the wall / 044
hang out the laundry / 043
hanging (toiletry) bag / 061
happy as a clam / 156
hard of hearing / 208
hard rock / 223
hardware store / 178
hard-working / 084
hare / 112
harp / 226
hat / 049
hate / 152
have a frog in ones throat / 109
hawk / 129
head / 097
headache / 103
headboard / 033
health center / 181
healthfood store / 181
heart / 094
heart attack / 099, 203
heart beat / 196
hear-to-heart / 108
heat / 250
heating contractor / 170
heating pad / 193
heatstroke / 099

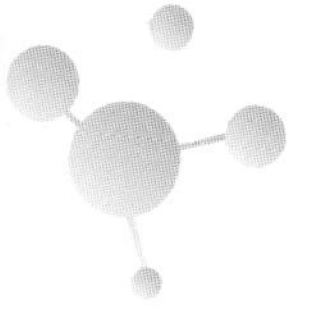

heavy metal / 223
hedge / 135
heel / 097
helpful / 083
hemorrhoids / 201
hepatitis / 203
herb / 014
herd (of elephants, horses) / 121
hernia / 203
heron / 127
herpes / 204
herring / 116
hiccups / 099
high blood pressure / 101, 204
high chair / 038
high heels / 054
high temperature / 101
high-rise / 029
high-top sneakers / 053
high-tops / 053
hiking / 212
hip / 098
hip hop / 224
hippopotamus (hippo) / 119
hit / 222
hit or miss / 219
HIV positive / 205
HMO / 190

hobby shop / 180
hockey / 212
hockey stick / 215
holly / 136
homeless shelter / 183
honey / 015
honeydew / 005
hook, line, and sinker / 218
hooked on drugs / 209
hope / 148
horn / 226
horror / 149, 235
horrors (withdrawal) / 208
horse / 113
horse of another color / 131
horseback riding / 214
hospital / 184, 191
host / 078
hot and bothered / 156
hot dog / 010, 025
hot water bottle / 192
hotel [motel] clerk / 167
house / 029
house detective / 162
(house) painter / 165
houseboat / 029
housekeeper / 162
housewife [-husband] / 167

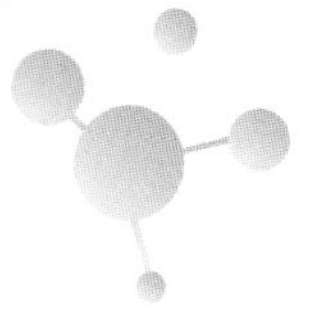

hummingbird / 127
humorous / 084
hunting / 212
hurricane / 244
hurt / 101
husband / 074
hut / 028
hutch / 120
hyacinth / 138
hydro-electric power / 247
hydrophobia / 100
hyena / 118
hymn / 221
hypermart / 178
hysterectomy / 196

I

ice cream / 012
ICU / 190
ID bracelet / 059
identification / 059
if the shoe fits, wear it / 055
igloo / 028
ill-mannered / 085
illustrator / 169
immunity / 203
impolite / 086
in a dither / 156

in a nutshell / 143
in one's blood / 107
in the doghouse / 133
in the pink / 208
in the rough / 219
Indian clubs / 215
indifference / 148
indigestion / 200
infant / 081
infection / 102, 201
inflammation / 201
influenza (flu) / 204
injection / 196
injury / 200, 241
in-laws / 075
inoculation / 197
insane / 086, 155
insane asylum / 191
insect bite / 100
instamatic / 229
insulation / 250
insurance agency / 180
insurance agent / 165
insurance claims adjustor / 165
insurance investigator / 165
intelligent / 083
intensive care / 196
interior decorator / 166

interiors / 231
Internal Revenue / 181
interpreter / 162
iris / 139
irritated / 155
itchy / 102

J

Jack knife / 059
Jack [Jill] of all trades / 176
jack of all trades / 167
jacket / 049
janitor / 162
jasmine / 138
jaw / 098
jay / 126
jazz / 222, 224
jealous / 086, 148
jeweler / 167
jewelry store / 181
jock / 078
jogging / 213
jolly / 154
journalist / 170
joviality / 148
joy / 151
judge / 165
juice / 016

jump out one's skin / 108
jumper / 051
jumpsuit / 051
junk dealer / 172
juvenile / 081

K

kerchief / 058
ketchup / 009
kettle / 019
key chain / 063
key ring / 063
key to the city / 064
kid / 123
kidney / 096
kin, kin folks / 075
kind / 083
kindred / 077
kinetic / 249
kingbird / 126
kingfisher / 126
kissing cousins / 090
kitchen / 031
kitchen chair [table] / 035
kitten (cat) / 124
kiwi / 005, 128
knee / 097
knee socks / 053

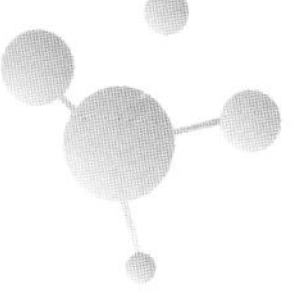

knife / 018
know where all the bodies were buried / 108
knuckle / 095

L

lab technician / 162, 195
labor room / 190
laboratory / 191
lady bug / 118
lamb (sheep) / 124
lament / 152
lamp / 032
lamppost / 041
landfill / 179, 248
landscape architect / 169
lane / 217
laptop computer / 058
large [small] intestines / 094
lark / 127
laryngitis / 100
last lap / 219
laughter / 149
Laundromat / 179
laundry room / 030
laundry worker / 166
law firm / 180
lawn / 031, 040
lawyer / 166

laxative / 198
lazy / 087
leader / 080, 231
leaf / 141
leather jacket / 049
leek sprout(s) [shoot] / 004
leg / 096
legislator / 163
lemon / 006
lemonade / 016
lens / 230
leopard / 119
leotard / 052
lettuce / 004
leukemia / 203
librarian / 171
lid / 020
life guard / 168
light classical / 224
light meter / 228
lightening contractor / 170
lighter / 059
like two peas in one pod / 025
lilac / 139
lily / 137
lime / 006
lion / 119
lip balm / 070

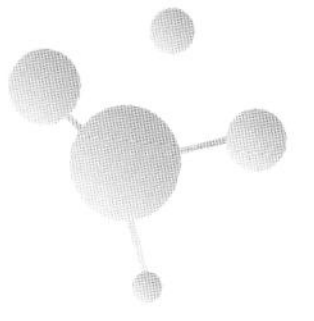

lip gloss / 068
lipstick / 068
liquor / 016
listen to one's heart / 105
little black book / 064
liver / 095
living room / 030
living together (living apart together) / 088
lizard / 115
llama / 112
load / 229
loan association / 178
loan shark / 165
lobbyist / 171
lobster / 011, 117
location / 233
locket / 060
loft / 029
log cabin / 028
logger / 172
long shot / 218, 232
longshoreman / 172
look over one's shoulder / 107
loon / 127
lotus / 140
lotus root / 004
loud / 083
love / 150

love will find a way / 156
loveable / 085
lovely / 083
lover / 079
loveseat / 032
low fat milk / 012
lungs / 095
lynx / 113
lyrics / 222, 234

M

ma / 076
macaroni / 008
mace / 059
machine operator / 173
magazine holder / 032
magnolia / 136
magpie / 126
mail carrier / 169
mailbox / 040
mailer / 228
mail-order / 182
maintenance worker / 171
make the bed / 043
make up / 066
makeup / 066
malaria / 205
male friend / 078

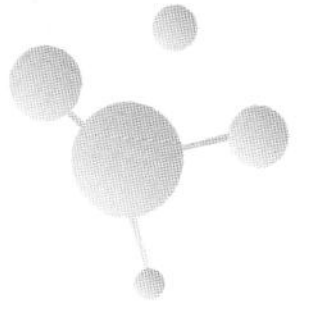

manager / 170
mandolin / 225
mango / 005
manor / 029
mansion / 028
maple / 139
margarine / 012
marker / 061
martial art / 235
martial art studio / 180
mary janes / 053
mascara / 069
mason / 163
masque / 068
mass transit / 247
masseur / 164
masseuse / 164
mat / 216
matches / 059
mate / 078
maternal / 074
maternity dress / 048
maternity ward / 190
matinee / 231
matte / 227
mattress / 033
mayonnaise (mayo) / 009
meadowlark / 126

mean / 084
measles / 101, 205
measure / 220
measuring cup / 019
meatball / 010
mechanic / 172
medicine cabinet / 037
melancholy / 155
melo-drama / 235
melody / 221
meningitis / 205
mental hospital / 191
mental retardation / 205
merchant mariner / 168
merry / 155
messenger / 167
meter reader / 164
method in one's madness / 157
microwave / 035
middle child / 076
middle-age / 081
military recruiting office / 182
minidisk player (MP) / 061
minimart / 178
minister / 165
mirror / 037
mittens / 051
mixer / 020

mob / 080
mobile / 038
mobile home / 028
moccasins / 054
modern / 223
moisturizer / 069
mom / 076
mommy / 076
monk fish / 116
monkey / 119
monkey business / 132
monkey on your back / 208
mononucleosis (mono) / 205
mood / 148
mood music / 223
moose / 114
mop the floor / 042
mope / 152
morning glory / 139
mosque / 178
mother / 074
mother-in-law / 075
motor / 248
mountaineering / 213
mourn / 152
mouse / 112
mouth / 097
mouthwash, oral rinse / 069

mover / 170
moving company / 182
MP3 player / 058
MRI / 197
mud room / 030
mud slide / 240
mudpack / 070
mufflers / 051
mug / 018
mug shot / 228
mulberry / 138
mule / 113
multiple sclerosis / 203
MUMPS / 102
mumps / 205
muscle / 095
mushroom / 003
music store / 184
music to one's ear / 237
musical / 223, 235
musician / 166
muskmelon / 005
mussel / 117
mustache / 098
mustard / 009, 014
mutton / 010
mystery / 235

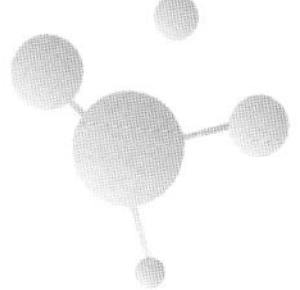

N

N.G. (No Good) / 232
nail clipper / 060
nail clippers / 067
nail file / 067
nail polish / 067
nail polish remover / 067
napkins / 193
nasal spray / 106, 198
natural gas / 247
nausea / 201
nauseous / 103
neck / 096
(neck) tie / 052
necklace / 062
nectarine / 005
needle / 141
NEET / 081
negative / 227
nephew / 075
nerd / 079
nerve / 095
nervousness / 150
nest / 120
nest (of snakes) / 122
nest egg / 134
net / 216

neurologist / 194
neurosis / 204
New Age [space] / 223
news reporter / 170
newspaper office / 182
newsstand / 181
newt (salamander) / 115
niece / 075
night light / 038
night stand [table] / 033
nightgown / 052
nighthawk / 125
nipple / 094
No sweat ! / 107
nomination / 233
non-aspirin pain reliever / 106
noodles / 008
nook / 030
nose / 097
not for all the tea in China / 023
not to move a muscle / 107
note / 222
notebook / 061
notebook PC / 061
nouvelle vague / 235
nuclear meltdown / 241
nuclear power / 249
nuclear reactor / 249

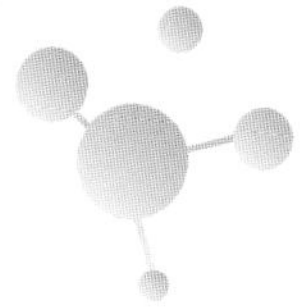

nurse / 173, 195
nurse practitioner (N.P.) / 195
nursery / 030
nursing home / 191
nutmeg / 014
nuts, nutty as a fruitcake / 209
nylons / 048

O

oak tree / 140
oatmeal / 007
obesity / 100
oboe / 226
observation / 197
obstetrician / 195
OD (Overdose on Drugs) / 100
office boy / 162
office hours / 207
oil / 248
oil drilling / 248
oil field / 248
oil production / 248
oil rig / 249
oil slick / 241
oil spill / 241
oil well / 248
ointment / 069, 199
okra / 003

old man [lady] / 088
olive oil / 009
olive tree / 140
ombudsman / 162
on a shoestring / 055
on call / 208
on one's back / 107
on pins and needles / 055
on the tip of one's tongue / 107
on the wagon / 208
one foot in the grave / 207
opera / 224
operating room / 190
operating table / 192
operetta / 224
ophthalmologist / 195
optician / 169, 181
optometrist / 174
(oral [rectal]) thermometer / 192
orange / 005
orchard / 135
orchid / 140
oregano / 014
organ / 226
oriole / 127
orphan / 075
orthopedic surgeon / 195
osmanthus / 138

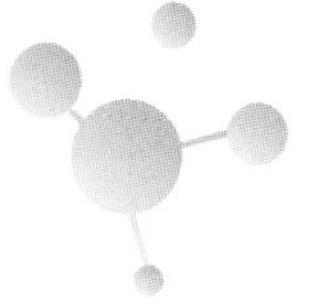

osprey / 128
ostrich / 128
otter / 113
out of sorts / 156
out on a limb / 143
out to lunch / 023
outlet store / 183
out-of-focus / 227
out-patient clinic / 190
ovary / 141
oven / 019
over one's dead body / 207
over the hill / 208
overalls / 052
overcoat / 048
over-exposed / 230
overnight bag / 058
overshoes / 053
owl / 127
ox / 112
oxfords / 054
oxygen tent / 192
oyster / 117
ozone (ozen layer) / 249

P

pa / 075
pack (of dogs) / 121

paddle / 216
pager / 063
pain / 149, 201
painful / 155
paint store / 180
pajamas / 052
pal / 080
palace / 028
palm / 094
(palm [pocket]) organizer / 062
palm tree / 139
pan / 019
pancake / 007
pancreas / 095
panorama shot / 234
panties / 048
pantry / 031
pants / 050
pantsuit / 052
pantyhose / 052
papa / 075
papaya / 005
(paper) napkin / 017
paper towel holder / 034
paprika / 014
parallel bars / 216
paranoia / 204
park / 135

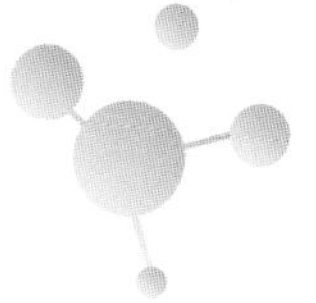

parka / 051
parking lot attendant / 167
parrot / 129
parsley / 014
partner / 080
partridge / 128
party / 078
passion / 151
passionate / 155
pasture / 120
paternal / 074
pathologist / 194
patio / 030, 041
pea / 004
peach / 005
peacock / 125
pear / 005
(pearl) onion / 003
peck / 129
pediatric ward / 190
pediatrician / 194
peel / 022
peeler / 019
pelican / 128
pelvis / 096
pen / 120
pen light / 062
pencil / 062

pencil sharper / 060
penguin / 125
penicillin / 198
penis / 096
penknife / 060
penthouse / 029
pepper / 009
pepper shaker / 017
perch / 115
perfume / 068
pest exterminator / 174
pestulence / 242
pet shop / 185
petal / 142
petroleum / 248
PG (Parental Guidance) / 236
PG 13 (Parental Guid-ance 13) / 236
phalaenopsis / 140
pharmacist / 173, 195
pharmacy / 185
pheasant / 127
phoebe / 127
photographer / 173
photography store / 182
physician / 195
piano / 226
piano tuner / 173
pie / 013

piece / 220
pig / 113
pigeon / 128
pig-headed / 132
piglet (pig) / 124
pike / 115
pill / 199
pillbox / 063
pillow / 033
pillowcase / 033
pilot / 167
pin / 059
pineapple / 006
pine cone / 140
pine tree / 137
ping pong / 212, 215
pipe / 061
pipe dream / 064
pipeline / 248
pistil / 142
pitcher / 017
pity / 150
pixel / 229
pizza parlor / 178
placement / 035
plain / 083
Planned Parenthood / 180
plate / 018

platform / 053
platter / 017
play room / 031
playing cards / 062
playing date / 232
playmate / 080
playpen / 038
playwright / 234
pleasant / 083
pleasure / 149
plum / 005
plum blossom / 138
plumber / 162, 178
pneumonia / 203
pocket calendar / 062
pocketbook / 061
pod (of whales) / 121
podiatrist / 164, 194
poeny / 137
pointy-shoe / 053
poison ivy / 138
pole / 215
police department / 185
police officer / 173
polio / 203
polish the furniture / 043
politician / 166
pollen / 142

polliwog / 123
pollster / 163
pollution / 240
polo / 213
pomegranate flower / 136
poncho / 048
pony / 113
pool / 212
pop / 075, 223
poplar tree / 136
poppy / 140
popular / 223
porch / 030
porcupine / 114
pork / 011
porpoise / 114
portable crib / 039
portrait / 228
pose / 230
positive / 227
possum / 114
post office / 182
poster / 232
potato / 003
potholder / 035
potter / 169
potty / 038
pour / 022

powder / 069
practical nurse / 194
prairie dog / 112
prawn / 010
praying mantis / 117
prejudice / 149
premier / 232
prescription / 198
press spokesman / 170
pressure cooker / 020
pre-teen / 081
pretty / 086
pride / 151
pride (of lions) / 121
priest / 165
print / 230
printer / 164
printing shop / 178
private room / 190
process / 230
producer / 234
professor / 168
prognosis / 197
program / 221
projection booth / 232
projector / 227
proof of pudding is in eating / 024
propane / 247

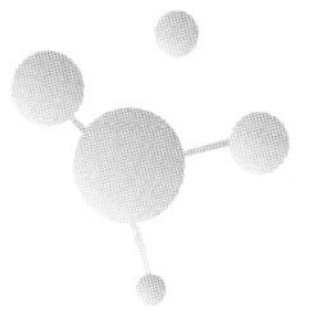

prune / 006
psychiatrist / 171, 195
psychoanalyst / 195
psychologist / 162
psychosis / 206
publicist / 165
publisher / 163
puck / 216
pudding / 013
puff / 013
puffin / 127
pulse / 197
pumpkin / 003
puppy (dog) / 123
purse / 062
purse snatcher / 064

Q

Q-tip (swab) / 192
quail / 128
quiet / 083
quilt / 033

R

R (Restricted) / 236
rabbit / 112
raccoon / 114
racket / 215

racquet / 215
racquetball / 212
radiologist / 194
radio-TV repair / 179
radish / 004
rage / 148
rain boots / 050
rain check / 218
raincoat / 050
raisin / 006
ranch house / 028
rap / 224
rash / 099, 200
raspberry / 006
rat / 112
rattle / 039
raven / 127
razor / 067
real estate agency / 179
real estate agent / 164
receptionist / 168, 194
recipe / 019
recital / 221
record / 221
recovery room / 190
recreation center / 179
recycling / 248
recycling center / 183

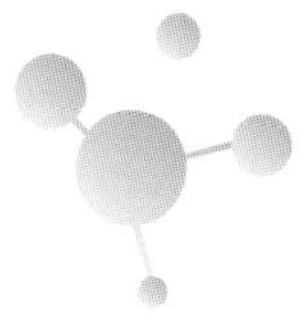

red cap / 172
red onion / 003
reduce / 230
redwood / 138
refinery / 250
refrigerator (fridge) / 034
reggae / 224
registered nurse (R.N.) / 194
regret / 151
rehearsal / 233
reins / 215
rejoice / 152
relative / 077, 080
release / 221, 233
relief / 242
religious / 223
relish / 009
renewable resources / 247
repairman [-woman] / 167
rescue / 242
reserved / 083
restaurant / 184
restlessness / 148
retake / 232
retiree / 082
rewind / 228, 232
rez (resolution) / 229
rheumatic fever / 204

rhinoceros (rhino) / 119
rhythm / 221
rhythm and blues / 223
ribcage / 096
rice / 008
Richter scale / 241
right off the bat / 218
ring / 141, 217
ringleader / 089
rink / 217
riot / 243
risk one's neck / 108
road hog / 133
roadrunner / 125
roadside vendor / 183
roast / 021
robin / 126
rock and roll / 223
(rock) climbing / 214
roll / 007
roll of film / 226
roller blade / 212
rolling pin / 019
romance / 235
romantic / 085
roof / 040
roommate / 079
root / 140

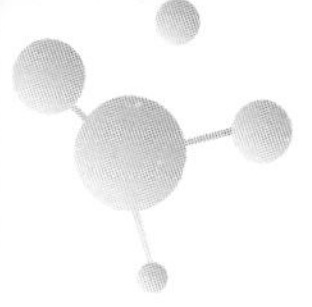

rose / 137
rosemary / 014
rouge / 068
roustabout / 172
rubber mat / 036
rubber tree / 140
rubbers / 054
rubbish collector / 164
rubella (German measles) / 206
rude / 086
running / 213
running nose / 200
running shoes / 054
running shorts / 051
running time / 231
runs in the family / 088
ruthless / 086

S

saddle / 215
sadness / 150
safe and sound / 207
sage / 015
sailor / 162
salad bowl / 017
salad dressing / 009
sales clerk / 168
salmon / 011

salsa / 009
salt / 009
salt shaker / 018
salt-box / 028
sample / 197
sandals / 054
sandpiper / 128
sane / 085
sanitarium / 191
sanitary / 192
sap / 141
satellite dish / 041
saucer / 017
sauté / 022
save one's breath / 108
saxophone / 226
scale / 021, 037
scallion / 003
scallop / 116
scallops / 010
scalpel / 192
scarf / 051
scarlet fever / 205
scene plot / 233
scent / 068
schizophrenia / 205
school (of fish) / 121
school administrator / 172

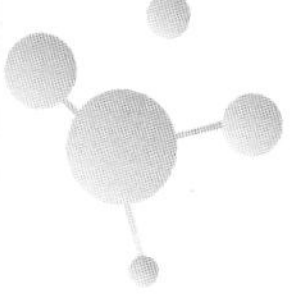

scientist / 166
sci-fic (science-fiction) / 235
scorpion / 118
scout / 232
scrape / 103
scratch / 099
screen / 229
screen door / 040
scrubbers / 248
sea cow / 114
sea urchin / 116
second wind / 218
secretary / 167
security officer / 173
sedative / 199
seed / 141, 142
(seeing through) rose colored glasses / 064
self-conscious / 083
selfish / 084
senior citizen / 082
senior citizen's center / 179
sensitive / 085
sentimental / 086
serious / 087
Service / 181
service center / 180
service station / 178
service station attendant / 163

serving bowl / 017
serving dish / 017
set the table / 043
setting / 227
sewing center / 184
sexy / 084, 154
shade / 032
shadlock / 137
shallot / 002
shampoo / 068
shark / 116
shaving cream / 066
shaving mug / 069
sheep / 113
sheet / 033
shelf / 036
shell / 130
shelter / 244
shin / 096
shipping center / 181
shipping clerk / 170
shipwreck / 242
shoe repair service / 180
shoe store / 184
shoe strings / 054
shoelace / 054
shoemaker / 172
shoes / 054

shopping mall / 184
shorts / 051
shot / 196
shoulder / 095
shoulder bag / 060
shower (shower curtain) / 037
shred / 021
shrimp / 010, 117
shrub / 135
shutter / 040, 227
shy / 086, 154
siblings / 077
sibling rivalry / 088
sick and tired of / 209
sideburns / 098
side door / 041
side-kick / 088
simmer / 021
singer / 221
sink / 034
sinking / 241
sis (sister) / 075
skates / 216
skating / 213
ski jacket / 051
ski pole / 216
skin / 095
skin and bones / 209

skin cancer / 203
skin cream / 070
skirt / 051
skis / 216
skull / 098
skunk / 114
skyscraper / 029
slacks / 050
slice / 021
slicker / 049
slide / 227
sling-back / 053
slip / 050
slippers / 053
smallpox / 203
smog / 250
snack bar / 183
snail / 117
snake / 115
snake in the grass / 132
snapshot / 227
sneakers / 053
sneeze / 099
snipe / 125
snowdrop / 139
snowsuit / 051
snuff / 059
soap / 067

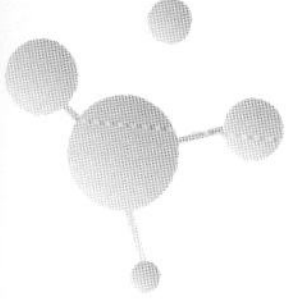

soap dish / 036
soap dispenser / 036
soccer / 212
socks / 054
soda / 016
sofa / 032
soft drink / 016
softball / 214
solar power / 247
soldier / 166
sole / 097
solo / 222
something fishy / 023
son / 074
son of a gun / 090
sonata / 220
song / 221
song and dance / 237
soprano / 220
sore / 200
sore throat / 101
sorrow / 149
soul / 224
sound track / 232
sour cream / 012
sour grapes / 025
source / 248
soy sauce / 009

spaghetti / 008
sparrow / 126
special effect / 232
specialist / 194
specimen / 196
speed / 229
speed skating / 214
spice rack / 035
spick and span / 045
spider / 118
spinach / 004
spinal column / 096
spinal cord / 096
spinster / 078
spirituals / 224
spit and polish / 056
spiteful / 087
spitting image / 090
sponge / 036
sport coat / 049
sport shirt / 049
sporting goods store / 183
spouse / 076
sprain / 099, 200
spruce / 139
spy / 169
square / 079
square meal / 023

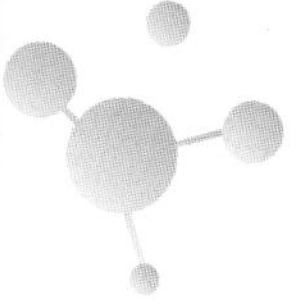

square-toe / 053
squash / 003
squirrel / 112
stadium / 217
stamen / 142
standoffish / 156
stand-offish / 084
starfish / 116
starling / 127
starring / 231
starvation / 242
state of emergency / 243
stationery store / 178
steady date / 090
steam / 022, 250
stem / 142
stenographer / 169
stethoscope / 193
stew / 022
stew pot / 020
stiff / 201
stiff neck / 101
stigma / 142
stir / 022, 153
stir-fry / 021
stockbroker / 180
stockings / 054
stole / 050

stomachache / 100
storage warehouse / 184
store clerk / 164
store room / 031
stork / 129
storm / 243
story / 234
stove / 020
straight from the horse's mouth / 133
strain / 200
strainer / 020
strap / 227
strawberry / 005
street cleaner / 168
strings / 225
stroke / 203
stroller / 038
strong / 085
stuck up / 085
student / 172
studio / 029, 230, 234
studious / 083
study / 031
stuffed shirt / 055
stump / 141
stunt / 233
stupid / 085
sturgeon / 116

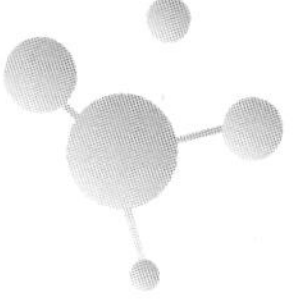

style / 142
subtitle / 231
sugar / 015
sugar bowl / 018
suit / 050
sun block / 066
sunburn / 100
sundae / 013
sunfish / 115
sunflower / 136
sun room / 030
sun screen / 066
suntan lotion / 066
super conductors / 250
supermarket / 182
supporting actor [actress] / 232
suppository / 198
surfboard / 216
surfing / 214
surgeon / 163, 195
surgery / 196
surveyor / 172
suspenders / 049
suspense / 236
swallow / 127
swan / 125
swan song / 131
swarm (of bees) / 121

sweater / 048
sweater pants / 048
sweatshirt / 050
sweet potato / 002
swimming / 213
swimming pool contractor / 169
swollen / 101, 200
sycamore / 138
symphonic / 222
symphony / 220
synagogue / 182
synchronize / 233
syndrome / 204
synopsis / 234
synthesizer / 225
syphilis / 204
syrup / 015

T

table cloth / 017
tablespoon / 017
tablet / 199
tadpole (frog) / 123
tadpole / 115
tail / 129
tailor / 169
take a chest X-ray / 104
take one's temperature / 104

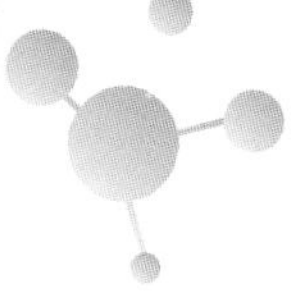

take out the garbage / 042
talon / 129
tambourine / 226
tangerine / 006
tank / 120
tank top / 051
tanning salon / 180
tape / 222
taro / 002
tax consultant / 169
taxidermist / 168
taxi driver / 166
TB (tuberculosis) / 100
tea / 016
tea kettle / 035
tea pot / 018
tea spoon / 017
teacher / 168
team / 080
team (of horses) / 121
teammate / 079
tear jerker / 156
tear-jerker / 236
tears / 149
technician / 164
tee / 215
teenager / 082
telephone company business office / 183

telephone lineman / 171
telephone operator / 171
telephoto / 230
teller / 171
temper / 148
temperature / 197
temple / 094, 178
tennis / 213
tennis shoes / 054
tenor / 220
tent / 029
termite / 117
tern / 127
terror / 149
terrorism / 241
that's just peachy / 143
the bluebird of happiness / 131
the blues / 237
the bottom line / 176
the flu / 200
the great unwashed / 071
the last straw / 143
the pill / 198
the shoe's on the other foot / 056
theme song / 231
thigh / 094
thongs / 053
thrift shop / 182

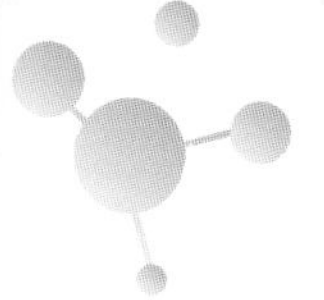

thriller / 236
throat lozenges / 106
throw one's weight around / 108
throw up / 102
thumb / 094
tidal / 249
tidal wave / 242
tie clip / 062
tied to someone's apron strings / 055
tiger / 118
tights / 052
time lapse / 229
timid / 155
tin pin / 059
tiredness / 149
tissue / 061, 068
titmouse / 125
to back the wrong horse / 132
to balance the books / 175
to be fired / 176
to be in one's shoes / 056
to be on diet / 025
to be punchy / 219
to be snowed under / 176
to beat around the bush / 144
to beat the band / 237
to beef about / 024
to beef up / 023

to bite more than one can chew / 024
to blow one's top / 156
to blow your own horn / 237
to break even / 175
to break the record / 219
to break up / 090
to bring home the bacon / 025, 176
to burn a hole in one's pocket / 055
to buttonhole someone / 055
to call it a day / 175
to cold call / 175
to collar someone / 055
to come by it naturally / 088
to cook one's goose / 131
to cough up / 207
to crack the whip / 176
to croak / 207
to cry over the spilt milk / 024
to eat crow / 132
to eat for two / 023
to eat humble pie / 023
to eat like a bird / 023
to eat one's cake and have it / 023
to eat one's heart out / 109
to egg on / 025
to face the music / 237
to fiddle around with / 237
to flip a coin / 064

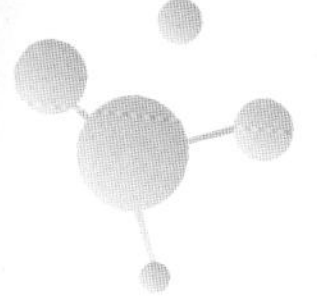

to gang up on / 090
to get on the ball / 219
to get one's goat / 134
to get the sack / 176
to give someone a dose of their own medicine / 207
to give up the ghost / 207
to go off the deep end / 208
to go through the motions / 088
to go to bat for / 218
to go to pieces / 157
to go to the dogs / 131
to handle with kid gloves / 056
to hang in there / 088
to hang it all out / 090
to have a crush on / 090
to have a lot of the ball / 219
to have a screw loose / 207
to have an affair / 090
to have one's cake and eat it / 024
to hit below the belt / 056
to hit home / 044
to hit the hay / 143
to hit the sake / 044
to hold one's horses / 133
to horse around / 132
to jump the gun / 219
to keep one's shirt on / 055
to keep the ball rolling / 219

to keep up with the Joneses / 044
to kick the bucket / 209
to kill two birds with one stone / 131
to know what the score is / 218
to let the cat out of the bag / 132
to look at a gift horse in the mouth / 134
to look for the needle in the haystack / 055
to look oily / 071
to lose one's shirt / 056
to make a beeline for / 131
to make a clean sweep of... / 044
to make a hit / 218
to make a monkey out of / 133
to make a scene / 156
to make heads or tails of... / 064
to monkey around / 132
to not worth a bean / 023
to pay lip service to / 108
to pepper with questions / 024
to pig out / 023
to pinch hit / 218
to pipe down / 237
to play possum / 133
to play second fiddle / 237
to pull no punches / 089
to pull one's punches / 218
to pull the stakes / 045
to put one's eggs in one basket / 025

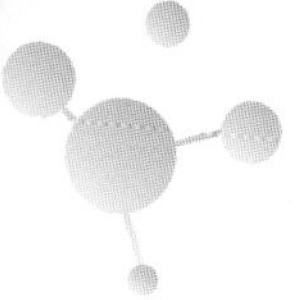

to put that in one's pipe and smoke it / 064
to raise the roof / 044
to rate a ten / 219
to reap what one sows / 143
to rest on one's laurels / 143
to ride the broomstick / 044
to shoot fish in a barrel / 131
to sing for one's supper / 237
to smell a rat / 134
to smell a trouble / 071
to soft-pedal / 237
to sow one's wild oats / 143
to spill the beans / 024
to spin a yarn / 055
to sponge off / 088
to sweat blood / 175
to take after / 090
to take one's medicine / 208
to take someone down a peg / 089
to take the bull by the horn / 133
to talk turkey / 132
to throw the bull / 131
to turn one's stomach / 207
to turn over a new leaf / 143
to turn the tables on / 044
to wait for the other shoe to drop / 056
to wash one's mouth out with soap / 071
to whitewash / 045

to win hands down / 218
to wolf down one's food / 024
to work one's finger to the bone / 175
toad / 115
toast / 007
toaster / 034
toaster oven / 034
tobacco pouch / 060
tobacconist / 182
toddler / 082
toe / 097
toenail / 097
toilet / 031, 036
toilet water / 067
tomato / 004
tonsillectomy / 196
too many cooks spoil the broth / 023
tool shed / 040
tooth powder / 066
toothache / 099
toothbrush / 066
toothpaste / 066
toothpaste gel / 070
tornado / 243
tortoise / 115
towel rack / 036
town [city] office / 178
town house / 028

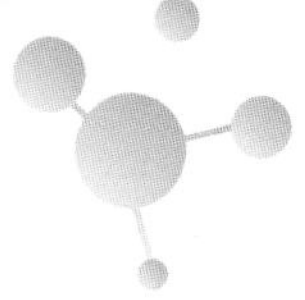

toy chest / 038
toy store / 180
track / 212, 217
tragedy / 235
trail / 217
trailer / 234
trailer house / 028
trampoline / 216
translator / 173
transplant / 197
trap / 120
trash compactor / 034
travel agency / 180
travel agent / 167
traveling salesman / 167
tray / 017
tree house / 029
tree surgeon / 169
tremble / 152
trench coat / 050
tribe (of goats) / 122
tripod / 226
trombone / 225
troop (of monkeys) / 121
tropical storm / 243
trouble / 150
troubled waters / 156
trousers / 050

trout / 011, 116
truck driver / 163
trucker / 163
trumpet / 225
trumpet flower / 139
trunk / 141
trustworthy / 085
t-shirt / 048
tsunami / 240, 249
tuba / 225
tuberculosis (T.B.) / 204
tuberose / 137
tulip / 140
tumor / 205
tune / 220
turbine / 249
turkey / 010
turkey / 125
turn your head and cough / 207
turnip / 004
turnover / 013
turtle / 115
turtleneck / 050
tuxedo / 052
TV antenna / 041
TV cable company / 179
TV [radio] repairman [-woman] / 171
tweezers / 067

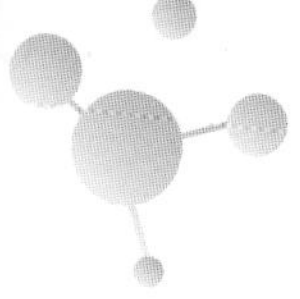

tweezers / 193
twig / 141
twist / 099
twister / 242
typesetter / 168
typhoon / 243
typist / 163

U

ugly / 087
ugly duckling / 134
ulcer / 206
umbrella / 060
unconscious / 099
under the weather / 208
underclothes / 048
under-exposed / 230
underpants / 048
undershirt / 049
undertaker / 173, 195
up to one's ears [eyeballs, neck] / 107
upholsterer / 166
upper crust / 023
upset / 154
up-tight / 085
up to snuff / 064
urologist / 194
used furniture clothing, car store / 184

utilities / 247
utility room / 030

V

V.D. (venereal disease) / 203
vaccination / 197
vacuum the house / 042
vanity / 036
vaporizer / 192
veins / 097
vest / 050
veterinarian / 173
victim / 244
viewer / 230
viewfinder / 227
villa / 028
vinegar / 009
viola / 225
violent / 236
violet / 139
violin / 225
virus / 200
vitamins / 106, 198
volleyball / 213
volunteer / 164
vomit / 102, 201
vulture / 125

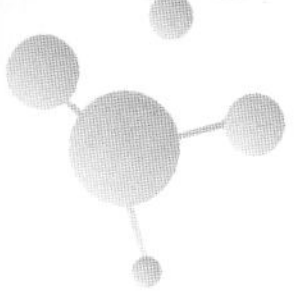

W

waffle / 007
waist / 096
waiter / 165
waiting room / 190
waitress / 165
walker / 038, 193
walking stick / 060
walkman / 062
wall unit / 032
wallet / 059
wallflower / 143
walnut / 138
war / 236, 243
warbler / 127
ward / 190
wart / 100
wash the window / 042
washed out / 230
waste one's breath / 108
wastebasket / 037
water / 016
watermelon / 005
water lily / 139
water off a duck's back / 133
water polo / 212
wax the floor / 042

wear and tear / 055
weariness / 148
weary / 154
weep / 152
weight lifting / 214
welding shop / 181
welfare office / 183
well groomed / 064
well-mannered / 084
wet blanket / 044
whale / 114
wheelchair / 193
wheeze / 101
whippoorwill / 125
whisk / 020
whiskey / 016
white elephant / 131
wicked stepmother / 089
wide-angle lens / 229
widow / 076
widower / 077
wife / 075
wig / 051
wildcat operator / 247
wildcat / 113
wilderness / 135
wild fire / 242
wild goose chase / 132

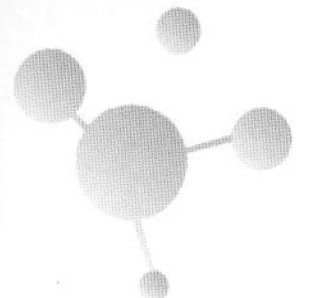

willow / 137
wind power / 248
windmill / 248
window / 032
window screen / 040
window washer / 166
windpipe / 095
wine / 016, 129
with open arms / 108
wolf / 114
wolf in sheep's clothing / 132
woodpecker / 126
woods / 135
worm / 117
wound / 201
wreckage / 242
wrestling / 213
wristwatch / 058
writer / 164

X

x-ray / 196
x-ray machine / 192

Y

yard / 031
yogurt / 012
yoke (of oxen) / 121

You scratch my back and I scratch yours. / 108
young adult / 081
youth / 081

Z

zebra / 119
zest / 151
zoo keeper / 168
zoom lens / 228

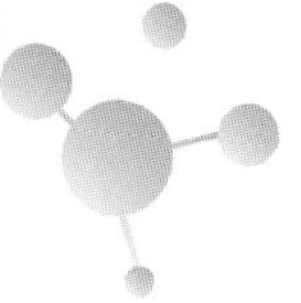

NOTE 筆記頁

NOTE 筆記頁

NOTE 筆記頁

NOTE 筆記頁

NOTE 筆記頁

NOTE 筆記頁

國家圖書館出版品預行編目資料

超實用生活英語分類單字／李普生著. ——初版.
——臺北市：書泉，2013.01
面；　　公分

ISBN 978-986-121-810-6（平裝）

1. 英語　2.詞彙

805. 12　　　　101025239

3AL0

超實用生活英語分類單字

作　　者　李普生
發 行 人　楊榮川
總 編 輯　王翠華
文字編輯　溫小瑩
封面設計　吳佳臻

出 版 者　書泉出版社
地　　址：台北市大安區106
和平東路二段339號4樓
電　　話：(02)2705-5066（代表號）
傳　　真：(02)2706-6100
網　　址：http://www.wunan.com.tw
電子郵件：shuchuan@shuchuan.com.tw
劃撥帳號：01303853
戶　　名：書泉出版社

法律顧問　元貞聯合法律事務所　張澤平律師

版　　刷　2013年1月　初版一刷

定　　價　320元整　

總經銷:朝日文化
進退貨地址：新北市中和區橋安街15巷1號7樓
TEL：(02)2249-7714 FAX：(02)2249-8715